PRAISE FOR *THE RULE OF ONE*

"Ava and Mira's world is an all-too-believable mix of advanced technology and environmental collapse. In their debut, Saunders and Saunders, themselves twins, lend an authentic voice to the girls' first-person narration . . . Readers are in for a fast-paced ride, poised for a sequel, as the twins embrace their father's call, in the words of Walt Whitman, to 'resist much, obey little.'"

—*Kirkus Reviews*

"Utilizing an SF-fantasy setting and a survival-oriented plot, the Saunders sisters are careful to promote growth and differentiation between the twins . . . There are parallels to current news stories, such as immigration, environmental resources, and an autocratic political system."

—*Booklist*

"The apocryphal nature, strong female heroes, and similar concepts to the movie *What Happened to Monday* and to Margaret Haddix's book series Shadow Children are reflected in this plot-driven book. Readers of the genre will appreciate the page-turning action, the close calls, and the authors' development of distinct personality differences between the twins."

—*VOYA*

"The descriptions of everything are incredibly vivid and make you feel as if you are running for your life . . . This story was completely compelling."

—The Nerd Daily

"Twin storytellers Ashley and Leslie Saunders are modern-day soothsayers who beautifully spin a suspenseful tale of the not-so-distant future. Pay attention—this could be what *1984* was to 1949."

—Richard Linklater, Academy Award–nominated
screenwriter and director

INTRUDERS

ALSO BY ASHLEY SAUNDERS & LESLIE SAUNDERS

THE RULE OF ONE TRILOGY

The Rule of One

The Rule of Many

The Rule of All

THE EXILES SERIES

Exiles

INTRUDERS

ASHLEY SAUNDERS
LESLIE SAUNDERS

Published by 47North, Seattle

www.apub.com

Amazon, the Amazon logo, and 47North are trademarks of Amazon.com, Inc., or its affiliates.

ISBN-13: 9781542032988 (paperback)
ISBN-13: 9781542032995 (digital)

Cover design by David Curtis
Cover images © Carabus / Getty; © Tuomas A. Lehtinen / Getty

Printed in the United States of America

This one's for our parents;
we're fortunate to call you ours

PROLOGUE

Iris Szeto gritted her teeth, indifferent to her epoch-making journey. A hundred feet beneath the Bering Strait's violent surface, the bullet train's lights flickered as it raced through the longest underwater tunnel on Earth, carrying Iris across the maritime boundary between Russian territorial waters and those of the States. She didn't bother to marvel at the cold, dark sea outside the train's ultramodern smart windows.

Iris focused instead on the bloody enamel pin held in her smooth palm. She ran her finger over three raised diagonal slashes that resembled claw marks, musing on the man she'd stripped it from. The Szeto family's enforcers had purloined the twentieth richest person in the world, known to have been in Los Angeles the night that Iris's aunt Poppy had been murdered, and discreetly transported him to their secluded property on Hong Kong Island.

It had been easy enough to get the man to talk. Stripped of his stocking mask and two-piece gray suit—the affluent armor he'd mistakenly thought would protect him—Iris had found that the man had no real fight. No firmness of purpose.

So Iris had shown him the strength of hers.

It wasn't that Iris particularly liked the sound of men screaming. At least, that's what she told herself, even now. But it had helped to drown out the bitter cries of her grieving family. To soothe, for just a moment, the biting ache of loss. And although it had come to light that the man was not the one who shot and killed Poppy, the interrogation had not been entirely wasteful.

Iris attached the bloodstained pin to the low neckline of her tailored blazer dress. It matched the shade of her dark red lipstick beautifully. The train suddenly slowed, and Iris rose on her stiletto heels.

Her father would forgive her for this clandestine trip. For taking the honor of being first to travel the groundbreaking high-speed rail that connected China, Russia, Canada, and the United States. The official inaugural passage of the Quartet Line wasn't scheduled until the following week, when the eyes of the entire world would behold the dawn of her family's latest masterpiece. Eight thousand miles of track, from Shanghai to San Francisco, in eighteen hours. Billions to be made in trade. Tourism. Harmony sowed between the world's superpowers.

A Szeto innovation set to rival Damon Yates's HyperQuest.

But Iris thought of none of that now. This unauthorized journey was personal.

The automatic door slid open, revealing a glass emergency walkway, wide enough for two. A figure stood staring into the murky abyss, his sharkskin suit the same cold gray as the pistol locked in his rigid grip.

"Used to be you wouldn't be caught dead wearing the color of ash and old age." Iris's red lips curled as she stepped from the train onto the walkway. "And yet it's your uniform now, I suppose."

The uniform of a Conservator.

Vance Yates, Damon's second son, kept his back to Iris, waiting for her to move first. To readily take the five steps to his side.

But Iris remained rooted, her dark eyes on Vance's pistol. "You're playing with guns now?" she teased.

He's filler, Iris's father liked to say about Vance, the rare times he ever spoke of him. *Dispensable. Why waste your time on a* middle *man?* Iris covered her father's disapproving voice with her own, a honeyed, forceful taunt she hoped would compel Vance to turn. To face her. "I didn't think you'd come. At least, not alone. You always need your older brother's approval, don't you?"

And Palmer Yates had *never* approved of Iris Szeto.

"Like you were any different with Poppy," Vance snapped, icy and frank. He remained facing the pitch-black waters.

Iris was on him before he took his next breath. She shoved the metal prongs of her palm-sized stun gun below his rib cage. "You so casually speak her name to me?" *Poppy.* Her father's sister. The treasured flower of the Szeto family tree. Her mentor, meant to show Iris how to be a worthy billion-heir. Iris had never made her proud.

She meant to now.

"I don't care which of you Conservators pulled the trigger," Iris seethed. "You're all answerable for her murder. The law might protect you from prison, but it won't save you from me." She thrust her stun gun deeper into his side.

She couldn't see Vance's face, but his pistol stayed lowered, and his tone was irritatingly measured. Controlled. "Maxen has already publicly confessed to matricide. Your cousin's lost."

"You mean *your brother.*"

"Only half," Vance muttered.

Iris knew he'd never quite taken to calling Poppy stepmother. "And *you've* got half a heart," she snarled.

"You should know. You were the one who broke it."

A half-truth, Iris thought. *Vance was broken long before I ever found him.*

She flicked off the safety switch, ready to shock him, when he finally turned, those pale blue eyes gaping at her, wide as open safes. For a second, he was twenty-one again: genuine, original, fresh-faced, and bold. He was the man she'd known at Oxford, where they had met and been together—free of family, of judgment. Often of clothes.

Vance locked a rogue golden curl behind one ear. "You really are stunning, Iris. With or without that *stun* gun of yours."

"With or without my last name?" Iris retorted, unmoved.

The crease between Vance's eyes returned, the practiced smile she'd grown to despise sliding up his hardened face. "An iris by any other name . . ."

Iris glided backward with her stun gun and with a click held the electric charge between them. "I'm here to tell you the Szetos will leave you to your affairs. Whatever new venture you and Palmer are operating with the Conservators is not our business." *Another half-truth.* "Simply order those government officials you have leashed to heel. Give us Maxen."

The judge on Maxen's case—on track to be reelected, she noted—had set her cousin's bond at ten billion dollars. It was a challenge, Iris knew, from Hariri, the infectious alpha of the exclusive Conservators. *Which would it be? The Szeto family's wealth? Or their flesh and blood?* She could almost see Hariri's billion-dollar smile. He'd had it out for Iris's father ever since it was leaked to the elite short list of contenders that Hoi Szeto was set to be named the next *Time* magazine's Person of the Year. Hariri was number two on the list. And he wanted her father cut down.

"Will you deliver the message?" Iris spurred, driving the blinding blue pulse of electricity closer.

Vance gave a maddening shake of his head. It was subtle. Sympathetic.

It was the wrong answer.

Poppy's murder was never going to be settled fairly in court. So Iris would have to settle it dirty now.

Vance's roving eyes found the enamel pin on her silk lapel. "Where did you get that?"

Iris answered with another click of her stun gun. A hologram shot upward, and the matching faces of Crystal Yates and Jade Moore hovered between them, real and sharp as Iris's grief.

Vance's pale blue eyes bulged before he locked them shut. The more he tried to swallow his cries, the harder he choked. The faster his limbs shuddered. The greater Iris's disgust became.

The Yates Empire is truly imploding. Explosions on Quest Campus, a vanished CEO, a murdered Adsum dean, missing students, a deserter billion-heir daughter, and now *this*? The fear gripping Vance was inexplicable, all-pervading, almost criminal in its potency and power.

What had Crystal, Vance's adopted sister, and Jade, her unscrupulous twin, done to him? It had been the same with the captured Conservator Iris had interrogated on Hong Kong Island. *It's their faces,* the wealthy man had rasped, cowering from their images on a news network. Iris had failed to get the *how* and *why* out of him before her phone vibrated, interrupting the interrogation with an encrypted message from her estranged amour.

Iris had named the place. Vance had named the hour. *The good times only begin after two, remember?*

"Please," Vance moaned now, a stark shadow in his gray suit, the leaden waters looming above and behind him. His gun clattered to the glass floor as he slumped to his knees. "Please, make it stop." His pleas were wet with tears, his voice stripped hollow from his irrepressible screams. Iris cocked her head, noting his thin brows and lashless eyes, both plucked nearly bare. Signs of stress, his trichotillomania, she recalled from their university days.

Vance Yates is crumbling, Iris realized. And from more than whatever fears his adoptive sister had seeded in him. Was it guilt for his role in his father's disappearance? Or a moldering resentment of his brother Palmer's sole claim of the Yates Empire?

"Please," Vance gasped, peeling open his lids. His eyes were wild, fighting to find Iris's. "Make it stop."

Iris extended the hand that bore her stun gun and charged closer, assailing his vision with the hologram of the sisters.

"Right now, *you* have the power to make it stop," Iris whispered. "Tell me who shot Poppy. Tell me where Hariri hid Damon's body. For once in your life, Vance Byron Yates, stand up to your brother. Shed that suit, rip off that vain facade you've withered under, and side with *me*."

Iris felt a sudden breeze at the back of her neck. She turned and found that the bullet train was speeding back toward Russia and Shanghai through the underwater tunnel. Had her family discovered her rogue plan and summoned the train's return? Or had Hariri tracked her surreptitious movements and callously left her stranded on the bottom of the sea?

No. Iris had been careful. Discreet, as always. She was a Szeto, a woman who knew how to cover her tracks.

Vance always did have a heavy tread, she thought, rounding on him. "Did you not—" But her remonstrations were cut short. A steel cord had wrapped around her delicate throat. Pulled her up to the tips of her stilettos. Iris gasped for breath, hanging in midair, and before she could comprehend the *how*, she understood the *who*.

Palmer.

His pet drone cruelly dragged her from the walkway and down onto the empty track, one of its clawlike arms pressing her face against the transparent tunnel, a second beginning to bore its way through the reinforced glass, a knife's edge from Iris's wide-open eyes.

Palmer meant to flood the tunnel. Destroy the Quartet Line. There was no way she could make it to the surface. Her body would freeze, her lungs crushed by the water's pressure.

Iris let out a strangled cry. The steel noose around her neck tightened, and she was suspended in the air again, swinging back and forth like a morbid pendulum, desperate to gain purchase on the ground.

Iris would either hang to death or she would drown, her body washed away alongside her family's fortune.

"Stop—" Iris rasped, black spots blurring the corners of her vision. Palmer's drone only squeezed harder.

She knew Palmer wanted *her* to stop. To give in. To stop fighting. But she couldn't bring herself to do it, to yield to a man like Palmer Yates. Dizzy and furious, Iris clung to her firmness of purpose, clawing at the cord locked around her throat.

I always said your stubbornness would be the death of you, Poppy chided her. Her body began to twitch.

Iris was a fool. She could not win. And yet she kept battling to break loose, even as her eyes rolled back, her oxygen-starved brain shutting down.

Distantly, she heard the *crack* of a gunshot, and suddenly she was free. She crumpled onto the cold track, gasping for air, the severed steel cord slipping from her neck. The sound of the drill had ceased.

"*Enough,*" Vance growled. He stood on the edge of the walkway, his gun aimed at his brother's predatory drone, which now hovered between him and Iris.

A cruel laugh emitted from the thing, sending shivers up Iris's spine.

Then a second steel cord dropped out of the drone's underside and lashed around Vance's ankle like a whip.

"*I* decide when I've had enough, brother," Palmer's voice jeered.

Before Vance could fire another shot, he was hauled into the air, head over heels.

Iris recovered the strength to stand, reaching out for Vance—

But the drone went flying down the tunnel, carrying him out of sight. Iris's knees gave way. Her head slammed against steel. Her father's voice echoed inside her skull. *Dispensable. Dispensable.*

An incoherent roar suddenly clattered out of the distant darkness. *Vance.* Then two distinct words hit her like an incoming bullet train.

"*Rarely ends!*"

Was Vance giving her a warning? A clue?

Rarely ends.

The phrase latched on to Iris's mind before her eyes closed and unconsciousness swept her away.

ONE

A great drumfire of hooves resounded across the dusty earth. Jade spurred her horse faster, kicking up a dust devil as she and Crys raced with flying speed.

The rocky valley of the Texas Hill Country stretched unendingly before them, rugged granite hills edging Jade's right. Her sister, atop her own lean quarter horse, a white blur on her left. Jade squeezed her thighs against the saddle, gripped the reins so hard her nails drew blood. Wind and sweat stung her eyes, but she still saw the felled live oak that obstructed their path ahead.

"Watch it!" she warned Crys. Her pulse pounding in her neck, Jade hesitated, cutting her horse around the tree, killing her momentum.

But Crys did not waver. She and her horse leapt over the hurdle with ease and took the lead. *You've got to be shaking me,* Jade swore. Despite all her undaunted efforts, every bruise and ache she'd acquired in the month since they'd fled the Golden State, Crys, the sheltered billion-heir—*former,* Jade reminded herself—now had more grit and guts than *she* did?

Jade Moore is afraid, she could hear the trolls taunt. *The slippery scapegrace has been unmade . . .* The beginnings of a new theme song.

The powerful beast beneath her could sense her rising panic. It whinnied and charged forward at a breakneck pace, sweat glistening off its muscular black shoulders.

Recklessly, Jade closed her eyes. Willing her nerves into steel. Baiting the intoxicating rush of danger to rise and meet her in the dark. Adrenaline crashed through her body—only it was not the thrill and vitality she was seeking, but raw fear. An unwelcome feeling Jade had come to know intimately since she'd been forced to give up her Quest Bot.

She snapped her eyes open. Somehow, she'd caught up to her sister. Crys must have purposely slowed. Anger blotted out all other emotion.

"Stop humoring me and *race*," Jade seethed, blood surging to her head. She spurred her horse's flank again, hard.

And then she was airborne, bucked from the saddle. She threw out her right arm, absorbing the fall, and rolled away from her horse with her hands raised. When the dust settled, a soft cooing reached Jade's ears, an audible teddy bear her mom used to deploy to soothe Jade and Crys as children. Jade turned to the sound, her heart slowing, her breathing more relaxed, but found it was meant for Jade's spooked horse, not her.

Of course, Jade thought, her pulse rising again. Crys spent more time in the stable these days than with her or the Adsum foster sibs they'd brought with them from the academy to the remote Texas hideout.

"Shhh," Crys continued to coo, calming the mare.

The disheveled fleece sweatsuit that Crys had worn like a uniform draped limply from her thin frame, her hair a tangled mess of golden curls. On her last venture from the ranch, Jade had bought a box of cheap hair dye that matched Crys's overgrown chestnut roots, but the box sat unopened on their makeshift nightstand. Was Crys still clinging to the last vestiges of her time as a Yates? *No,* Jade assured herself. It was just that Crys rarely showered these days, or even glanced at a mirror. Which was perhaps even more troubling . . .

"Break anything?" Crys asked, sliding from her saddle with the fluid grace of a practiced equestrian.

Jade checked the glass vials she kept wrapped inside her skull-patterned handkerchief. Crys was always edgy about the welfare of their fear fragrance, Crys's former Quest Bot turned nanoweapon that made people terrified of their identical faces.

"Don't worry, the only thing shattered is my ego," Jade said, stuffing the kerchief back into her pants pocket. "What's new?"

"I meant your fragile bones," Crys clarified, offering Jade a hand.

Jade stifled a moan as she lurched to her feet. She set her dark clothes and tousled curls back to rights, reaching for the silver chain and its mangled bullet that hung permanently from her neck, as much a part of Jade as her own eyes or hands. It was her reminder that she'd challenged death and won, her steadfast souvenir, her luck charm.

And it was gone. The necklace must have slipped off somewhere on their ride.

"Did you lose something?" Crys asked.

You mean besides my Quest Bot and steady nerve? Jade thought miserably, but she muttered only, "In Extremis." *At the point of death.*

"Let it go," Crys insisted, attempting to hand Jade her horse's reins, not even pretending to search for the necklace. "You don't need it."

Yes, she shaking well did. In Extremis was the only thing convincing Jade she could be utterly, wholeheartedly fearless. She *needed* it.

Jade's horse nickered beside her as she dropped to her palms and knees, desperate to feel the warm metal, the reassurance, the instant boost of self-possession as she held the spent bullet in her grasp. Instead, she felt her sister's touch, forceful and impatient.

"Jade?"

She shrugged off Crys's hold. Resumed her search.

"Jade?"

They were miles from the ranch. It could take days to retrace their steps. The chances of finding it were abysmal. Jade used to smile at such odds.

"Jade!"

Sighing, Jade finally turned and followed Crys's eyeline to a nearby willow thicket. Inside the dense brush, a rectangular trap lay broken, its mesh gravity door cut clean off.

"That's the second damaged cage we've come across today." Crys pointed to the far side of the thicket to a third. "This doesn't look like the work of a clever animal."

"More like sabotage," Jade grunted.

Crys shook her head, disbelieving. "You think one of our sibs would deliberately destroy the traps? I can't imagine any of them would still be loyal to Quest . . ."

"Me, either," Jade groaned, kneading her sore back with her knuckles. Poppy, their dean and foster mother, might be dead, but the exiled Adsum students were still a family. And all of them understood the importance of every hare. Each one they caught meant the possibility of answers. The chance of a cure for the Unfortunates infected with the Conservators' nano reform. The promise of returning to their home cities without fear of laying eyes on three diagonal slash marks that signaled *this is not a safe place.*

"Then who could do this?" Crys asked.

"Gen 1, those two adoptive brothers of yours, comes to mind . . ." Jade made herself shrug, a show for herself and Crys that she was unalarmed by the prospect. Had Palmer and Vance somehow tracked the Exiles here? Been watching their every move?

"I filed a special petition, by the way," Crys whispered, her russet eyes roving the still valley. "To revoke my adoption as a Yates."

Jade froze. She'd been waiting seven months, since she'd first learned that her sister had changed her last name, to hear Crys speak those words. But by the hard look on Crys's face, now didn't seem the time to celebrate. "Thank you for sharing that with me," she said simply.

Crys nodded, her untidy head tilted skyward, presumably searching for Palmer's drone, while Jade resumed her frantic search for her necklace among the rocks.

"I'll find you, I'll find you, I'll find you," she whispered, with a conviction she didn't feel. It was a trick her uncle Willis had taught her, a tactic he'd used whenever he misplaced his Medal of Valor, a decoration he'd been awarded for his heroism in the Greater LA Fire. *You gotta let what's lost know that you're confident, or it will disappear.*

Crys sighed, her fear fragrance making a soft *clink* inside a pouch at her belt. "I hear you whispering yourself to sleep with those words. Are you talking to Damon Yates?"

I'll find you, I'll find you.

"It's like he doesn't *want* to be found," Jade mused, her fingers scraped and bloodied as she crawled toward the thin dirt road the horses were now grazing beside.

Or they were all too late, and Yates had already forgotten why he'd hidden in the first place. He might be truly lost. The man he was—the rogue tech pioneer with enough fortune and clout to put a stop to the Conservators—had disappeared.

The sound of tires cracking against shattered limestone suddenly filled the lonely landscape. A pickup sped toward them, glinting like a polished garnet in the afternoon sun.

Jade shot to her feet, spotting two lithe, tanned arms waving wildly from an open window. A tremendous smile cut across her face, her necklace dropped from her mind in an instant. "Ani. And is that Rhett behind the wheel?"

"They found us," Crys gasped, smiling for the first time in days. "Good news. For once."

Ani Agassi and Rhett Wood took in the Exiles' impressive hideout, a lavish Spanish-style ranch house with an elaborate U-shaped courtyard, a clay tile roof, and grated arched windows. Jade stared at the new earring dangling from Ani's left ear as it sparkled blindingly in the Texas sunlight. The deep burgundy of her leather jacket offset the gemstone perfectly.

Crys noticed it, too. "Is that a jewel from the Soaring Precious?" she asked, moving closer.

The exquisite stone must have dislodged from the ancient saber and slipped into Ani's blood-soaked clothing the night Hariri stabbed her in the hyperloop pod, as they'd fled Quest Campus to San Francisco.

Jade rubbed her hands together, the visceral memory of pressing into Ani's gushing wound returning like a punch to the gut. There had been so much blood, Ani's hemophilia a death sentence without her Quest Bot.

She's here, Jade reminded herself, stilling her hands. Crys had found Ani's nanobot before Yates's lab blew up. Saved her from bleeding out.

"Your own 'morbid memento,' as you like to call mine," Jade said, stopping herself from reaching for her own absent souvenir. Ani fingered the ruby, a self-assuredness edging the curves of her round face. "Let's hope I haven't started a trend."

"I was thinking of fashioning one for myself," Rhett said, pushing up a pair of shades that vanished into his wheat-colored hair, exposing several thin scars that ringed his eyes like bloody lashes. Yates's former elite enforcer scanned the empty horizon before he followed Crys through the heavy plank front door. "If—*when*—I get my hands on Palmer's drone and its damnable claws, I'm open to suggestions."

Ani gripped Jade by the shoulders, her thick dark brows slammed together, her wide eyes boring into Jade's, and tugged her backward from the threshold. "I can see it on your face, Jade. You don't have to pretend, you know."

For a horrifying moment Jade thought Ani could see through her steely mask and was clocking her washed-up nerve. "Pretend what?"

"That you don't blame me," Ani insisted, her husky voice low. Tears tracked down her cheeks, drowning her assuredness with guilt. "You blame me for forcing you to get rid of your Quest Bot when it turns out you didn't need to."

Jade unclenched her jaw, her lips curling into an easy smile. "Ani, the only thing I blame you for is my *deplorable* taste in television."

That won a quiet laugh from Ani. "Reality TV is fast food for the soul. And you eat it by the mouthful."

Jade's grin broadened. "Crys was always the one with the refined palate." She wiped the teardrops from Ani's face with the back of her hand. "But seriously, how could I blame you when you thought you were saving my life?" She shrugged. "And the only bots I care about now are the ones spreading the Conservators' nano reform."

Ani's eyes narrowed, scanning the half-healed bruises along Jade's forearms, the splint on her right ankle, the fresh cut along her sharp jawline. "Then how do you explain all those?"

Jade hesitated. She never could hide her scheming, her *deceiving*, from Ani. But what could she say? How could Jade explain the desperate pull that made her leap off an eighty-foot cliff into the clear blue waters of Devils Bluff? The need that compelled Jade to taunt her daring to return by pulling wildly dangerous stunts on an ATV and pilfering an egg from the property's ostrich farm, narrowly missing an alpha's vicious kick to the chest?

"Well—" Jade started, but then Crys's head popped through the open door, and Jade's pathetic excuses died on the tip of her tongue.

"The manhunt," Crys lied for her. "The quest for Damon Yates hasn't been gentle, I'm afraid." That part was true, at least.

Jade threw a small, grateful nod to Crys. Was she covering for her to assuage some guilt for not taking part in the manhunt herself? Crys hadn't once left the retreat's grounds, leaving the search for the billionaire—Crys's legally adoptive father, Jade noted, even if Crys no longer utilized the familial term—to the rest of the Exiles. Whatever the case, Jade couldn't meet her sister's eyes. She'd taken great pains to keep her after-hours pursuits a secret, even from Crys. *Did everyone know?* The thought made Jade's mouth dry, her palms sweat.

When all the others at the ranch were asleep, or away tracking down the seemingly untraceable Yates, Jade would slip away, seeking her old spirit, chasing after risk, desperate for her reward. Weeks of training and countless efforts, of pushing herself to face her fear. It wasn't simply the cold panic of neck-snapping heights, speeding past tight corners, or stealing from hostile birds that drove her. It all led to the fear of losing Crys, the Exiles, the Adsum sibs. Her family.

How could she protect them if she was a coward? How could she admit she had never been more terrified?

Jade's phone suddenly vibrated with a barrage of messages.

Apparently so did Crys's. "Living room," she said. "Now. *Rfa.*" She lifted her gaze to Jade, fiddling with the pouch on her belt that held her fear fragrance. "It's from Eli."

Red fucking alert.

Rfa, rfa. The letters and their meaning taunted Jade as she charged past the hulking door, leading the way through the circular, white-washed foyer. With Crys and Ani at her side, she joined Rhett at the entrance of a spacious living room with intricate handcrafted tiles, a few squares chipped where Jade had taught the Adsum third-years how to ensnare a fully grown man with her police-issue BolaWrap. Urban calf-roping, a few had coined it.

Rhett's focus was glued to a large screen that hung from the floral-papered wall, four separate news stations delivering voting results from across the country. It was Election Day. The day to determine if Hariri's grand threats and theories held weight. Governors, mayors, judges—how many would be reelected thanks to the nano reform, the "remarkable remedy" so cunningly provided by the Conservators to cure the homeless pandemic in the cities? How many were now beholden to Hariri and his invisible weapon, just as he had predicted and promised?

"How's it looking?" Jade asked Finn Whitlock, who'd sprinted over from a cluster of fifth-years huddled by the screen when he'd caught sight of her. Strong and narrow as a needle, Finn had been a track star at Adsum Academy. Now he choked on his breath, wheezing as he discreetly clasped a glossy inhaler to his lips, fighting to pull oxygen into his inflamed airways. Without the aid of his Quest Bot, his severe asthma had returned. He wasn't supposed to run with his chronic condition, but Jade pretended not to notice, repeating her question. "How are we faring?"

Finn pulled a face. "Zero for thirty so far." Pocketing his inhaler, he handed Jade a stack of unopened letters. "On more than one account."

Jade reached for the heap, tucking it beneath her arm before either Crys or Ani could get a good look at the name and address scrawled across the top envelope. She was too slow.

"*Maxen Yates?*" Ani exclaimed. "So you send handwritten letters to a billion-heir in prison, but you could barely text your poor friend in the ICU?"

This time, Crys didn't spring to Jade's defense.

"They aren't letters, per se," Jade answered hotly. "They're various coded strategies. Plans of attack to get him out of San Quentin. He needs something to keep his spirits up, keep his mind busy . . ." She trailed off, catching the tense glances passing between Crys, Ani, and Rhett. Even Finn looked distressed.

They thought Maxen was lost to them—physically, of course, he was wrongfully locked in a cell for Poppy's murder, but mentally as well. Now that he lacked the Quest Bot that effectively cured his childhood schizophrenia, they were in the dark as to the current state of Maxen's mind. He had lawyers from Quest—the family empire now controlled by Palmer, the brother who tried to run him off a cliff—and crooked prison guards to watch over him, which meant there was slim chance Maxen was receiving any sort of medication or therapy to help control his disorder. He was likely isolated in a padded room, unable to interpret her coded letters, even if he did have the mind to.

Rhett cleared his throat, rubbing the sharp bones of his cervical vertebrae. Jade wondered if he could feel the cracks where his neck had snapped all those years ago when he'd fallen from a garden wall while snooping on Yates. "I've learned through my back channels," Rhett finally muttered, "that Maxen has been transferred."

"Topple it all," Jade cursed, a bit louder than she'd intended. She expected Crys to balk at her growing concern for her adoptive brother, but Crys just kept her impassive gaze leveled on the screen that now bore Damon Yates's missing face. "Tell me you know where they moved Maxen," she pressed Rhett. She wouldn't put it past Hariri or Palmer to relocate Maxen anywhere from a graveyard to the moon.

"Pelican Bay."

The pit of Jade's stomach twisted. Pelican Bay was a supermax prison that housed the state's most violent offenders in its bleak, X-shaped structure. Why had Maxen been transferred? Why now? Were the Conservators playing their next move?

Rfa.

And things just kept piling on.

"Wait, what's with the traps?" Ani asked as Eli Jones and Cole Riggs strode toward them, holding busted animal cages. She flashed a wry smile. "I thought we already worked out that Crys was one of us and didn't need restraints? Or did I miss something while I was in a coma?"

Cole set a damaged cage at his feet, which were wrapped in ocean-blue silk slippers. "Well, we for sure missed *you*." He pulled Ani into a side hug, avoiding the bandage that peeked below her half shirt. His voice lowered to a playful whisper. "Our sibs are getting your surprise party ready, I'm not supposed to tell you . . ."

Cole's coffee-colored curls caught on his long lashes, dancing with every blink. His smile had a stimulating effect on almost everyone in his orbit, though it seemed to make Crys jittery. She looked away. Jade thought the two would've revived their courtship by now, shacked up in one of the guest bedrooms. But for the past weeks, Crys had slept beside Jade on a pallet on the living room floor. It reminded Jade of the pre-quake days, before LA and their whole world were shaken apart and rebuilt, when as children they'd create blanket forts on the floorboards of their parents' motor home, pretending to live in a high-tech mansion that shielded them from the dangerous outside world.

"Welcome back, sis," Eli said to Ani, slamming his cage against the tile, the metal ringing like an urgent alarm. *Rfa. Rfa.* His large frame was outfitted in a knee-length lab coat, a medley of whites and creamy pearls with a bone-notch lapel of his own design. Only a month ago, Eli had been a premier fighter in the underground rings, doing what he could to help his crew survive. Now he'd taken his fight to the labs, becoming Hema Devi's right-hand man in the battle for the cure. Both he and Cole were infected with the nano reform, like a grenade hidden in their bloodstream. Everyone pretended it wasn't there. No one spoke of it. But Jade could hear the nanobomb ticking.

"I checked all my traps this morning," Eli said, his face slack with exhaustion. "Every one of them was trashed."

Jade shot Crys a look. "The western valley traps were sabotaged, too."

"But there are still the rabbits at the lab, right?" Crys asked. "Last I counted we had, what, a hundred? That should be more than enough."

"About that . . ." Eli snarled, spinning on his heel. "The reason for the red alert." Without another word, he marched for Hema's laboratory, tucked away in the east wing of the ranch house.

Rhett whistled when the lab door slid open at the swipe of Eli's thumbprint. "How did Hema swing *this*?"

It was no Asclepius, the world-class laboratory below Yates's Castle in the Air that Crys had described to Jade, but the repurposed three-car garage sure beat the tiny basement lab Hema had made when they were living like a hermit in NYC. "The ranch, the lab, it's all courtesy of one of Hema's Brainious clients," Jade explained. "The dad owed a favor after Hema's Smart Bot juices got his two Fortunate kids admitted into their Ivy League school of choice."

"Mastermind," Rhett admired, a smile dangling on the corners of his lips.

"Let's hope," Eli whispered, sighing as he hastily led them around a block of biosafety cabinets. He stopped, gesturing to the wall where the stainless-steel cages were kept.

All of them were empty.

The AI clean-bot that the fifth-years had taken from Adsum powered on and wheeled toward Eli. It cleared its robotic throat and recited a proclamation from the Adsum sibs. "Just as it was wrong for Damon Yates to use *us*, his students, as test subjects for his own experiments without our consent, it is immoral for us to continue to stand idle as you do the same to innocent rabbits. They, too, deserve autonomy."

Swallow the Earth whole, Jade cursed. So the vandalized traps were a protest. She understood their good intentions, admired the fifth-years' dogged humanity. But so far, no rabbits had died. Jade liked to think of the rabbits as noble foot soldiers in the war that the Conservators had waged against the Unfortunates. Each animal was "challenging" the nano reform Hema injected into their bodies, the front lines in the fight to find a cure. The true side effects of the nano reform bots were still unknown: Was it more than just an engineered fear of a simple symbol driving the unhoused out of their cities? Or was there a second phase to Hariri's grand plan? How many more people would end up dead like their foster sisters Khari and Zoe?

Any delay in discovering the cure meant potentially thousands more displaced Unfortunates, kind and tenacious people *terrified* and kicked out of their own homes. Banished from the cities that made and shaped them. People like Cole and Eli.

How could such a big man cower from such a small symbol? Jade thought of Eli, not for the first time.

Eli growled. "Cole, get this mutinous *thing* away from me before I melt it down to bullets."

As if on command, the clean-bot raced out of the lab, rolling right over Cole's toes.

"Cole, your foot," Crys exclaimed, jumping to Cole's side with a burst of energy Jade hadn't seen for weeks. Bloody track marks cut into his right foot, deep enough to require stitches.

"You noticed," Cole said, smiling down at his silk slippers. "They're just like the ones we used to wear at Adsum." When he peered down, he blinked, as if mystified by the sight of his lacerated toes. He hadn't even flinched.

Curious, Jade thought.

"Let's go and see Hema," Rhett offered Cole, using his fingers to smarten up his scruffy beard. "They'll get you squared away."

"I'm fine," Cole replied, even as blood soaked his slipper. "Honestly, I don't even feel it."

More than curious. Was he experiencing some type of side effect from the nano reform?

"Can't we just buy more rabbits from a pet store or something?" Ani asked, a bit breathless as she clutched her bandage.

"It's not that simple," Crys said. "We've already purchased enough within a hundred-mile radius to be flagged by every major animal rights organization. That's why we're catching them here on the ranch."

"We'll just have to buy more traps and keep a careful eye on them," Rhett said. "Back on my family's farm in Kansas, we had an influx of cottontails one year. I could be of use."

And how long will all that take? Jade thought. They needed help *right now.* In this moment, Jade understood more than ever why Maxen had given himself up to the navy suits, sacrificing himself for the good of his Adsum family.

When you think of me, think of me like this, he'd asked her.

And she did. Every day.

They found Hema hunched over a lab table, absorbed in their work. Their short black hair was unkempt, the patchwork lab coat that Eli had made for them disheveled. Jade watched as Hema huffed and rubbed their forehead before deftly placing a glass vial onto a white tray the size of a personal pizza box.

"Is that your latest batch of attack bots for the nano reform?" Jade asked. So far, none of Hema's engineered nanobots had been able to locate and disable the nano reform swimming around in the rabbits' brains. Fifty-one rabbits, fifty-one different formulas, fifty-one amygdalae going haywire when three red slash marks were placed in front of the rabbits' beady eyes.

Hema didn't look up. "It is. Goddess knows when I'll be able to administer them."

"How about right now?" Jade snatched one of the vials with the speed of a pickpocket.

"The attack bot would be wasted on you," Hema sighed. "You aren't infected."

"Oh, but I will be," Jade said, plucking a piece of chewing gum from her inner pocket.

Crys understood her latest stunt immediately. "Topple it all, Jade, is that what I think it is?"

The Conservators had expanded the market for laced goods, moving beyond handmade quiches to common junk food and chewing gum. Jade had discovered and carried this spiked pack of gum since her last expedition to the outskirts of LA in search of Yates.

"Don't," Crys demanded.

"*Shit*," Hema yelled, slapping their hands on the steel table, making the glass vials tremble. "I made it unequivocally clear that I would have *no* human test subjects."

Jade grinned. "Nothing I haven't been before." She held the stick of gum to her lips.

All shouted their protests, but Crys the loudest.

Eli was the only one to whisper encouragement. *"Do it."* Although he and Cole were infected with the nano reform, they had both declined to volunteer as test subjects for fear of losing their Quest Bots, which staved off Eli's paraplegia and Cole's major depression.

Do it, the lost scapegrace in Jade echoed.

A savage, desperate recklessness quickened her blood. She didn't even try to rein it in.

Crys must have seen a flicker of the counterfeit boldness in Jade's eyes. "Jade, if you do this, I will leave you."

That gave Jade pause. Would Crys really abandon her when she most needed her sister? *Leave before you're left,* the orphan in Jade answered coldly. She shoved the gum into her mouth and smacked loudly before swallowing it whole.

Hema spoke with quiet fury, a finger pressing into Jade's chest. "Even if this foolish exploit of yours works, I want you out of my laboratory and off my ranch by morning." Jade had been thrown out of plenty of homes in her lifetime, but somehow this one stung the most.

She downed Hema's untested attack bot formula. No going back now. "Lucky number fifty-two."

Before the liquid had even made it past Jade's throat, Crys was halfway to the door. "I won't," she yelled. "I won't stay and watch you try to get yourself killed all over again."

"I'm trying to help *save* us," Jade snapped back. Her fingers itched for In Extremis. *At the point of death.* She'd been there, conquered that. She'd do it again.

"Keep deluding yourself," Crys fumed. "I hope you find what you're looking for." Her eyes were dark slits, her hands fidgeting with the pouch where she kept her fear fragrance. "I thought it was me." She stormed out of sight.

And out of Jade's mind.

Act now, feel later, Jade goaded herself onward. "Ani, if you'd be so kind as to draw up the Conservators' symbol." She knew Ani always kept acrylic pens on her, along with her pocket knives. Ani nodded, clearly unwilling to challenge Jade's decisions a second time when it came to bots and her own body.

With a deep, grounding breath, Jade prepared to face three red slash marks, so powerful they could clear out entire cities and upend millions of Unfortunate lives by stripping people down to a single emotion: inescapable fear.

She lifted her chin. "Now, let's see what all the fuss has been about."

Two

Crys's patience was waning. She stood in a parking lot beside Cole and Eli, a quarter mile outside the Coachella Music Festival's gates. The tips of her fingers strummed a zipper on the insulated cooler bag she wore strapped across her chest as she stared out at the seventy-eight acres of sun-drenched desert cluttered with palm trees and boho chic festival goers. The iconic music event had been pushed to early autumn after the 2040 Quake delayed the customary spring dates, an alteration that still riled the pre-quake generation. *Tradition gives us our only sense of permanence,* they grumbled.

Shaking fools, Crys thought, biting on fingernails already gnawed to the quick. *There's no permanence in this life; 2040 should have taught them that. Should have taught* me.

Or *Crystal Yates*, at least.

Crys flicked her eyes to the impossibly high mountain peaks looming beyond the stages. Back in LA, she had called such a place home. Millions had looked up to her. Wanted to *be* her. If they saw her now, with her grimy, unmade face, in her soiled secondhand clothes, they would only pity her fall. Was she a Fortunate? An Unfortunate? Crys was neither. Crys was both.

Pity. It was why Cole and Eli had joined her on her first venture outside the ranch. Why they said nothing of the insulated bag at her chest, though there was little doubt they'd known where—and *who*—she'd stolen it from, and suspected what was within. *How desperate my act must seem to them,* Crys thought. Their presence at her side was a charity.

Billion-heir to beggar in a matter of weeks, Crys thought, before a heart-stopping scream erupted from her memory, jolting her out of her own self-pity.

The harrowing sound of Jade's fear incursion had followed Crys all the way to the Coachella Valley.

Hema's latest attack bot formula had failed. Jade was now willingly infected with the nano reform, her mind occupied by an engineered intruder, weaponized to make her afraid. To compel her to flee, to feel unsafe, unwanted. Exactly how Crys felt when Jade placed the contaminated chewing gum into her mouth, choosing another reckless stunt over the bond they'd worked so hard to restore. *I'm trying to save us,* Jade had proclaimed.

"More like save your scapegrace reputation," Crys whispered now, drowning out her memory of Jade's wild screams echoing from the lab.

Crys refused to stay and watch Jade tremble, a terrified cry ripping from her throat as her eyes locked on to the Conservators' symbol, her face a perfect mirror to Crys's own when she herself had been trapped inside a fear incursion of Damon Yates's making.

Swallowing the nano reform, Jade had thrown herself in the spotlight and, somehow, garnered every Exile's admiration. Well, Crys had her own exploits in mind. A way to steal Jade's thunder, to make the others see Crys in a new high-voltage light.

She was going to track down Yates, drag him back, and make him answer for what he'd done. To the Adsum sibs, to Hema. To *her.* *Crys Moore.*

"This music could cause a toothache," Eli said, popping a pair of headphones out from his ears. "But you look like you could use a pick-me-up."

"You're one to talk," Crys huffed.

Eli was back in his streetwear, his broad shoulders hunched, the fight in his amber eyes dulled now that Hema had banned him from the laboratory alongside Jade. "Here," he insisted, "take my buds, listen in. Maybe join Cole? Bust out that Argentine tango you two learned for our fourth-year awards gala?" His mouth curved into an ironic smile. *It takes two to tango.* He wanted Crys and Cole to face each other. Own up to their part in the silence, the strained distance that stretched between them, wide as the Texas countryside.

Cole was dancing alone, the concert pumping through his high-tech earbuds. His hips swayed to a beat specially calibrated for his unique "hearing fingerprint." Crys couldn't help but smile. Instead of cramping his style, the bulky ortho-boot Hema had strapped onto his injured foot to protect his stitches somehow enhanced his spry, carefree movement.

In the early Adsum days, she and Cole used to share earbuds. Close their eyes and lie on the grass, her head tucked into his shoulder. Grounding themselves in the same rhythm, drowning out the rest of the world until it was just the two of them, connected. In sync, riding the same sound wave. Now, Cole was happily riding solo: his injury, the nano reform in his bloodstream, the lack of Crys at his side—none of it could kill his vibe.

Crys's smile suddenly vanished. She snapped her neck toward the sky as two dozen people-shaped objects dropped from the heavens. Her lips twisted in distaste. "Space divers."

"They jumped from a Quest-made spacecraft," Eli said, shoving in an earbud. Crys took the other. "I'd put money on it."

Cole's body stilled, his gaze locked on the sky. The space divers' helmets shimmered like falling stars, bulky suits and gyroscopic boots moving with the synchronized grace of a flock as they whirled and weaved around two central figures in perfect time with the beat pulsing from Crys's earbud.

With great effort, she kept her eyes from straying, searching for the satellites that memorialized their two Adsum sibs. She wondered if Cole and Eli felt the same struggle. Like them, Zoe and Khari had been victims of the Conservators' nano reform. Only their bots had proven fatal.

That would not be Cole's or Eli's fate, Crys told herself, even as her blood froze. A male's voice, polished and clipped, spoke above the music in her earbud. She knew that voice. It came from one of the two divers at the core of the extravagant performance. They'd opened their parachutes, descending closer to the main stage on the far side of the valley. He was making an introduction, but whatever he said was buried beneath the threats she'd last spat at him. *You better hope you never see my face again.*

"No." Cole gaped. "Is that . . ."

Crys unholstered her phone, tapped the camera app, and zoomed in with binocular-quality clarity on the space diver in the pressurized silver suit. Her breath catching, she ripped out her earbud, just as the biggest rock star in the world belted her first note, still airborne and flipping in her harness like a trapeze artist, beside the man Crys had once called *brother.*

"Palmer Yates," she seethed. The eldest son of Gen 1, from Yates's first marriage.

Eli squinted at her phone's screen, gripping the spot where a bullet from Palmer's gun had grazed his shoulder. "What's he even doing here? Trying to out-dare *Jade?*"

Crys's skin prickled. *Can I never escape her?*

"Palmer's just doing a bit of grandstanding," Cole said, raking a rogue curl from his eyes. "Hoping his dive through the stratosphere will snatch the media's attention from Maxen and their MIA father. But we're not going to let the new CEO of Quest sidetrack us from recovering the *old* one . . . right?"

Neither Eli nor Crys answered. Absently, her fingers slipped to the magnetic pouch wrapped around her belt loops. She itched to hold the glass perfume vials, to count them—estimate how many milligrams of her fragrance remained, how many sprays.

How much power. How much fear.

With a glazed numbness, Crys watched Palmer's parachute disappear behind the massive metal ring of the festival's famous Ferris wheel. In her pitiable isolation at the ranch, Crys had realized she'd wasted most of her life seeking love, from strangers, the internet, her guardians, her kin. But seeking admiration and applause was also a kind of servitude. She knew that now. There was another path to influence and recognition, and she held it in her hand.

"It's a shame, isn't it?" she lamented out loud. "That my late adoptive brother didn't burn alive during atmospheric reentry?"

Eli laughed. Cole sighed.

"Palmer was never going to go out in a blaze of glory," Sage Parker's matter-of-fact voice shouted behind them. "The Quest spacecraft was never even in orbit."

A black six-seater golf cart pulled up, quiet as a shadow in the late morning sun. Behind the wheel, Wily Lee grinned at Sage in the passenger seat, an unopened heart-shaped box gripped tight in her lap. "See," he said, "you *can* pull random facts from that big brain of yours even without that overhyped Quest Bot."

"Condescend to me again," Sage threatened, holding up the box of sweets with an equally sweet smile, "and I'll shove the chocolates that you *refuse* to eat down your throat."

"Let's keep our foreplay to the bedroom," Wily jested, his grin widening even as his jaw tensed. He side-eyed the tacky box as if it housed a flash grenade.

"Are you two . . . dating?" Crys asked. She knew that Wily, fearful he'd gain back the weight he'd come to Adsum with, had practically quit eating since he lost the Quest Bot that granted him high metabolism. The Exiles had been attempting to ply him with food at every turn. But judging by the romantic air that clung to him and Sage like one of Crystal's perfumes, this struck her as something more. How had she missed this development?

Wily's scarred brow shot upward. "What? It's not weird; we're not blood-related. We might be a bit *unconventional*, as some of the other sibs put it—"

"But you and Cole did it," Sage insisted. "*Are* doing it. Whatever your status is." Her long, acrylic nails rapped against a pale thigh under her torn trousers, her gray eyes rimmed red, like a Soot junkie hankering for her next fix.

"Sage," Cole said delicately, "I'd never be so moronic as to say you look tired, but . . . when's the last time you slept?" Empathy bloomed across his face. Cole knew firsthand the struggle that came with functioning without the support of a mind-enhancing bot.

"Between memory training," Wily defended, "and searching for a needle in a quakestack, Sage hasn't had even time to blink." He turned to Crys, his mischievous gaze like a microscope on her overgrown curls, the shabby sweatsuit that had become her grown-up version of a security blanket. "What's your excuse? At least Sage has *actual* pants on."

Had Crys really let herself go that badly? She hadn't looked in a mirror in weeks. *Old habits die hard,* she could hear Jade quip.

For the past week, Wily and Sage had been out foraging the fringes of LA for clues of Yates's whereabouts. They were to alert the Exiles with a group *rfa* if they found any hot tips, but Crys had gotten to them first. She'd made a deal with the crafty pair to give her a "first look" at any leads, a part of her knowing even then that she'd need a fail-safe with her sister. Jade was now in the dark about this rendezvous, and about whatever move Crys would make next.

Sage perked up as she noticed the cooler bag at Crys's chest. "Those for me?"

Crys hesitated before moving for the golf cart, debating whether it was right to supply Sage with a quick fix to her addiction for greater brainpower. *Sage doesn't want pity,* Crys thought. *She wants respect.*

30

"The Smart Bots are yours if you give me your end of the deal," she said, yanking the thick strap of the insulated bag over her head. Crys's neck jerked to the side, her scalp searing. One of her knotted curls was caught in the zipper. She tugged and ripped at the tangled mess, to no avail. *What a piteous sight I must be.*

Then Cole's hands were in her hair. His calloused fingers brushed hers before he pulled away.

"Sorry," he mumbled, shuffling back. He stuffed his hands into the deep pockets of his shirt. "I didn't mean to touch you."

Why would Cole apologize for that? Does he think he gave me the wrong idea?

Crys shook her head free and held the bag out to Sage, who hastily snatched it, slinging the straps across her curvy waist. Her restraint surprised Crys, who had expected Sage to rip out the Brainious juices and down every bottle immediately, desperate for an instant intelligence boost. What was holding her back?

Eli eyed the exchange warily. "I just hope you're still smart enough to know what you're doing."

Sage shrugged, smoothing back her auburn locks. "A bottled redhead and a bottled genius, what's the difference, really?"

Wily reached for her hand, their pinkies interlocking. For a fleeting second, Crys wished for Cole's reassuring touch, the soft stroke of his fingertips vibrating like lightning against her palm. *Don't go dark,* he used to tell her. *Don't go quiet.* Crys scraped the sensory memory away with what was left of her chewed nails. Lately, she had come to embrace the silence. The dark.

"Get in," Wily shouted, shaking Crys out of her reverie. "And we'll take you to him."

Cole bent his long neck toward the empty sky, as if the "him" that Wily referred to could drop from the stratosphere at any moment. "Yates is *here*?" For all they knew, Yates *was* hiding among the stars. It seemed the Exiles had looked for him everywhere else.

"Well, here-*ish*," Wily amended.

Cole and Eli relaxed into the golf cart's plush second-row seats. Crys climbed onto the back bench and gripped the roof, preferring to stand and feel the wind on her flushed face. She wanted to be the first to see her one-time father, her *savior*, her former controller.

"We just need to get past a few initial gatekeepers," Sage said.

Wily punted the box of sweets onto the grassy lot, and the wheels crushed the heart-shaped cardboard as they sped away from the festival toward the freeway.

They zipped past gated suburban neighborhoods and several exclusive golf courses, which Crys suspected were the source of their top-of-the-line transport, before turning into the parking lot of a palm-tree farm that showcased a giant knight holding a shield that read Shields Date Garden.

"You've got to be kidding me," Eli scoffed. "So I really am a fifth wheel."

"Date as in the stone fruit," Wily replied, parking the cart beside a stocky date palm, its large feather-shaped leaves providing little cover from the sun. "This place is known for its date *shakes*."

Cole laughed. "There he is, thinking with his stomach again."

"Fat chance," Wily countered. "Do you know how many calories are in one of those things? Diabetes in a cup."

"Four o'clock," Crys warned, staring at the two bedraggled strangers who emerged from the thick trunks of palms, heading straight for the golf cart.

"This is our guy," Sage said. She stepped out with Wily. "My end of the deal."

Crys shook her head, jumping to the pavement, heat rising up her neck. "I asked for Yates. If this is some trick—"

"Just hear the guy out," Wily said, cutting her off.

Eli and Cole exploded from the cart. Eli held a hand up to the strangers. "That's close enough."

The taller one tossed a shawl over his angular shoulders, the tattered linen reaching the ends of his threadbare, high-water pants. "*Five* Exiles in one place," the man said, smiling. "I consider myself fortunate."

Crys didn't recognize the face, but she knew the voice: sweet, yet potent, like a craft whiskey, intoxicating millions of listeners every week, Crys included, reluctantly. Nolan Ortiz, the famous podcaster, was *rich*, so why was he wearing rags?

"I'm here to be of guidance." Nolan spoke slowly, seeming to expect Crys to savor his words. "There's no need to be afraid."

Crys spit out a laugh. "It would take *much* more than a scandal-monger to scare me."

Nolan turned to the slender, tattooed woman that Crys guessed to be his co-host. "Is that what the kids are calling podcasters these days?"

Eli stepped forward, towering over an unperturbed Nolan. "Who you calling kid, old man?"

The only thing old about Nolan Ortiz were his eyes. There was an ancientness to them, a finely aged shrewdness that made Crys want to look away, but she held his gaze as he sidestepped Eli and moved toward her, his gait straight-backed, his movements lithe and deliberate. Relics of his days as a dancer, before his body wore out, his livelihood stripped down to his voice. The voice of the biggest scandal in generations. The voice of *The Adsum Atrocity*.

He's a has-been, Crys thought cruelly, *an amateur*. Who cared if he had the number one true-crime podcast in the world?

For weeks, tens of millions had been subscribing to Nolan's investigations on the lives and deaths of Questers. His listeners wanted dirt and blood, and Nolan would gladly be their supplier.

Crys had always loathed him. He profited from tragedy. He rose while others fell.

"If I earned a commission every time my name spilled from your lips," Crys said, "I'd still be a billion-heir."

The co-host's mouth dropped open. "It's true then?" the woman probed. "You've lost out on your adoptive family's fortune?"

Fortunes change, Crys mused, glowering at the woman. She jammed all her emotions into one hard frown. This pitiless duo would get nothing from Crys. She was here to *get* answers, not give them.

Nolan moved in on Cole, who'd returned to the back seat of the golf cart. "What about you, Cole Riggs? Has Crys lost *you*, too?" He scanned Cole's bright, open face, which betrayed no hint of longing or regret, before zeroing in on Cole's boot. "Oh dear, I bet there's a story behind *that*—"

Eli lunged between Nolan and Cole, raising balled fists. "Nobody talk to this prying piranha. I bet my most valuable shirt he's miked."

To Nolan's credit, he didn't flinch. "Eli Jones. Known to many as 'the Knockout.' Not only for your striking looks, which, after meeting you in person" he threw a disappointed glance to Crys—"I'll be more than happy to confirm for my listeners, but also for your ability to render every opponent unconscious in LA's underground fighting rings." Nolan took a step back. "You've been a ghost in the rings of late. Care to share what you've been up to?"

"Let's chat about what *you've* been up to," Eli growled, rubbing the deep brown skin of his unblemished knuckles. "You leaked Khari's burial site. Our sib's final resting place is a tourist trap now, thanks to you."

Crys remembered the morning *that* particular episode dropped. Nolan had roamed the rolling hills of the Forest Lawn cemetery, dissecting in gruesome, fabricated detail *how* and *why* an Unfortunate Exile wound up dead and entombed inside a secret niche.

It was lucky that Ani, Khari's still-grieving ex, wasn't present for this meeting. No doubt she'd seen the viral videos, mobs of sightseers desecrating the once peaceful crypts. Many more threats and knives would be added to the flash of steel Crys saw peeking from pockets and fists around her. Even Wily clasped his pen blade. A precaution in case of an outside ambush, or a measure to protect the podcaster from a violent protest within the ranks?

Nolan raised his arms, showing his smooth, flat palms. *Empty hands, open minds.* Had he learned this street greeting from his study of the Exiles, or had Sage and Wily offered this truce sign, knowing Nolan would hit trouble?

"Khari's fate should not be hidden away," he said with his strange, languid urgency. "Now instead of collecting dust like the thousands of dead girls like her, Khari's grave collects the flowers of mourners demanding to know what happened to her . . . and what *is* happening to each of *you.*"

How much did this investigator, this burglar of privacy, already know? In his podcast, there'd been no mention of Quest Bots, Conservators, or conspiracies as to how LA's elected officials were managing, block by block, to rid the city of its chronic homeless epidemic. What—and *why*—was he withholding?

"It's charming you think being a stalker is a form of public service," Crys mocked with a saccharine smile. "But I won't be giving you material to sensationalize for your next episode. I won't share our lives—the *atrocities* we've faced—for strangers' entertainment."

"Then this will certainly be a dilemma for you," Nolan mused. "Since I know how zealously you must be searching for your father."

Crys kept her face neutral. Indecipherable. *I have no living father.*

Nolan narrowed those intoxicating eyes of his. "I also know of Damon's dementia, how he's long kept hidden his early-onset Alzheimer's disease. *And,* what must be a relief to you, I'm sure . . . I know where he's mislaid himself."

Crys held Nolan's gaze for several long beats. She felt dizzy, euphoric. Was Yates truly still alive? Had Nolan really uncovered him?

I'll find you, I'll find you, Jade had repeated in her sleep, so confident, so sure. Crys swayed, drunk on the possibility that she'd get there first.

"Skip to the big idea," Sage pressed, gesturing toward a line of RVs that had turned off the freeway's access lane and were now heading for the gardens. "The charity shuttles are on time."

Wily had grown distracted, analyzing his face and pinching at his swollen cheeks in the cart's side-view mirror, but now he snapped his head to the caravan, his scarred brow lifted in delight. "The scandal-monger has told a truth for once." He grabbed Sage by the shoulders and kissed her, hard. "I never doubted that gorgeous mind of yours for a second."

Sage sat primly, a satisfied pink creeping up her alabaster cheeks. "Episode five, minute fifty-four. Nolan all but told us he'd discovered where Yates was hiding."

Eli screwed up his face. *"What?"*

Sage rolled her eyes. "Was no one else listening?" She flicked a furtive glance at the red ink scribbled across her wrist—Sage hadn't memorized it, Crys noted—and read aloud. "The future for the orphans was a *desert*, but the *winds* of change were coming. Yates had to *work* for forgiveness. But would any of his children *listen?*"

Crys squinted at the four driverless class-C motor homes that pulled to a halt along the curb beside them. She read the decal: **GOLDEN STATE WORKFORCE SERVICES**. Had Nolan lured them to some kind of pickup spot for a state-run jobs program?

"You're looking at your tax dollars in action," Nolan explained. "California claims one of the largest public-employment service operations in the world."

Clumps of men—grungy and shifty eyed—began to emerge from the scant patches of shade, hurrying toward the newly arrived motor homes. They shouted and shoved one another, trying to pack into the open doors.

"These government-sponsored RVs give Unfortunates a place to reside while traveling from place to place, chasing wherever work leads them. Mostly menial and seasonal farm labor. But not for our enigmatic Damon," Nolan teased with a sly smirk.

"Where is he?" Crys pressed. She stepped forward, gripping Nolan's tattered shawl.

"My price is access," Nolan said, peering down at her. "My co-host and I will accompany the Exiles on your search, and you will allow us to continue our undercover journalism without hindrance or sabotage."

"Explains the getup," Eli sneered, scrutinizing the podcasters' terribly mismatched clothes. "Just so you know, we might be strapped for cash, but that doesn't mean our sense of style is broke."

Crys let go of Nolan and nodded.

"I'll need a verbal confirmation," the co-host insisted.

Were they recording this exchange? It didn't matter, Crys told herself. The only important thing right now was finding Yates, whatever the cost.

"I agree to your price," Crys said. One by one, the others repeated the agreement. Only Cole was silent. *Nothing new there.*

Nolan's eyes glimmered. "There are warehouses all over this valley," he revealed. "Factories for assembling wind turbines. There are rumors—"

"Just rumors?" Cole interjected.

"Son, I make a killing off rumors," Nolan scoffed.

"I'm no one's son," Cole fired back, without heat.

Nolan continued, unfazed. "I've learned that a man known as the twins' guardian, a man considered to be a savior, is working as a shift leader in the valley's biggest turbine factory. It appears that even lying low, Damon can't help but rise above his fellow man."

Savior. Guardian. Once more, Crys's head swam, her heart racing with hope.

It was *him.*

"We better get a move on," Wily urged. "Our new digs—for today, anyway—are filling up quick."

Sage checked to make sure the Smart Bots were secure around her waist and made off with Wily and Eli as Nolan and his co-host disappeared through the entrance of the last motor home.

"I don't like this," Cole said, rising from the golf cart. He eyed a cluster of brutish men as they emerged from the stocky palms, sprinting in a rough-and-tumble free-for-all for the overcrowded RVs. "We should do reconnaissance. Find our own way into the warehouse."

"I thought that Quest Bot of yours was meant to keep you happy," Crys threw at him, "not *tame*." She didn't know why she'd said it. Maybe to see if he could still *feel*. Still *hurt*. She glanced at the thick boot that hid his wound. He hadn't even winced. *It's like he feels nothing at all.*

"You two, hurry and get in here!" Eli shouted, standing guard at the last RV's door.

More desperate men had arrived. Crys saw metal glinting at their hips.

"They have guns," Cole warned.

Crys closed a fist over her glass vials. "And I have my own weapon."

What are you going to do, Jade's voice taunted her, *make the whole world fear you?*

Maybe, Crys shot back. She made it halfway to the RV door before Cole spoke again.

"Crys," he called, his voice resigned. "You told me the night you first used your fear fragrance that you were going to make your own path." He paused, reaching for her. To grab hold of her vials? Her hand? He dropped his arm. "I'm sorry, but I don't think I can follow you down it anymore."

She searched his face for traces of anguish. Resentment. Anger.

Instead, she saw patience, an imperturbable tranquility that made her want to scream. She thumbed the fresh nail marks in her palm to keep her voice steady. "Do you not trust me?"

If it was Jade here instead, would he join her?

Cole stared down at his feet. "I don't trust myself."

Crys strode into the RV, and as it began to pull away, Cole didn't move to follow.

THREE

Jade stepped out of Cambridge's HyperQuest portal, careful to remember that she'd just entered a hotbed of Conservator activity. She couldn't lose track of her marks, but she couldn't chance spotting their symbols, which no doubt saturated the ads and artwork on the city's buildings, buses, and sidewalks. It was a delicate balance, an intricate dance.

This isn't a safe place. This isn't a safe place.

Don't get lost in a fear incursion, Jade willed herself. *Don't scream.*

She fell into a memory, its terror still raw, her muscles still sore from the mental fight to stand her ground against the three slashes. Three simple lines that could—did—bring her down. Sent her crying, flying across Hema's lab, where she collided with a concrete pillar and dropped unconscious. She'd come to drenched in shame.

Crys had been terrorized at the sight of her own face, her fear incursions virtually inescapable. Yet she'd adapted, rallied. If she could survive, *thrive*, in all those years as a test subject, then Jade could spend a few hours in Massachusetts.

Jade was now doing damage control, a way for her to rebuild her confidence. Jolt her daring back into action, like she'd failed to do at the ranch.

She adjusted the brim of her suede bucket hat, confident, at least, that she hadn't been recognized or reported, either by the mass of students and tourists or, most importantly, by Ani and Rhett, who were barely identifiable themselves. Ani wore oversize shades, her thick black hair freed from its usual whip of a ponytail, glossy tresses bouncing at her waist above hidden knives. Rhett had traded his favored patterned suit for a trucker hat and patchwork denim, a lethal enforcer in farmer's clothing.

They were only ten paces ahead.

Hema may have kicked Jade out of their lab, but she'd refused to be shut out of *all* investigations. She wouldn't be sidelined from Hema's latest plans. While they thought Jade had been cowed, off licking her wounds and preoccupied by Crys's desertion—*the first time Crys leaves the ranch, and it's to leave* me?—Jade had actually been sharp-eyed and suspicious, keeping tabs on the remaining Exiles. She hadn't stopped Eli or Cole when they'd set off with Crys, grateful that whatever her sister was up to, she wouldn't be alone. But when Jade spied Ani and Rhett speeding from the ranch in the pickup, she couldn't help but tag along.

Jade wasn't privy to the exact details of their afternoon field trip, but she had her guesses. Why else would the pair turn off the paved path that rimmed the Charles River and trek toward the heart of MIT's campus?

Hema wanted assistance. A helping hand. *And mind.* But MIT was the most prestigious science university in the world—it wouldn't team with a blacklisted genius, even if it *was* one of Hema's alma maters. The Exiles' garage experiment was a rogue clinical trial, unsanctioned and floundering, using nanotech that wasn't even on the path to FDA approval. They were bleeding money and no closer to locating Yates, who had created this ever-expanding mess they were struggling to reengineer their way out of. It was obvious why Hema felt it time to bring in new blood.

Yet what professor would believe that some future-tech, both life-saving and society-destroying, was currently circulating through the unhoused population? The scientific community would be forced to accept that the miraculous "cleanup" of cities nationwide was a dirty secret. That it wasn't a natural remedy, but an engineered solution. Nanotech run rampant.

The genie had left the bottle, and Hema needed help stuffing it back in. No professor would come willingly.

They would have to be coerced. Stolen.

And everyone thought I *made poor decisions,* Jade thought curtly, clenching her agile fingers. *She* had the flair for thievery, a talent both Ani and Rhett should have utilized.

Suddenly her veins felt like lightning, her nerves fried. *Leave,* her mind screamed at her. The fear symbol. On the wooden deck of a young woman's skateboard.

Jade stumbled back, retreating three steps in wide-eyed panic. But the bold design peeking out from beneath the skater's right sneaker wasn't three slashes, but two fingers. "It's a peace sign," she laughed bitterly.

You're paranoid. Susceptible, she chastised herself. *This is what the Conservators want.*

Stop. Living. In. Fear.

She crushed her weakness in her fist. *Body over mind, body over mind.* Sharper, steadier, she looked up to find that Ani and Rhett had sauntered onto Killian Court, a large patch of lush grass that stretched in front of Building 10. Jade remembered a campus tour Poppy had organized when Jade was still at the academy, and she calculated they'd be heading straight for Building 46, the Department of Brain and Cognitive Sciences.

So why did Ani plop down on a bench, her face lazily turned up to the sun? And why had Rhett parted from her, leaning against a **NERD XING** sign ten yards ahead?

Jade stalked closer, grumbling as she passed a pack of mini robotic dogs racing through an intricate obstacle course that a group of students had set up on the lawn. The things were creepy but somehow cute in their limber, metal uncanniness. One of them sprang into a backflip after successfully maneuvering through a tunnel and a series of weave poles, its human controller whooping in triumph. "My algorithm *destroyed* you bitches."

That's how you accelerate research, Jade mused. *Competition.*

Had that driven Jade to take the nano reform? To volunteer as an experiment? To stalk around a campus with ridiculously high IQs and massive bank accounts, asking to be caught?

Competition.

Crys had always called Jade a show-off. But was it not obvious? Their entire lives were a contest, a rivalry. A challenge to be seen. Crys had always had all the firsts: first born, first steps, first to fall in love.

Well, I'll be the first to bring back something useful for the cure, Jade vowed.

She spotted a large sculpture of a disjointed bronze figure near Ani's bench. Jade had never found much use for modern art, but now she felicitously concealed herself behind what she assumed to be a headless torso.

A wiry man suddenly charged through the marble-clad pillars of Building 10's front steps. With a quick scan, she realized he had caught half the court's attention, including the robotic dogs. Thin copper hair was tied in a knot at his sun-browned neck. Beaded bracelets and patterned dress socks protruded from the cuffs of his indigo suit. A fat diamond was nearly buried in his exposed chest hair. Jade pegged him as an "eccentric intellect."

She whipped out her eight-generations-old phone and quickly matched the man's face with a headshot on MIT's online faculty roster.

EARL SNYDER, PhD

PROFESSOR OF BIOLOGICAL ENGINEERING; BRAIN & COGNITIVE SCIENCES; NANOSCIENCE AND NANOTECHNOLOGY

Was this the mark Hema sought to capture?

Straightening the chunky lenses of her cat-eye shades, Ani rose and wandered toward him. With a hasty jerk, she pulled at the front of her sweater that flaunted Tim the Beaver, MIT's mascot, "nature's engineer," and pushed up her cleavage.

Jade chuckled, despite herself. Did Ani hope to distract the man from the tanto knife up her sleeve?

The professor drifted onto the court and was half seated on the trimmed grass, a doorstopper of a book cracking open, when Ani arrived at his side. Instantly he snapped shut the book, and he stood erect, regarding Ani with a wide grin.

Jade flicked her eyes to her phone. Five seconds into scrolling the man's social media accounts, and she registered that Professor Snyder had a taste for undergrads. Again, she laughed. Some men just made it too easy. Jade grasped that the plan was to seduce the professor off campus. She looked in Rhett's direction. He was gone. *Likely moving to Phase Two,* Jade theorized. Heading for the parking lot, toward the professor's AV, lying in wait to sweep the man away, leaving behind no spectacle, no trace of struggle for campus surveillance to stumble upon later.

Back on the grass, Ani allowed the man to reach for her handsome earring, his slick excuse for intimate proximity. With curious fingers he caressed the ruby memento that dangled from her left lobe. He leaned in, whispering, and Ani hooked her elbow around his. The man's dimples deepened in a clueless, hungry grin.

Jade stood tense. Watchful. She didn't trust simple. She waited, on the balls of her feet, for the other shoe to drop.

As a salty breeze picked up from the river, the tiny hairs on her arms shot upright.

A rush of movement from atop Building 10's concrete steps drew her focus. A beautiful woman in a bright red silk suit had slid something out of the folds of her tailored jacket. There was an elegance to her bearing, a purpose in her dark eyes, that instantly made Jade think of Poppy. Jade's heart twisted, then jumped to her throat as she spied the palm-sized stun gun the woman held against her slender thigh. Jade clocked the woman as the woman clocked Ani and the professor, her red lips coiling into a smile.

Was she a Conservator?

Jade panicked. Were there more of them skulking about? Her suit was the wrong color, and she hadn't spotted a lapel pin on the woman's jacket, but Jade's eyes cut to the ground nonetheless, too fearful to scan the court for other potential threats.

Topple it all, she cursed, speed-walking toward Ani. *Don't cause a scene. Don't run. Don't scare off the professor.* Her legs couldn't chew up the ground quick enough. The mystery woman got there first.

Jade blinked as a handheld taser jammed into Ani's stomach, dead on her mending saber wound. In less than a heartbeat, two steel blades glinted in Ani's fists, their high tips hovering just below the rib cages of both the woman and professor.

Why didn't the professor raise his voice in alarm? Surprising everyone, he instead raised his tome of a book and whacked it hard across Ani's face. She fell back against the mystery woman, both of them toppling to the ground, triggering the military-grade taser. Jade cringed in empathy as seventy billion volts of electricity surged into Ani's bandaged stomach.

Jade was torn between helping Ani, who was writhing in agony, or chasing after the man, who was booking it across the court toward Building 4.

"Ani, you good?" Jade shouted.

She needn't have bothered with the question. Ani had already revived and rallied, straddling the red-faced woman, two knives at her delicate throat.

The brief hesitation cost Jade precious seconds. She broke into a sprint, no longer concerned that the court was watching. The professor, surprisingly fleet-footed in his leather Oxford shoes, yelled a quick command to the mechanical engineering students before he whipped out his keycard and disappeared into the safety of the marble building. Next thing Jade knew, a dozen robotic dogs were bounding toward her, frighteningly agile roadblocks whose new purpose was to protect Professor Snyder.

Repeating to herself that these were *robot* dogs, and *robot* dogs couldn't feel, Jade swung back her leg and started kicking.

Two of the robots—decidedly no longer cute—fell to the ground, a leg each flying across the grass. Within seconds, the bots restarted, righting themselves into a preprogrammed crouch, then trotted toward her on three metal legs.

The things were unstoppable, Jade realized.

Shifting strategies, Jade beelined for a cluster of students playing croquet. Snatching one of the players' mallets with a hasty "I need this more than you," she whirled the stick like an airplane propeller, creating a defensive shield as she made her way to Building 4.

With no time to think, she acted on instinct when she reached the locked doors. Pulling the brim of her bucket hat low, she grabbed the nearest body and pushed it against the card panel, betting that a key was stashed in one of the person's pockets. There was a soft *ding*, and the door slid open. Jade bolted inside and slammed the door shut just as the robot dogs attempted to leap into the building, their metal bodies smashing into the glass doors with such force that they broke apart like Lego pieces.

Jade didn't linger to see if they were programmed to put themselves back together. She turned and spotted the professor's copper ponytail weaving through a bevy of students before slipping out a side exit. Jade raced after him, chasing the man along Memorial Drive. She was slower than usual, her injuries causing her to run with a limp.

What she wouldn't give for her BolaWrap right now.

A silver, bullet-shaped AV shot up beside them. Its roof lifted, like metal jaws opening, and two thickset bodies launched out, their heads wrapped in beige stockings.

Jade staggered forward, fingers sealed around her perfume vials. Before she could spray the vermin down, she homed in on a glossy pin affixed to the collar of one of their polo shirts.

The transformation was instantaneous. She felt as though she'd been dropped in a tub of boiling water. She drowned in panic, flailing to break free. She heard the professor's screams before her own overtook them.

Leave! her mind cried. *This isn't a safe place.*

She turned to run and knocked into something sturdy.

"Jade," Rhett whispered, shaking her by the shoulders. "Snap out of it; they're gone."

Jade rubbed at her eyes, glancing to the empty street. The professor was gone, too. Had they taken him?

Ani materialized behind Rhett, along with the taser-wielding woman in red. Jade fumbled for her vials. A few slid from her grasp, landing in the folds of her fallen bucket hat.

"Don't worry," Ani assured Jade. "The woman's not a Conservator." She bent to help retrieve the glass vials. Thankfully, none had cracked. "Though she's not much better," Ani added under her breath.

The familiar stranger stood over Jade, her head cocked in amusement. "Are you the fearless scapegrace my cousin wouldn't shut up about?"

Cousin? Jade thought distantly. *What cousin?*

"No" was all Jade said.

"We better split and head for the portal before the real security comes," Ani panted, gingerly touching her wounded side. Blood in the shape of a saber slash dotted her bandage. *She has her Quest Bot,* Jade assured herself. *Ani's blood will clot. She's fine.* In fact, Ani was aiming a healthy glare at the fair-skinned, dark-haired woman who, Jade had slowly come to realize, was none other than Iris Szeto. The obvious wealth, the brazen arrogance, the stoic grief—all added up to Poppy's infamous niece.

Iris scoffed. "Don't be silly, I'm not taking a *Quest* hyperloop." She pressed a button on her diamond-plated smartwatch. "We'll take my private jet."

Rhett grumbled, crossing his arms. Clearly not so keen on trusting another Szeto after Poppy's betrayal. "How did you know we were after that scientist?"

"I didn't." Iris lifted a padded shoulder. "I was given an anagram that led me here. *Rarely ends.* The rearranged letters form the name Earl Snyder."

The professor.

"And you were told this anagram *by?*" Ani pressed.

Iris touched her throat, where a thin bruise shaped like a noose peeked above her lapel. "Vance Yates. I believe he wants to jump ship."

"Vance Yates . . ." Jade repeated. She let the name wash over her blistered mind.

"Come," Iris beckoned as a new AV pulled to a stop beside them. "I'll explain in the air."

But Jade already felt like she was flying.

They may have lost the scientist, but they just might have gained two billion-heirs.

Fortunes changed, indeed.

FOUR

Crys sat at an empty dinette table, heavy eyes fixed on the smudged glass of the motor home's screen door. The view outside was uneventful, the massive wind turbine factory that loomed beyond the RV park still as an overexposed photograph.

It was approaching noon. Crys should be resting, restoring her body for the midday shift that the work program had assigned to the new arrivals. Preparing her mind for the possibility—no, *the guarantee*—of seeing Yates. *Soon.* In a matter of hours. Minutes.

The wait felt like years.

She rose to stand beside the door. Gazed at the stern reflection that stood out against the glass. For an instant, her eyelids shuddered, her feet jerked to flee. But the fear incursion never came, and Crys stared boldly at her mirror image. Although she was no longer terrified of her own face, she was still scared of what she'd see. Jade? Crystal? Crys narrowed her glare at the reflection's sharp cheekbones, its hard mouth and stony eyes. Who was this woman? It was the face of no one she knew. The face of a stranger.

No, Crys corrected silently. She gripped her fingers around her vials. *It's a face to inspire fear.*

Eli cleared his throat, sliding into the bucket seat behind her. "Sorry for interrupting."

Crys turned from her reflection, rubbing at her eyes. "I was just watching for the shift change."

"It's nice to finally see you in some fresh clothes," Eli said, nodding to her graphic tee that read EVERYONE CAN AFFORD A SMILE. Crys had found the shirt in a donation bin below the bunk beds. She liked the dark humor of it: a billion-heir who now couldn't afford to buy her own clothes. "Don't know the last time I've seen you smile, though."

Crys shrugged. "Maybe when we find Yates."

"Will that really make you smile?"

She let her silence answer. They'd checked every one of the thirty-odd motor homes that lined the RV park adjacent to the factory. Most were vacant, and scattered food cans and sacks of clothes piled atop claimed bunk beds were the only sign that other transient workers were here.

Crys had thought she'd spot evidence of Yates's presence: a pair of house slippers beside a door, a discarded wrapper of sweets, little prizes he'd use to reward himself after completing certain tasks throughout the day.

He's trying to disappear, Crys reminded herself. Of course he wouldn't leave traces.

Yates was likely off with other employed Unfortunates on a morning shift. She knew from one of the "Discovery Discussions" at Adsum that the fabrication process for wind energy was extremely labor-intensive. The average utility-scale turbine contained roughly eight thousand parts. The mega-factory was probably a twenty-four-seven operation.

A sharp bell cut through the RV park, drawing Crys's gaze to the factory's roll-up entrance, where a neon sign blinked **REGISTRATION**.

Her body thrummed with anticipation, her mind racing with uncontrollable *what-ifs*.

What if Yates wasn't inside the factory? What if he no longer recognized Crys? What if he refused to leave? To help them in their fight with the Conservators?

"Can someone turn that thing off?" Wily grumbled from the bunk he shared with Sage. On the ride to the work camp, he'd gulped down three glasses of water before crashing out cold for hours.

"You're fatigued because you're not eating," Sage said, putting aside her phone and tossing Wily an energy bar. Crys noticed that the small cooler bag stuffed with a variety of Smart Bots was still untouched at Sage's waist. She'd been tirelessly scouring the internet for articles and e-books on wind power, attempting to cram enormous amounts of information into her mind, desperate to recover the extraordinary brainpower she'd lost through sheer force of will.

The fantasies we sell ourselves, Crys thought, unlatching the door.

"I'm fine," Wily insisted as he slid down the bunk, smacking his dry mouth. "I just need another glass of water—"

Bam. He dropped to the floorboards.

Crys dove for him, unfastening the collar of his shirt, which he had buttoned all the way up to his throat. *Since when did Wily cover up so much?* Crys thought, realizing just how insular she'd become. Wily was usually shirtless, eager to show off his lean muscles and abundant scars.

Crys's hand brushed against something poking out of his chest pocket. One of his syrettes laced with sedatives, like he'd jabbed her with at Husk Row? No, it was larger, with a rigid glass tube. Curious, Crys started to pull out the capped syringe, but Wily suddenly came to, snatching it out of her hand.

He comically pushed away from Crys and slid it stealthily back into his pocket before Sage could see. "Whoa, whoa, whoa, the only one giving me any mouth-to-mouth resuscitation is Sage."

"Maybe you shouldn't take this shift," Sage said, grabbing his hand. "Stay here and rest."

In answer, Wily gave her a quick kiss, popped to his feet, and headed for the door. "Best get a move on before all the noon slots fill up."

Nolan and his co-host emerged from the loft's staircase, and Crys took in their faces, which they'd painted with dirt, and the dented beer-bottle caps they wore around their necks on cheap chains.

Eli shook his head. "I thought we went over this . . . being needy doesn't mean you have to be starved for taste." He pulled on one of his patchwork overshirts, brushing down his short, tight curls with his palm. "And be sure not to point those damn things my way, old man." He shoved past the podcasters to join Crys and Wily at the door.

Nolan laid his necklace, which hid a miniature microphone, over his shabby shawl. "Remember my price?" he broadcasted to the Exiles. "No hindrance or sabotage."

"That goes both ways," Crys said, bolting down the motor home's front steps, hoping to be the first in line for registration. But the ruffians from the date farm pickup had already gathered around the factory's locked doors, their broad shoulders and balled-up fists daring someone to get too close.

Were these the people Yates was overseeing on the factory floor? Without his money and Rhett to protect him, Crys wondered how Yates had gained their respect.

By controlling fear, she thought, resting her fingertips on the magnetic pouch at her belt loop. She walked straight into the huddle of wayward men, cutting short their crass banter when she came to a stop at the head of the line.

Crys heard knuckles pop, guns cocking. But before she could draw her fear fragrance, the steel roll-up doors hoisted open, revealing a long row of rectangular compartments separated by metal barriers. Each had a touch screen attached to the front wall, reminding Crys of high-tech voting booths.

The men rushed the compartments. "They better not be askin' for no bona fides," one of them jeered.

"I assure you that they will not," Nolan said quietly to Crys. They hadn't had time to fabricate IDs, and there was no way they were going to register under their true identities. But if neither the factory nor the state workforce service required documentary evidence for new hires, what was the point of the registration booths?

"Maybe there's a test," Sage speculated, a glint in her eye. She stretched her fingers, eager for the challenge, and stepped inside one of the compartments. She pressed the screen, but nothing happened. "Hurry," she said when loud cursing erupted from the other compartments. "It looks like registration won't open until everyone has entered a booth."

Crys nodded to Eli and Wily before she claimed the booth beside Sage's.

The moment both of her feet touched the metal-plated floor, a door shot up from the ground, sealing her inside. An image appeared on the screen, and Crys went cold with shock.

She blinked, hard, but there was no mistaking what she saw. Three red diagonal slashes stood out against a stark white background.

The Conservators are here.

Though she couldn't see them, Crys knew cameras and sensors were tracking her smallest moves, testing how she would respond to the symbol.

She reacted on impulse. Folding her dignity in on itself, she cowered, imitating a woman gripped in the maw of a fear incursion. An artificial cry tore from her throat, and the steel wall before her split in two, the floor shuddering forward.

There was no time to second-guess her decision. The compartment had already resealed behind her, and she was deposited into a small room inundated by a harsh floodlight. Her retinas felt on fire. Tears sprang to her eyes, but she scraped them away, anticipating the familiar screams of Eli, Wily, Sage.

But the honeyed voice that spilled out beside her belonged to Nolan Ortiz. "I always tell my listeners that a good scream can be therapeutic."

A vial of Crys's fear fragrance was in her hand before her mind even thought *pounce*.

"How did you know what that symbol meant? You better start talking, or I'll have you *really* screaming this time."

The fine lines of Nolan's forehead twisted in curiosity at the sight of Crys's perfume. "I hazarded a guess. Same as you, no?" He swept his gaze up to Crys's slitted eyes. "I heard the man in the stall next to mine cry out. I figured it was in response to the symbol. Some sort of secret password for admittance."

More doors thundered closed. Eli, Wily, and Sage formed a spearhead around her, Eli at the tip, fists raised, chest heaving. Unlike the others, Eli's fear incursion had been real. He blinked back tears, trying to hide them from Nolan. "You knew," he choked out. "You knew who ran this charity workhouse, didn't you?"

Calmly, Nolan twisted his torso, one arm held out behind him. "As you can see for yourselves, my co-host did not meet the requirements for whatever test we all just passed. If I had been wise to this, as you claim, do you not think she would be here by my side?" For a second, his composure sank with his shoulders. Was he *scared*?

Not nearly enough. Nolan seemed to have only the barest clue what they had freely walked into. He straightened his shawl. His smile. "But if you care to elaborate more on who you believe to be running this program . . ."

Sage broke ranks, moving for a line of tall doorless lockers. Crys watched a gnarled-looking man with a face full of scars yank neon-green coveralls from a hanger. "These look like the right PPE," Sage called back, holding up a pair of plastic safety goggles.

Crys's heartbeat slowed. She stored away her vial. This could still be a turbine factory. This could still be a work detail. The Conservators might be supervising, but maybe that's why Yates had come to this place. To study what his sons and Hariri were assembling behind closed doors.

Turning from Nolan, Crys jostled her way to a locker, choosing coveralls that seemed her size. She suited up, placing her bag of vials securely around her wrist, goggles stretched across her cheekbones and obscuring her features. She inhaled a steadying breath. Emptied her mind. A ritual she would perform before any fencing match. She imagined a saber in her hand. The Soaring Precious. The sword she'd promised to win back from Hariri. She felt grounded. Calm.

"Let's get to work," she said, nodding to the Exiles. She pushed her way to the wide double doors labeled FACTORY FLOOR.

Reckless, Jade's sibilant whisper poisoned her mind. *Leave, like the symbol warned. This isn't a safe place.*

"No," Crys hissed back. The reaction test was to weed out the botless. Those they couldn't control. And Crys was in full control of herself.

With her vials, *she* was the one who controlled fear.

A harsh siren blared, and the double doors gaped open. Instantly, Crys was hit with such an overwhelming wall of sights and sounds that she took a step backward. They all did.

Three men from their caravan tried to turn back and bang loose the compartment doors. But there was no escaping the horror that awaited them. The conveyor floor beneath them jerked forward, and Crys's stomach dropped. *Cole was right not to follow me.* Loud music pulsated through her body—the same bass beats from the music festival—as her eyes locked on the transparent vertical tube at the center of the cavernous room.

A mega wind tunnel, her mind grasped. She forced herself to narrow in on the details. Sixteen fans with razor-sharp blades housed at the top, generating wind that circulated down to the ground floor before being forced back up by turning vanes. Blood was splashed against the walls. Tunnel fliers in neon coveralls struggled to manipulate their bodies against the powerful airflow.

Just as the conveyor floor spit the new arrivals onto the platform haloed around the tube, the crack of a gunshot rang out from inside the tunnel. The recoil sent one of the fliers spinning. The shooter lost control of his movements, and he soared, screaming, all the way to the top of the hundred-foot ceiling, straight into the fan's exposed blades. Crys looked away when his dismembered limbs dropped into the tunnel, hovering on the wind.

Cheers erupted from the third and fourth floors of the enormous warehouse. Platinum suits lounged against the metal railings, chins lowered on the lethal blood sport.

"What on shaking Earth did we just fall into?" Wily gaped.

Crys looked to Eli. "We're in an underground fighting ring, aren't we?"

Another warehouse door rolled open. A landslide of neon green hurtled forward, burying her question beneath a mass of violent shouts. Bodies, reeking of sweat and fear, fled frantically for the walls, scouring for a way out.

Wily unsheathed his blade. Eli raised his fists. Sage downed her Brainious juices.

Nolan's slurred whisper came hot in Crys's ear. "Tell me you have a plan." He paused, his breath as sour as his words. "Or did I partner with the wrong sister?"

You shouldn't have left me, Jade whispered cruelly. *You need me, don't you?*

Crys curled her fingers around her vials. "Your microphone won't protect you here," she told Nolan, nodding to the necklace tucked beneath his coveralls. "Find a weapon, or your podcast ends today."

She set off for a copse of neon-green bodies that stood rooted to the floor beside the glass ring, heedless of the chaos around them. These were the seasoned roundups.

She'd start her search for Yates with them.

FIVE

The monster fans cut off, and the victor hit the ground with a nasty *splat*. Her oily hair covered her face like tentacles. Blood exploded from an artery in her neck. She wasn't moving.

Streets take me, Willis cursed. He rubbed a calloused hand over the bristles of his shaved head.

"Yeah, looks like that bullet got Bambi," a rickety man named Geezer grumbled behind his mangy beard. "Don't think you can save this one, Good Sam."

Willis's league of miscreants had taken to calling him that. They said it was short for "Good Samaritan." He liked it just fine. Others were stuck with tags like Six Foot—not for his height, but for how far you had to stand from the guy to avoid catching a whiff of him—or Manic or Prosthetute, the boy with a prosthetic leg that the roughnecks liked to pick on.

The one you didn't want was Corpse. That's what the fighters called you when they pegged you as next on the chopping block.

Chopping *roof,* Willis corrected himself.

He spat and charged through the wind tunnel's small opening, dragging Bambi out before the platinum suits could restart the bloody fans. Her body vibrated with the pulsating electronic music, so Willis put his ear to her nose to check if she was breathing. Deathly still.

This was the fourth one he'd lost this week. Good thing his heart was already as numb as his legs.

A scrap broke out nearby. The roughnecks had a newcomer pushed up against the plexiglass tunnel. One of them took the necklace that was rattling above the man's collarbone, and squeezed, crushing the newcomer's windpipe.

"We've got ourselves a fresh Corpse!" the roughneck announced.

Look the other way, Willis advised himself. *Save your strength for the tunnel.*

But the Good Sam in him couldn't look the other way. That's what he'd been doing since the quake shook his life to hell. Only looking out for number one, oblivious to anyone who needed help around him. But if he kept this "Good Sam" business up, he was going to become *zero.* The next Corpse.

Willis tramped toward the scuffle, peering down to make sure he was, in fact, walking. Sometimes he wasn't sure what his body was doing unless he looked, and this wasn't the place to fall flat on his ass. He'd come to the warehouse plenty burned and broken, but winning matches in the tunnel had awarded him with stab wounds to the torso, bruised ribs, and fractured fingers.

Somehow none of it bothered him, pain-wise. Same went for most of the fighters, actually.

Unlike the newcomer, who was screaming, blood trickling down his throat.

The roughneck released the man, and the newcomer tumbled to the floor. The onlookers snickered, pointing and thanking their fortune it wasn't them. Willis picked up his speed, but before he could reach the bleeding man, four neon jumpsuits appeared at his side.

Odd. No newcomers turned up with chums. Odd, too, that one of them clutched a shiny new phone. Who were they kidding, thinking they'd get a signal? And did they really have someone who'd care enough to answer? Odds were low.

Overhead, the spotlights cracked on. Fat, dazzling beams sliced through the dusty air, shining down on pockets of beggars, their hands lifted to the gods on the upper floors, pleading to be passed over.

Willis kept his eyes on the unusual newcomers.

Three of them had found scuzzy bits of cloth to use as head covers to compress their hair. That was crucial for success in the ring. Bambi might still be alive if she'd hacked off her hair like he'd told her. So these newcomers were smart. And *young*. How did they wind up in a place like this? The turbine warehouse was home to wastrels. Menaces to society. Ruffians on their last legs who'd burned every bridge.

Even through their large goggles, Willis could see there was something about them. A stamina. A spark. A reason to live.

These newcomers would be hard to match in the vertical ring.

The spotlights were flashing faster now. He should go. Slip himself into the center of a knot of gray-haired hooked backs, where the light was less likely to spot him. The slow-moving elders were too quick to die. And the platinum suits would want a long-lived grand finale.

But a desperate shout grabbed him by the ears. It came from the newcomer on the ground, who'd pulled out a large wrench and was brandishing it at the roughneck that had stolen his bottlecap necklace.

The craving for a beer hit Willis like a bottle over the head. *No*, he snapped at his brain, suddenly furious. He was fifteen days sober. Forced withdrawal had almost killed him before the fighters ever got the chance to. He'd seen his sister Emmy in the fevers, the hallucinations. And the flames. Always the flames.

The newcomer's commands snapped Willis back to sober reality. "Give me my necklace. Give it back, or your deaths will go unknown."

Was the man drunk? Then Willis realized he knew that voice. Had run from it once. Before he could align the name and face with the man's puzzling threat, the spotlights flashed colors in blinding succession. Blue. Green. Yellow. Willis tried to step back from the attraction before the searching light solidified red, but his nerve-fried legs froze on him.

His old burn scars still slowed him, even if painlessly. He was quicker in the air.

It was too late, anyway. Red spilled over him as the spotlight's wide oval flooded around him, trapping him, along with the newcomers and two roughnecks, in its bright beam.

There was no use for guards. No need for the laser point of a sniper to force the selected fighters into the ring. The ones passed over, reprieved for this round, did the dirty work for them.

Willis didn't blame the Unfortunate bastards. Didn't even push back against the hands that shoved him into the vertical tunnel. He put his mind and energy into what really mattered right now: keeping his head.

The giant fans switched on, and the 185 mph wind blasted the eight fighters into the air. The newcomers went reeling, ramming into the cylinder's walls, clueless how to maneuver their bodies. They shouted at one another, their strategies or goodbyes swallowed by the ruthless roar of the indoor gale.

Belly to the earth, Willis arched his body. Threw his arms above his head, palms flat, elbows partially bent. He hovered, controlled, at the bottom of the tunnel, ready for the signal.

Stay focused, he prodded himself. *Don't lose your head.* He kept his eyes on his opponents' backs and off the fans above.

In concert, they all lit up. Round sensor patches the size of fists blinking at the center of their spines.

None of these fighters were his. Four of them were still kids, but he reminded himself that this was a game of tag, or you leave in a bag. He didn't like it, but he had his league of miscreants to think of now.

Overhead, the two roughnecks collided. Willis watched, weightless, time moving slower inside the ring as they struggled to push their fists through the punishing air current. The one who'd stolen the necklace tried a different tactic, shoving his opponent's head straight down and raking his mouth open with his fingers. The man screamed, inhaling a Category 5 hurricane. Sputtering, he slammed against the glass wall, stomach first. His back exposed, the other roughneck struck his sensor with a fist.

A small-scale parachute ejected from the collar of his jumpsuit, and the man was launched up the tunnel, a heel catching his opponent square in the back. The roughneck's sensor light blinked red, and another parachute discharged.

Tag, you're in a bag.

Willis held his gaze straight forward, but he heard the *snip-snip* when the roughnecks' bodies caught in the blades.

It was just the newcomers now. Judging by how chummy they'd been before, they were going to band together against him before they inevitably turned on each other.

Willis went for the biggest one first. Relaxing his hips, he cupped the air with his chest and stretched out his limbs to make himself as large as possible. His speed slowed, and his body rose.

Twenty feet from the top, he straightened his legs and tipped forward, headfirst, moving for the young man who had fists the size of Willis's face. He hoped to overwhelm the man with his speed, but one of the man's chums flew in, her strong arms blocking Willis's attack. She clutched a small vial in her fingers, battling against the current to raise it to Willis's face.

Pepper spray? he guessed. That might be the smartest weapon he'd seen brought into the ring. And he was going to take it for himself before he sent her soaring.

He thrust out his arms, latched on to her wrist, and pulled her close, intending to steal the vial and then strike her sensor in one controlled movement.

61

But those russet-brown eyes behind the clear goggles gave him pause. He'd know those eyes even in the dark. He had seen them every time he'd closed his eyes for the last twelve years.

"*Emmy?*" Willis gasped in disbelief. Had all the time spent in the wind tunnel rattled his brain? His sister was dead. Killed in the quake.

Then he saw a look of pure hatred twist the young woman's rounded brows, and he knew.

It clicked for his niece, too.

"*Uncle Willis,*" she spat. She recoiled, and the vial slipped out of her grasp, spiraling to the opposite side of the tunnel.

Before he could even think of how to react, how this reunion was even possible, the large man's fist connected with his nose. His own blood spewed into his eyes, blinding him. By the time he blinked them clear, his niece—it must be Crys, judging by the golden strands of hair flapping out of her head wrap—and her chums were flying up toward the ceiling. Toward the deadly fans.

"No!" Willis choked out, going after her. If he got sucked in and chopped up, so be it.

But then he saw something that made him blink again. Hard.

One of the high-powered fans had been immobilized, its blades stilled. Willis had guessed these kids were smart, but outsmarting the rich sadists who built this death ring?

Another young woman, auburn brows hugging the tops of her goggles, had hold of the paralyzed blades and was using the wind to hoist herself up through the fan's metal blades. Crys and her other two companions followed close behind, but the third, the one who'd had his necklace stolen, remained hovering in the tunnel, staring back at Willis.

A second realization hit him. He knew this man, too. It was the podcaster who'd made Willis's sad life even more of a joke. *Worse.* A viral one. His voice, his words, had sent vloggers to Willis's Beverly Hills tent, who then sent Willis running bare-assed in front of the cameras down Rodeo Drive.

It was the hobo warning that had you turning tail, Willis thought. *The same one that got you entrance into this tornado of hell.*

But the symbol wasn't an enemy he could get his hands on, like this podcaster floating in front of him.

"You son of a bastard!" Willis shouted, his curse lost on the wind.

Anger licked his insides, hot as the flames the night of the quake. Willis stretched out his limbs and prepared to rocket toward the podcaster, but the wind speed suddenly slowed. He felt himself free-falling.

The platinum suits had shut off the remaining fifteen fans, aiming to stop the escape. *And watch me plummet to the ground and splatter.*

Thinking fast, Willis slapped his own back, initiating the sensor. His parachute released, buoying him on the last dregs of the wind current.

He had about two spits' worth of time to make it to the ceiling before a gun started firing. Using his body weight to steer his movements, he guided his way to the jammed fan. The podcaster had already made it through. But there was no air current to help haul Willis's body up, and no chums to lend a hand.

Willis grunted as he threw his arms up and clung to the blade. More blood trickled out from his palms. His grip was too slippery, and he began to slide. His stomach flipped.

He felt his whole hundred fifty pounds battling gravity, fighting not to hurtle to the ground.

Forty years flashed by in a blink.

Willis and his baby sister, Emmy, chasing ducks at the lake. Willis in a borrowed suit, the best man at her wedding. Willis gazing down at his two perfect nieces, wondering how he got so lucky. The rumble of the quake. The heat of the fire. The pills that came after. The booze. The loneliness.

The terror.

A hand clamped around his wrist.

It was Crys. She'd come back for him.

But he was still slipping. And he was going to take her down with him.

"I'm too heavy!" he shouted, steeling himself for the fall. "Let go!"

"I don't abandon people!" she rasped back, and with a grunt, she dug in her short nails.

Dimly, he noted that he didn't feel the sting.

The podcaster grabbed hold of Crys's left leg, the guy who'd cracked his nose, her right. In one tremendous heave, Willis was on top of the metal blade, his limbs spent, his mind running wild.

"How?" he croaked. "Why?"

Crys's mouth twisted in a grimace as she yanked him up to stand. "I was told there was a man here that people call a 'savior.'"

Without thinking, Willis's hand moved to his Medal of Valor, tucked safe beneath his jumpsuit. He'd rescued seven families from the Greater LA Fire. Half a dozen miscreant victors from the vertical ring. Had Crys really come now to save *him*?

Crys backed away. "I thought you were someone else."

Disappointment burned through Willis. He had no right to feel anything but gratitude. Shame. He'd deserted his nieces. Let the world swallow them whole, even after the quake. What did he expect? Absolution?

"Where's Jade?" he asked, searching as the others tore off their head wraps and goggles. He recognized Eli, Sage, and Wily, even without all that corpse makeup. He'd seen the Halloween photo of them in their Adsum uniforms that went viral after their classmate was found dead. "She's with you, right?"

Suddenly bullets ricocheted off the steel ceiling. Howls of anger from the platinum suits echoed up from below. Without a glance at Willis, Crys turned to bolt with the others down the industrial catwalk.

Willis scrambled after her.

The podcaster fell back beside him. "In case you're unaware, you're bleeding profusely." He ripped off a piece of his jumpsuit and held it up to Willis's nose. The bottlecap necklace was around his neck again. It must hold a mike, Willis figured. What else would a man like him die for but scandal? "Press it tight."

"Thanks, asshole," Willis muttered.

"The name's Nolan, but I suppose I deserved that." The tall, elegant man laughed, and the smooth, warm sound was so inviting, it made Willis want to join in.

An earsplitting whistle sounded from their right. There, at the end of the floating walkway, stood a platinum suit. Extracting the fingers he'd used to whistle from his mouth, he waved them down.

Why wasn't he *shooting* them down?

Willis flinched, prepared to see the enamel pin on the suit's lapel, the hobo warning, but instead he saw that the young man had no shoes. And his foot was bleeding, bad.

When he ripped off his nylon mask, he was smiling, not grimacing.

The platinum suit couldn't feel pain, just like the tunnel fighters, Willis realized, confused.

"Cole, brother!" Eli exclaimed, rushing forward. "How'd you lose your boot?"

Wily stopped running and leaned against Sage, his chest heaving. "I knew you wouldn't leave us hanging. Or leave us *flying*, I should say—"

"What happened to your head?" Crys asked, joining Eli at Cole's side.

Cole shook his head hard, grabbing at his temple. "What do you mean? There's nothing wrong with my mind."

Crys shot Eli a troubled look. "There's a gash above your eye—" She tried to reach out for Cole, but he jerked back.

"Please," Cole cried. "Just stay away from me."

Crys's face burned redder than a flame. Her hand squeezed around a vial like the one she'd lost in the tunnel. "If you wanted me to stay away from you, then why are you here?"

A bullet drove into the railing, dangerously close to Cole's skull.

"Let's continue this love spat somewhere with fewer bullets, shall we?" Sage suggested. "Or Cole really will have something wrong with his head."

"Quick, up here." Cole spun toward a thin emergency ladder only a few strides away. "We can steal the ride that brought me and the platinum suits from the music festival. They're all Hariri's."

"Of course this is all him," Eli growled.

They scaled the five rungs of the ladder, Cole leading, Willis coming up last, and emptied out onto the warehouse roof that doubled as a heliport.

"I've got the codes for the middle copter," Cole yelled over the storm of boots.

"No go," Willis shouted back, sprinting toward the line of helicopters. "The owner will just reroute its AI pilot . . ."

"We don't need an autonomous pilot," Sage assured him. "We have me." She flung open the door and strapped herself into the captain seat.

"Don't fret," Wily said to him. "Sage is a genius."

"Are you trained to fly?" Nolan asked suspiciously.

Sage flashed a coy smile, patting the bag strapped around her waist. "I just learned."

Everyone piled in, as if that were a normal statement. Willis remained on the roof. *Streets take me,* he cursed. *What if we crash?* He might not feel pain anymore, but what good was that if he was dead?

He squinted into the copter's cabin, at Crys, who glared hard at him as she gripped the small pouch tied to her wrist. In a spit's worth of time, he remembered what was worth living for. Jade. Crys. *Family.* What good was never crashing if he wasn't truly alive?

He leapt on board with a groan, sealing the door with a bang. Or was that the thump of bullets driving into metal?

The rotor blades overhead started spinning, chopping at the air, and they were up and off, his league of miscreants left behind. No chance of rescue. They'd be gone within the hour, all traces of the warehouse and its tunnel of terror stripped clean.

"Good Samaritan," they had named him.

Willis wondered what they'd call him now.

Six

Hema slipped out of their lab coat. With a concentration reserved for observing the molecular self-assembly process of their nanobots, Hema folded one sleeve, then the other, creasing the sacred uniform in half and resting it calmly atop the workstation.

For several measured heartbeats, Hema stood there. Hands braced on the steel table, trying to hold back their impending panic.

Hema hadn't been in Los Angeles in 2040 when the Big One shook the City of Angels and Dreams. At nineteen, Hema had been away in their third year of biomedical engineering school. But now, Hema was experiencing their very own internal quake. Faith and conviction collapsed inside of them, the foundation Hema had built their life upon splitting apart.

Quietly, internally, Hema repeated the inspirational quote from the poster above the workstation. *Nothing in life is to be feared, it is only to be understood.*

At present Hema understood nothing except their own limitations, and it shook their chakras to their core. They stood very still, like riding out any quake. Hoping to avoid the worst of the destruction. But Hema knew they were going to crack. Truth always found its way into the light. And the secret they'd been sitting on was too powerful for one person to keep buried.

Hema stuffed the hem of their white coat into their mouth and screamed.

"Uh . . . Hema?" Finn asked tentatively.

Hema spat out the cloth. Took a moment to regain their composure before they spun around. "Yes?"

Finn leaned against the lab's doorframe, out of breath, a look on his narrow face that meant he was about to tell Hema something they weren't going to like. "Rhett is back."

Hema took a shuddering breath. *Only* Rhett?

This shit day is about to get even shittier, Hema thought, scrubbing a hand across their tired eyes. "Let him know I will meet him on my bench outside in the garden." When the boy lingered, Hema understood there was more bad news. "And what else?"

"I can't find Jade anywhere on the ranch . . ." Finn probed. His bitter tone suggested that he took it personally, like he'd been left behind on purpose. *He doesn't realize that I banished Jade from the ranch.*

Hema noticed the outline of Finn's inhaler in his pants pocket and felt another pang of guilt. Finn, like many of the other Adsum sibs, was finding it difficult readjusting to his life after Quest Bots. But even if Hema had time to try and reproduce the unique bots Damon had created for them, Hema wasn't sure that they would.

The morality of using human-enhancement technology was so gray, so complicated between good and evil, that Hema was no longer sure which side they stood on.

"Thank you for informing me," Hema said. "Please return to your classes. I'm counting on you to set the example for your year."

Hema had managed to recruit an online tutor, but without Adsum Academy, the students lacked accountability. They needed structure. A guardian, someone to look after them.

But Hema was no Poppy. And Hema was certainly no Yates.

Most days, Hema barely even felt like an adult. How could they be entrusted with the futures of these kids, who'd been promised a gilded life at Quest, only to face the real possibility of ending up back at the very shelters Damon had plucked them from?

It started off weekly, then daily. Now hourly, Hema wished they could go back to being a hermit in their old Brooklyn basement. They weren't a foster parent. They weren't the scientist who could single-handedly stop a fear plague that was spreading across the country.

When Finn had left, Hema crammed their white coat back into their mouth and finished screaming.

Hema sat on their oak bench, eyes on the big Texas sky. A pair of ruby-throated hummingbirds zipped past, dancing above them. The male darted high, his tail feather whistling, until he was almost out of sight, then dive-bombed back down, directly at a seemingly unimpressed female.

Hema whistled, mimicking their sharp trills. The dramatic aerial courtship helped to settle Hema's hyperactive mind, until they felt a change in the vibrational energy around their little garden oasis.

Rhett emerged between two giant century plants. His dirty-blonde hair stuck out at odd ends, a contrast to the stark military style he'd worn before his exile.

"Professor Snyder proved more evasive than I remembered?" Hema asked, fiddling with the buttons on their collared button-down.

"The Conservators got him first," Rhett explained with a grunt. He flashed a sheepish grin, setting a cage down at Hema's feet. "There were no 'I'm sorry I lost your scientist' cards at the portal gift shop, so I brought you some rabbits instead."

Hema didn't laugh. "Where is Ani? And I'm assuming Jade followed you to Cambridge. Finn informs me that no one has seen her on the ranch."

"I . . ." Rhett mumbled. "I'm not so good with heights." He rubbed the sharp bones at the back of his neck. "I took the hyperloop back, while Jade and Ani chose a private jet."

"Really?" Hema replied, only half listening. "Whose?"

"Iris Szeto. She said Vance Yates might be turning. Jade and Ani should have beat me here . . ." His head swiveled, scanning the ranch's dusty drive, the empty courtyard. "They aren't back yet?"

Hema shook their head. "And no word from Crys and the others, either."

Rhett took this news in silence. Hema had observed that Damon's former enforcer was always reserved, closemouthed when it came to his own opinions or feelings or fears.

One sunrise over yoga—the fifth-years insisted that the overtaxed Exiles, Hema in particular, needed to reharmonize mind and body—Jade had related Rhett's story to Hema. He'd grown up on a Kansas farm, had lost the land, and then his father and, not long after, his mother. Then he lost himself. For six years, he was under Damon's employ, his magnetizing spell. He'd loved and loathed his mentor, the guardian figure he was secretly working to destroy. He was late to his revenge, but in the end, he'd had a hand in bringing down a titan. And now he was seeking him again, hoping to help restore him.

Hema could certainly relate. "You can have a seat if you want," Hema offered, squinting up at Rhett's dirt-stained fingers and scratchy beard. The polish that Rhett had exuded when they'd first met had grown coarse. Hema thought he wore this roughness rather well.

Rhett hesitated, glancing at the gold plate on the back of the wooden bench. "You put your name on it. Figured you didn't like people messing with your spot." He plopped down, the oak creaking beneath his sturdy weight. "I've run off a few sixth-years fooling around here. Can't seem to keep them away."

"I don't mind," Hema answered. "It's good for them to focus on something other than their suspended lives."

Some of the older ones had begun to act out. Or else they were trying to emulate Jade. Either way, it was a problem. It felt like every few hours an academy student was standing in the doorway to Hema's laboratory, asking if they'd discovered what their terminated Quest Bot had been used for. Some of the spiteful students had told the first-years they were all in for agonizing deaths without their Savior bots. And it was Hema's fault they didn't have them.

Nothing in life is to be feared, it is only to be understood.

Don't they understand? Hema thought wearily. *I understand nothing.*

Rhett cut in on Hema's thoughts. He was up, one knee in the dirt, crouching beside waist-high shoots of grass. "Is this my winter wheat?" His slanted grin burgeoned into the smile of a wonderstruck child, decades shedding off his hard-edged face. "How in the hell did you get these stubborn bastards to grow?"

Everything was going to shit, but Hema couldn't stop a smile. "Wheat. Is that what those are? I found the loose seeds scattered on a couch cushion." Had Rhett been carrying them in his pocket? A piece of home, always within grasp? "I thought I'd plant them and surprise myself with what would emerge."

"Well, I hope you aren't disappointed," Rhett said, standing to wipe the soil from his jeans. He raised his eyes to Hema, his blush-red scars highlighting the curves of his long lashes.

"No," Hema answered a little too quickly. "I eat gluten." Sweat beaded their temples. *It's stress,* Hema rationalized, ignoring their flushed cheeks. *The Texas heat.* "What I mean is, carbohydrates can be restorative."

Rhett's smile grew. "I'm glad you think so."

Hema moved to gather their things. Remembered they had no things. "I have to get back to the lab."

Rhett sat before Hema could stand. "I know you're a science mas-termind and all . . ."

And a social dunce, Hema thought. After six years hiding alone in New York, with their discoveries their only companion, Hema had forgotten how to converse properly. Now they just wanted to flee before they said something senseless. Or wholly unwise.

"But I want you to know," Rhett continued, his lips in a firm line, "you can talk to me."

The seismic secret inside Hema rumbled up their chest and out their throat. "The nano reform cannot be stopped. It's not just a single bot attacking its target, it's a *swarm.* It could be that each bite of contaminated food contains hundreds, thousands, even *millions* of them, each with its own payload, some to instill fear of the Conservators' symbol in the amygdala region of the brain, others programmed with the ability to sense an invading synthetic protein, catalyzing the release of a substance that can act against it, just like my attack bots. My formulas don't have a chance."

Rhett leaned back hard against the bench. Hema was sure he'd gotten much more than he'd intended with his offer to lend an ear, but now that they'd started, Hema could no longer hold in the truth.

"And there is no cure," Hema continued, raking their bangs from their eyes. "The nano reform is generating a prion disease in those infected. Healthy proteins in the brain are misfolding into unhealthy proteins that cause clumps, killing neurons, ravaging entire systems of the body, and triggering a complete shutdown. The disease could lie in wait for years, or progress rapidly, with devastating effects. Either way, there's nothing I or any scientist can do to stop it."

Rhett closed his eyes, taking in this cruel reality with a deep, stoic breath.

"As you can now understand," Hema said, "I really could have used Professor Snyder's assistance."

Rhett opened his eyes, coming to grips with impossible news. "According to Iris," he said, "it seems like Snyder was already busy assisting the Conservators."

"You don't think Hariri or Palmer had the professor abducted, to ensure we had no allies? To keep me alone in the fight?"

"Hmm," Rhett grunted. "My gut tells me different. I played the enforcer for many years. And that slimy profess-*whore*—" Rhett stopped short. "Ah, sorry if you liked the guy . . ."

Hema shook their head, waving him on. Professor Snyder had one of the world's most superior minds, but his cheap morality had been the leading reason Hema had chosen Damon Yates as their mentor. And Earl Snyder had grown a firm animosity toward them both for the slight.

"The professor didn't bat an eye when the hosiery-heads nabbed him," Rhett continued. "He knew them. His screams were just a show for the campus cameras."

Hema's brows shot high, although nothing should have shocked them at this point. Rhett went on to explain Vance's unexpected alliance, his coded revelation.

"Rarely ends . . ." Hema mused. Dread filled the catastrophic cracks their confession had left behind. "I'm afraid the Conservators are only getting started."

Nothing in life is to be feared, Hema repeated again. *It is only to be understood.*

"Any guesses what—or who—might be their next target?" Rhett asked hesitantly.

"Nanotech is the most powerful tool humanity will ever create," Hema sighed. "Left at the disposal of a nihilist, the scenarios in which Hariri's nano reform could be utilized are frighteningly endless."

"There's still the option of partnering with the Feds," Rhett offered, his tone neutral. His fingers grazed the back of his neck again.

"No authorities, please," Hema said. A cold shiver racked their small frame. Goddess save them if the government with the largest military budget in the world got its hands on Hema's technology. "On the topic of authorities, Jade told me it was *you* who led her to me."

Hema remembered that day, clear as the sky after a hard rain. Sitting on their bench in Central Park. A shadow. A prodigy gone astray. Known only by a nickname. "If you had always been tracking me, knowing who I was, what I was illegally selling, why didn't you rat me out? Have Damon come and stop me?"

"Because I knew it was you who really saved me." Rhett prodded the ridges of his spine as if probing for the nanobots that had healed his paralysis. His hand slipped from his neck, and his clear azure gaze leveled with Hema's. "It was your initial discovery, your mastermind that got me moving again." He stood up and stretched his legs, as if to prove the point. When he sat back down, it was closer to Hema, a hand's length away. "And if you wanted to stay invisible, it was my only way of thanking you."

A ghost, Hema once called themself. With the way Rhett was looking at them, they felt far from invisible now.

Suddenly Hema's phone rattled from inside their chest pocket. Thinking it was Jade or maybe Crys, calling with a status update, Hema plucked it out. A message, like an emergency alert, flashed across its lock screen. No phone number. No name.

Rhett must have seen the bewilderment creasing Hema's brow. He scooted closer, reading the text aloud.

It begins in the peaks

And ends where it began

Over vast valleys and shallow creeks

It is wise to time your plan

Look high, seek low

75

And you'll find your fortune grow

Do all I have told and if you are bold

You will find riches greater than ~~gold~~

"This is that poem with clues to Damon's hidden treasure," Rhett said confidently.

Hema blinked, squinting down at the words—some circled, one crossed out—trying to make sense of what they were seeing. "The one every Quester was after?" Hema had thought of the silly challenge as merely a game, a device to gain Damon popularity and press. A way to make his Questers and the public search for something other than his unlawful bots . . .

Rhett's elation radiated off him in waves. "For about a year, everyone from the top engineers to the custodians went haywire over searching for the chest. Hell, even *I* tried."

The entire world had known about the hunt. Hundreds of websites and social media accounts were dedicated to theorizing and arguing over what the treasure might be—and where it might be squirreled away on campus.

To Hema's knowledge, no one had ever found it. Damon Yates alone knew its true location.

"Do you think . . ." Rhett pondered, a bit breathless. "Do you think *Damon* sent you this message?"

It would mean that Damon was still alive. Still out there somewhere—a ghost, like Hema had once been. Why wasn't he here, with them, helping to fix the medley of mistakes they'd cocreated?

"It's a good hypothesis," Hema muttered. "He's unwilling, or *unable*, to join the fight. But he wants us to have something . . ."

"A secret weapon, maybe?"

A burst of laughter shook Hema's slight body.

Rhett's neck went red, and not from the sun. "Did I say something stupid?"

"No," Hema said, wiping tears. "That's brilliant. You're *brilliant*." Hema zoomed in on the poem's markings. On Rhett with his rugged scars and soft smile. Something ignited inside of Hema, like the fires after a quake.

Nothing in life is to be feared, only understood.

Lost in the exhilaration of discovery—of possibility—Hema closed the gap between them and grasped Rhett's cheeks, then paused. "Oh," Hema spluttered. "Can I . . ." *Shit.* This was awkward. Hema pulled away, mortified for thinking . . . for *asking*.

Then Rhett's lips smashed into Hema's. Sealing joy into joy. The moment was brief, but lasting. Hema released their grip on Rhett's shock of wheat-colored hair. Cleared their throat. Settled their mind. Grounded to their renewed purpose.

"I know why no one has found the treasure," Hema said. "It's not on campus."

Rhett stared, puzzled. "Oh?"

"It's *above* it."

SEVEN

Jade's right eye twitched as she considered Iris Szeto. Perched on the luxury AV's white leather seat across from Ani and Jade, the billion-heir had been quiet since the private jet had landed in San Francisco.

Like her aunt Poppy, Iris possessed an ethereal beauty, and an uncanny resemblance to her namesake: tall and slender-stemmed, though she wore a vivid red instead of deep purple. And Jade knew Iris was far from delicate, also like her aunt. She was ruthless, unforgiving, and skilled with the world's most powerful stun taser besides.

Fooled by a Szeto twice, shame on me, Jade warned herself. She kept her eyes squarely away from the window, not risking a view of the fear symbol. Jade knew the Szetos had an arm of their empire in the city, but Jade didn't like returning to such a Conservator hot spot. Not at all. Right now, she wondered if Iris brought them here to find information on Hariri's whereabouts, as she'd promised, or if she was playing Jade, just like Poppy had.

One thing Jade hated more than being pitied: being underestimated.

Iris's cutting stare scrutinized Jade's ripped jeans and patchwork tee, her most recent bruises and lacerations. *Likely assessing the value of her acquired strays,* Jade thought, nettled. What did she care what some overindulged blue blood thought of her?

Yet Jade found herself posturing. Spine straight, jaw clenched, sharp glare meeting Iris's obsidian eyes. Jade toyed with the cold chain of the zipper pocket that held her vials. Iris absently stroked the faint abrasion that wrapped her neck, the only mar on her flawless skin.

"So you and Vance Yates, huh?" Jade said. "I bet Poppy *loved* that."

On the jet, Jade had recounted Poppy's double-crossing, her fatal undoing, her son's extravagant sacrifice, her final warning: *beware the cities.* When Jade had gotten to the part about the Conservators' invisible weapon, she studied Iris closely, aiming to learn how much Poppy's niece truly knew of the nano reform and its Yates-made predecessor. But Iris's porcelain face never cracked.

Jade figured she'd just have to prod a little harder. "Your forbidden romance was a whopping secret," she goaded. "But I guess secrets must be a family trade." She avoided Ani's *you're one to talk* glare. "Poppy had a mountainous secret of her own."

Iris unsealed her red lips. "You'll have to change," she said, dodging Jade's scrutiny. She pointed to two large mint-green boxes, thick and made of a shiny cardboard. Had Iris ordered *clothes?*

Ani reached across the aisle, the blood-colored gemstone on her left ear swinging as she opened each box. Two oversize silk cashmere suits were folded inside. She scattered the boxes to the floor, crossing her arms over her upcycle leather jacket, careful to avoid her wound. "I like my own clothes just fine."

"You told me that you wanted answers and would do anything to get them," Iris said, waving to the crumpled finery already wrinkling by Jade's feet. "If that's true, then you will put these on. We'll be attending the soirée of the season."

Jade perked up. "Are we party crashing?"

"Something like that."

The AV came to a stop, and Jade peered out the window. They had parked alongside the waterfront, next to a building with a dramatic 245-foot clock tower at its center.

"This is the Ferry Building . . ." Ani said, her eyes wide, like she was on the verge of piecing something together.

Jade was connecting the dots, too. The Ferry Building was San Francisco's iconic, turn-of-the-century transportation hub, and Jade remembered that the much-anticipated Quartet Line was scheduled to debut that week. Had they just turned up at the launch party for the Szetos' momentous intercontinental rail line? *A symbolic setting,* Jade thought, glancing out at the soaring Bay Bridge. Celebrating the future of travel on the foundations of the structure that had paved the way.

But why would Iris have to crash her own party?

"Don't bother changing shoes," Iris said, frowning at Jade's worn-out boots. "If you move fast, like me, the stiffs will hardly notice." She swept a finger across the glass console beside her armrest, and the door lifted upward. She was gone before Jade could ask any follow-up questions.

Jade and Ani quickly slipped on their respective luxe suits, Ani choosing the double-breasted jacket, Jade the no-collar V-neck blazer. They exchanged approving once-overs—Jade hadn't donned something this soft since her Adsum days—and then stalked to the rear of the venue, where Iris stood waiting outside the staff entrance.

"You both clean up well," Iris said, shrewdly sizing them up.

"Was that meant to be a compliment?" Ani asked, whipping the long sheet of her hair behind her shoulders.

Iris shrugged and pulled open the back door, revealing a massive industrial kitchen teeming with cooks in tall chef hats and waitstaff in white tuxedos. Iris adjusted the lapel of her red suit and strolled into the bustling room like she owned the place. *Maybe she does,* Jade thought, following.

They hustled down the food prep station, Jade gaping at rows of silver trays laden with lobster-tail, foie gras, gold-leafed macarons. Crates filled with hundreds of bottles of Cristal champagne. All, without question, pure—devoid of the Conservators' nanobots. Jade's upper lip lifted with disdain. The Fortunate guests could gorge themselves on gourmet food blissfully free of worry, while the unhoused had to cross their fingers over a cheap pack of chewing gum.

"And do we have any misgivings about running into your family?" Ani asked, her voice stripped with concern. Jade didn't blame her. She couldn't say she was up for encountering Iris's father, either. Hoi Szeto loathed Damon Yates, all things Quest, and his sister Poppy's Unfortunate Adsum fosters in particular.

Iris released a contemptuous chuckle, her amusement cutting through the babble of the kitchen. "My family was blacklisted from this little *ceremony*."

"What's that supposed to—" Jade started to ask, but then the answer rolled right past her.

A towering, ten-foot wedding cake, with an elaborate purple-and-pale-pink peacock draping across one side, was being whisked out into the lobby.

"Holy Quake." Ani stiffened beside Jade. "Are we nuptial crashing *Qin and Song's* reception?"

"*Who?*" Jade asked, confused as to how Ani could possibly know these billion-heirs. "And why do you suddenly look so adrenalized?"

"I had a lot of time to kill at the hospital, and reality TV treated my soul," Ani replied, unabashed. "This is supposed to be the wedding of the century."

Iris scoffed. "It would have been, had I not thrown my engagement ring from Andy Song into the middle of the Bering Strait *months* ago."

Ani's thick brows lifted in veneration, her big brown eyes eager with questions, but Iris tracked after the showstopper of a cake, escorting a wary Jade and Ani into the expansive Grand Hall, which had been transformed into a reception fit for royalty.

The extravagance took Jade's breath away. A quarter million roses adorned the walls and arched ceiling, the tops of hundreds of circular tables set for a thousand of the bride and groom's closest friends. A purple carpet lined with candles ran down the center of the Grand

Hall, leading to a holographic castle projected behind the newlyweds' elevated head table.

As if these people aren't already living a fairy tale, Jade thought scornfully. She scanned the lively party, full of Fortunates dressed in crisp white ties and elegant ball gowns, finding no sign of the bride or groom. *Who should I be on the lookout for?* From the sides of her eyes, Jade searched the silk lapels for pins. Surely there was a Conservator or two present. Was Iris here to interrogate one of them?

Iris moved for the smooth stone staircase that led to the entryway, but the crowd suddenly gasped, turning Jade's attention back to the cake. The peacock's tail feathers had burst into pink flames, crackling and sparking in a kinetic, fiery display that got Jade's heart racing.

Then she saw something that stopped her heart completely.

Maxen Yates.

Jade didn't think to ask how or when or why, she just ran to him. Her body flooded with relief, her vision tunneling in on the dark tousled waves of his mane, the loose-fitting two-toned suit, identical to the one she last saw him in, at this very city's portal.

"Maxen?" Jade said—*shouted.*

He didn't hear her. He strolled away from the pyrotechnics, farther from Jade. She picked up speed and tripped on the glittering train of a woman's dress, flew forward, arms flailing, and landed shoulder-first onto the wedding cake.

A scream rent the air.

It was Maxen—no, it wasn't Maxen at all, just another young man with the same cavalier swagger. The face was a stranger's. His mouth gaped at Jade in horror. Had Jade spilled her fear fragrance? No. She looked down to her arm. It was on fire.

For a few breaths, Jade didn't react, overcome with the strangeness of the non-sensation. She didn't feel a thing. Was it shock? Or something else? She remembered Cole's numb reaction when the AI robot sliced his foot open in Hema's lab.

Then a jolt of cold water brought Jade back into her body. Ani had come to her side and doused the flames. "Gotta make haste," she said, trying not to grimace at the gruesome burns as she hauled Jade to her feet. "Security's coming." Ani escorted them quickly out of the Grand Hall, the crowd's attention now drawn to the dance floor and the beats of a famous DJ.

"You all right?" Iris asked Jade when they rejoined her at the bottom of the staircase. Her words were civil, but the shrewd look in her dark eyes suggested that Jade had better say yes, wounded or not.

She nodded, and shoulder to shoulder, they smuggled themselves into a long, thin room where an intimate few—family only, Jade swiftly worked out—were smack in the middle of a traditional Chinese tea ceremony.

The bride and groom, the only ones in red besides Iris, were kneeling on pillows, presenting tea to their elder relatives. No one noticed the new guests' presence, except a long-faced man in a peach-colored suit.

Iris flicked her eyes to the open door on the far wall. The man gave no indication he'd understood—or would follow—but Iris moved for the threshold without a second glance.

A stack of red envelopes, doubtless stuffed with cash worth a billion-heir's ransom, sat unguarded atop a marble end table. Jade shoved her hands inside her pockets to keep herself from snatching a few. It was the least she could do, seeing how she'd already wrecked the newlyweds' exorbitant cake. She considered it her wedding gift.

They entered a wide hallway, smart lights overhead awakening at their appearance. Upholstered chairs with circular backs like white pupilless eyes were scattered about the plush carpet. Iris deposited herself into one. Jade and Ani remained standing.

"I haven't worked it out just yet," Jade said, scanning for exit points, "how you expect this guy to offer up any information." She crossed her arms, forgetting her recent burn. "I assume the disengagement wasn't an amicable one?"

The peach-tuxedoed man rushed in, corroborating Jade's suspicions.

"Showing up in a bride's red, expecting to win my son back?" The man's face went scarlet, fighting to keep from shouting.

"Sadly it appears I'm too late for that," Iris replied, looking the antithesis of dejection. With her pointed stiletto heel, she kicked a nearby chair to face hers.

The groom's father didn't take it. His heavy glare landed on Ani, then Jade. "Are these the delinquents your aunt raised? The ones that Hariri wants?" He shook his head. "I see what you're after now. You want the codes."

"Yes," Iris said evenly.

"No," the man answered with a twisted smile. "There is an etiquette, and if the Szetos were not notified of the upcoming high-ground market, then the Exhibition is closed to you. There's nothing I can do . . ." His eyes shone with a fiendish satisfaction. "We are not family, you see."

Jade had no idea what "the Exhibition" was, but it sounded promising.

Ani seemed to agree. As the man turned to leave, one of her blades whizzed through the stuffy air, sinking into the hand-painted wallpaper with a sharp *thunk*, impeding the man's escape. A thin line of blood trickled along his high cheekbone where steel had caressed skin. He didn't move to wipe it.

His head snapped to Iris, his trigger finger toward Jade. "You've made a poor alliance, Ms. Szeto. Your family might be the Golden State's richest, but your social standing is beggarly. Your crazed cousin Maxen locked away for matricide—"

"Don't call him that," Jade spat, venom stinging her veins. Her hand shot to her zipper pocket. To her vials.

"Why is this tearaway speaking to me?" the man snapped. "I'm tainted even listening to you. Leave. There is nothing that will make me help you."

Iris looked to Jade. "I believe you have something that can change his mind . . ."

So Iris knew of her fear fragrance, the power Jade could unleash with a single spritz.

"Use it," Ani whispered. And that was all Jade needed.

The groom's father fumbled for something inside his tuxedo jacket, but Jade was already an arm's length away, the nozzle of her vial aimed at the man's flared nostrils. His hand clamped around the fresh burn on her forearm, and he tried to force Jade back, but she only pushed forward, not screams but laughter bouncing up the walls of her throat.

She sucked in a deep breath, sprayed, and watched, numb as her arm, when the man's furious eyes stretched wide in horror at the sight of her face.

With a swift swipe to his legs, Jade had him flat on the carpet, the heel of her palm pressed into his windpipe, fingers peeling back his eyelids. Nose-to-nose with him.

"The codes, the location, and the date," Iris spoke from her chair. "I think you understand now that we are not asking."

He answered through his shrieking, though it sounded like drivel to Jade, whose heartbeat pounded in her skull, her mind suddenly lost to the sound of someone else's terror. She heard Crys screaming, trapped in a fear incursion. Her own. The tortured screams of the banished Unfortunates torn from their homes by a nanoweapon, so similar to the one she was employing now.

Ani grabbed her uninjured arm and pulled her from the hallway, out of the building, and into the chilly afternoon, with Iris right behind them.

"Tell me the Conservators will be at this Exhibition," Jade panted, shaking off the screams as she inhaled gulps of the damp air.

"They're the ones *leading* it, Jade," Ani answered, breathless herself.

"Hariri is a businessman, above all else," Iris said, tapping her watch to summon the AV. "When you told me the truth behind the success of our metropolis's restorations, I had an inkling that Hariri would seek to capitalize on this exclusive new product of his."

The high-ground market, the groom's father had said, a fancy way of referring to the Fortunates' underground trade in stolen and highly illicit goods. The realization hit Jade with the impact of a hyperloop pod.

"And when is this Exhibition?" she asked, hurrying into the AV's cabin.

"Tomorrow," Iris said.

Of course it was tomorrow.

"Where?"

Ani sighed. "Monaco."

Crys had always wanted to visit Monaco. Yates had never taken her. Well, Jade would take her now.

"We're going to squeeze in a quick layover before crossing the Atlantic," Jade said, a statement, a command. She wasn't asking. "To Texas, to pick up a few sibs."

Iris nodded, staring fixedly at the singed flesh of Jade's arm. Bright magenta icing from the cake mixed with the sickly yellow ooze of her burns, making Jade think deliriously of Ani's paint palettes.

"Do you really not feel it?" Iris asked.

Jade shook her head, her eyes on the vicious wound that felt so disconnected from her body. Her mind.

"Jade, something is seriously wrong here," Ani said, radiating anxiety.

Jade knew what she was thinking. An unexpected side effect of the nano reform.

But Jade wasn't anxious at all. She felt a new kind of power surging through her body. For the first time since losing her Quest Bot, a thrum of adrenaline—the good kind—quickened her blood. She felt like she had suddenly returned to herself, and she didn't care if it was manufactured. She may no longer be fearless, but she was now impervious to pain.

Jade laughed, drunk on the possibilities.

EIGHT

Maxen Yates came to, recumbent in a luxury hardwood bathtub. He opened his eyes, noticing himself before noticing his surroundings. His immensely dry mouth. His settled mind. How the obsessive, racing thoughts had ceased. How out of place his orange prison jumpsuit looked against the sculpted mahogany, how wrong.

He sat up, gaping incredulously at the lushly appointed bathroom that for a second gave him double vision: twin marble sinks, twin cabinets, twin faucet heads in the glass-enclosed shower built into the center of the room. He breathed in lavender and eucalyptus, became conscious of soft instrumental music. It felt like he'd awakened from his stark cell in Pelican Bay to a plush day spa.

Maxen gripped the tub's smooth wooden sides, suddenly dizzy.

He'd been drugged and moved—he understood that much—but *why*? Denied meds or any form of jailhouse psychotherapy, he'd spent the past month sequestered, twenty-three hours a day, in a single cell, cut off from the outside world. Alone with his unbalanced mind. It seemed like a direct order from the Conservators, his *brothers*: lock him up and throw away the key. Out of sight, out of the public's mind.

Where had they tried to bury him now? *A luxurious coffin is still a coffin,* Maxen thought, rising to his bare feet. Ignoring his thirst, he pressed his ear against the dark mahogany door. Silence. Who knew if there were guards on the other side? Or a camera watching his every move? But he'd learn nothing by sitting still. If there was a chance he could break out, he'd take it.

The door slid open to a full-blown VIP suite, complete with a king-sized bed, lounge area, and private office. No guards, no windows from which to espy his location. He moved for the computer on the sleek desk, not holding much hope that his new jailer would be so indiscreet as to keep a device with Wi-Fi at his disposal.

This assumption proved true. The motherboard wouldn't even boot up. He turned and surveyed the room for something to arm himself with. He'd only been granted a half hour for outdoor exercise in a small, highly secure area with one other inmate, but Maxen was a quick study. He wasn't in Quest Campus anymore, with his father, his *name*, to protect him.

He could still remember the crack of the correctional officer's rifle just as the inmate's shiv reached his throat.

Maxen shook his head, clearing it. Finding nothing useful, he flattened his ear against the door. More silence.

With nothing but a clenched fist, Maxen threw open the door, ready to swing, duck, or run, but he was met with a long, empty hallway. He roved down the champagne-colored carpet, checking the doors on each side of the corridor. All housed lavish beds and gilded dressers, but no people.

Undeterred, Maxen kept walking, finding himself in a central lobby, split into two lounges by a grand spiral staircase. One was filled with velvet blue sofas and a rosette-patterned rug that gave the illusionary effect that it was vibrating every time Maxen moved his head. The other contained a circular bar and professional-grade home cinema complete with reclining leather seats.

A shiver snaked up Maxen's spine. This mansion was fit for a billionaire, a *Conservator*. Another crack sounded in his mind, another gun firing a bullet into his mother's thigh.

A fresh swell of rage rose in him. At the red-haired Conservator for killing Poppy, at Hariri for betraying her. At his mother for betraying *him*, for ever having joined their side. At himself for his rash sacrifice, rendering himself utterly useless in the larger fight.

His fists clenched once more, but he was going to need more than his hands if he wanted to break out of here and be of use again. Eyes raking his surroundings, Maxen detected a fire extinguisher on the wall at the bottom of the grand staircase. He moved stealthily, descending the bespoke maple steps on the balls of his feet, then lunged for the weapon before anyone occupying the ground floor could stop him.

But like the bedrooms above, this floor was outwardly empty. Holding the extinguisher out in front of him, his thumb hovering above the release nozzle, Maxen peered into a stylish home gym, a fourteen-seat dining area designed inside a tranquil orangery, and a spectacular paddle tennis court. Still no sign of his jailers.

It wasn't until he stood still in the center of the vast living room, staring up at the hand-cut glass ceiling, that Maxen registered that all the mansion's curtains were drawn. His sense of dislocation suddenly skyrocketed. The only clue to his current location was a bright, sunny sky. He strode for the nearest door, swung it open, and immediately staggered backward, overwhelmed.

He'd somehow traded supermax for a super*yacht*.

One hand braced over his eyes, Maxen padded onto the bow's helipad, taking in the infinite cobalt sea. There were no other people inside the mega vessel, and no land in sight. Reeling, Maxen stumbled to the deck's stainless-steel handrail, gripping it tight as he peered into the water's depth, desperate to find any sense of bearing. Judging by its color and the lack of light reflecting off the bottom, Maxen estimated he was somewhere far out at sea, but he could have been *anywhere*. And he was alone. *I might as well be stranded on a desert island,* he lamented.

Panic flooded his mind, making him forget himself. He started to unbutton his jumpsuit before remembering that the anti-abduction microchip embedded in his arm had been cut out after his arrest. Not that anyone at Quest would have answered his call for help. He'd chosen the Exiles, *Jade*, over his family.

He had to get to the helm. Find the yacht's coordinates, send out a distress signal, program a route to the nearest seaport. The vessel might be empty now, but that helipad meant someone could arrive at any moment. Holding on to the rail—his legs felt wobbly despite the smooth sea—Maxen made his way to the center deck.

He found the wheelhouse's door already open. He stepped inside, running his hands over the sleek control system. This model looked similar to his father's *Aurora*, which meant the vessel was AI-captained, equipped with twin radars, a navigational sonar that could capture a huge field of view at long range every two seconds, and a GPS with built-in chart plotters, all of which could give Maxen an indication where in the briny deep he was. But even if he did know how to command the controls, the complex system was locked to whatever course his jailer had set.

He scoured the wheelhouse for alternative distress signals. The cord to the radio was cut, and the emergency locator beacon, air horn, and flares had all been cleared out. He'd have to hope for a plane to fly over and resort to arm signals.

Frustrated, Maxen pounded one of the nineteen-inch touch screens. Surprisingly, it popped on, and a movement tracker appeared, a Doppler radar system that detected the presence of persons within the vessel. Maxen's blood froze.

The interior of the yacht may have been empty, but there was someone on the sky deck. According to the radar, whoever it was stood still, breathing slowly. Relaxed.

Apparently his jailer *wanted* to be found.

Curiosity burned through Maxen. Anticipation at being unexpectedly thrown back into the fight. He climbed the deck's stairs, telling himself that whoever he was about to face had already had a chance to kill him.

Still, he gripped tight to his makeshift weapon as he stepped onto the landing, his eyes going directly to the starboard side where the tracker radar had placed the passenger that awaited him.

Maxen struggled to conceal his utter shock.

A bare-chested man in mid-length marble-print swim shorts rested on a deluxe daybed, surveying the monotonous ocean blue. A bottle of añejo tequila settled in one hand, an empty stemless glass flute in the other.

"*Vance?*"

His head of excessive golden hair swiveled, dull aquamarine eyes rolling over Maxen with grim appraisal. "Brother," Vance greeted.

"*Half*," Maxen countered. He toggled between relief and disdain at discovering the minor Gen 1. He fiddled with the nozzle of the fire extinguisher, calculating whether to douse Vance with the jet of freezing carbon dioxide or hit him over the head with the tank.

Where was Palmer? Gen 1 rarely divided.

Vance nodded toward Maxen's fire extinguisher, amused. "Hoping to quench some flames, little brother?" he mocked, filling his flute to the brim and knocking back the golden liquid.

Maxen skipped over his first and obvious question—*Why in Savior's sake am I on a yacht?*—in favor of query number two. "Why in Savior's sake are *you* on a yacht?"

"I'm in quarantine," Vance sighed, refreshing his glass. "I was jettisoned here"—he lifted his ringed fingers disconcertedly toward the open horizon surrounding them—"wherever in high hell *here* is, to reconsider my sins. And make certain they don't spread."

They were both on a floating prison, Maxen comprehended. *Vance is my cellmate, not my jailer.*

"Glad to see you didn't piss yourself." Vance smiled. "The soaking tub seemed preferable to the floor . . . I was willing to play doctor, but changing soiled linens is well below my pay grade."

Maxen kept his face neutral, his tone patient. "You were *doctoring* me?"

Tampering with my mind.

Vance's grin faded. "Before Hariri's rabid wolf pack besieged the Castle in the Air, I had the foresight to take a few of Father's Quest Bots into my custody. *Your* Quest Bot, more specifically."

Maxen supposed he should be grateful, indebted even, but he felt only indignation and ire. "How long?"

"How long have I been stranded here?" Vance answered. "Two days—"

"No," Maxen snapped. "How long have you known of my diagnosis and Father's *prescribed* choice of treatment?"

Maxen himself hadn't ascertained the full scope of his childhood schizophrenia and its "cure" until the night he'd lost everything. His Quest Bot, his family, his freedom. His mind.

"Cool your jets," Vance replied languidly, scrubbing a hard hand over his bloodshot eyes, which were plucked mostly bare of lashes and brows. His *tricho* had returned, Maxen realized. Vance was more distressed than he was letting on. "Father never shared much of anything with me and Palmer, either. When that seventh-year went missing—"

"Zoe Reeves," Maxen interjected. After their father had adopted Crys Moore, essentially stealing the Adsum superstar from his mother— the dean's—foster family, Zoe Reeves had filled Crys's place as Poppy's favorite. There had always been a steady pressure by his mother and the Quest CFOs to push him and Zoe together. *It was a fairy-tale narrative,* they liked to say. No one had fully grasped they were all really living a horror story.

Vance swatted at the air in front of him, as if spooked by something that wasn't there. Maxen thought he caught the muttered names

"Crys" and "Jade," but his half brother drowned any future words with a mouthful of tequila.

Maxen cast his eyes over the calm sheet of sea. He was struck by an overpowering curiosity to know where the sisters were. Was Jade still joined with Crys? Had Maxen flitted across her thoughts? Or had Jade moved on, ever the lone common swift, solitary in her constant flight?

"When Zoe went missing," Vance continued, "Palmer and I initiated our own investigations." He paused, targeting his gaze on Maxen. "Father never really trusted me, did he?" *Was he expecting an answer? Sympathy?* "He never really gave me a chance." Shoving on a pair of square rimless sunglasses, Vance reclined heavily on his daybed. "Things could have ended up differently for all of us had the old man not aspired to be a walking *safe*."

That was one thing the Gens could agree on.

"The man had many lives," Maxen confirmed, "many secrets." Their father had seldom spoken of his life before he was taken in—*chosen*, as he was wont to phrase it—by his adoptive parents. He'd been Damon Hicks, Damon Yates, Damon the Savior. What was he now? "Tell me the truth," Maxen whispered. "Is he dead?"

Vance stared up at the sun, his brow creased intently. "I don't know if anyone told you, but our father had early-onset Alzheimer's." Maxen shook his head. "*Has*, I should say," Vance amended. "Hariri disabled his Quest Bot."

"Do you know where he is?"

"No," Vance admitted. "Although apparently, our father put up a fight before the end. An authentic duel. I would have given my inheritance to have been at his side. But he was alone, taken down by his own saber, and is now in exile, like all his heirs save Palmer."

Vance lifted the bottle of premium tequila and waved it enticingly toward Maxen. "Set down that useless tank, dear brother, and pull up a seat. We're in a Class-G wildfire, and there's nothing either of us can do at this point but lie back and acclimate to the burn."

Maxen shook his head, holding fixedly on to the fire extinguisher. "So you're just giving up?"

Vance hiccuped, stammering out his words. "There's honor in accepting defeat." He poured himself another full glass. "And after I finish off this tequila, I'm certain I will find it."

"*You* might not have anyone else wondering where you've disappeared to," Maxen countered, tugging at his ear, realizing, discomfited, that Vance was unconsciously showcasing the same Yates quirk, "but my other half, the Szetos—"

"*Ha!*" Vance shouted, suddenly surging to his bare feet. The golden tequila splattered over Maxen's naked toes. "Poppy's relatives are why we're *on* this yacht, don't you get it?"

Maxen shuffled closer. Plunked himself down on the splattered daybed. "They were trying to break me out?"

"Of course they were," Vance said, tearing off his square shades and depositing the half-full bottle on the floor as he sat. "Iris is on a rampage."

"So they know that I'm innocent?"

"You're still a federal inmate," Vance grumbled, reaching out a pale finger to flick the collar of Maxen's orange jumpsuit. "Hariri worked out a deal with the governor. This way the Conservators can ensure your safekeeping and captivity, all while saving the precious taxpayer's dollars, you see?"

Maxen rolled up his sleeve. Centimeters from where the family doctor had inserted his missing subcutaneous microchip into his upper arm, there was a second, more recent injection site. He'd been tagged. Now not only Palmer and Hariri could track and monitor his every move, but the government as well.

"I'm never getting off this yacht," Maxen said. He could feel the inferno licking at his neck.

Vance lay back, closing his eyes as he raised his empty glass. "Acclimate."

Maxen pulled off his bright orange jumpsuit, overcome with the impression that he'd been set aflame. *You* chose *self-immolation, martyrdom,* he imagined Palmer taunting from the ship's invisible speakers. *Do you regret it?*

"I'm going for a swim," Maxen whispered, before charging for the edge of the deck. He scaled the steel railing and leapt, for a moment feeling like he had wings.

A lone common swift, he thought ruefully.

When he hit the salty surface, the endless ocean hid his tears.

NINE

Crys closed her eyes, breathing in a lungful of sea breeze. She smelled musky sand, hints of brine and petroleum, sulfuric base notes. Not exactly the fresh scents of Silicon Bay, but close enough for her to feel the magnetic pull of Quest Campus, only thirty-five miles up the coast. Thanks to the Smart Bot that Sage had ingested, uploading a commercial pilot license instantly to her brain, she was able to fly and land the stolen Conservator copter expertly along a deserted beach on the southwest edge of LA.

During the short flight, Willis divulged that he'd learned from a few of the infected fighters of a place where a band of Unfortunates, all too sick to flee the city's fringes, were whispered to be gathering. That was all Crys needed to hear. As soon as they touched ground, she'd grabbed Nolan's phone, using his rideshare app, and his money, to order an AV to take them straight to Point Fermin Park.

Yates could be there, hiding among the ill. It was a long shot, but Crys knew one thing for certain: she wasn't going back to the ranch where *she* had been hiding out from the world all these weeks.

You failed, Crys imagined she heard Jade's voice on the salty breeze. *You already failed to find him. Just come back. Admit that you need me.*

A shout shook Crys's mind back to Shepard Street, where she stood kitty-corner from Point Fermin Park. "Shove off, *intruder!*"

She opened her eyes. Took in the stopped AV at the streetlight, the rage twisting the passenger's mouth as he glared at her cheap, mismatched clothes, her grimy face and wild hair.

"Go back to where you came from!" the man in the AV growled. The city, he meant. Far away from the sanctity of his Fortunate suburb.

Crys drew her fear fragrance from the pouch at her wrist, just as the man uncapped his thermos, steam swirling about his self-righteous smirk. He launched it at her, but before the scalding liquid reached its target, Willis stepped in front of her. Bare arms raised to shield his face, he took the hit without a sound or a grimace. He didn't seem to notice the spritz of perfume on the back of his neck. *A wasted spray,* Crys thought irritably.

"Just add these to the burns I've already got," Willis yelled at the man, holding up his pant legs to show the third-degree burn scars he'd received during the Greater LA Fire.

"You think you're so *privileged,* don't you?" Cole spat. "Well, I've got some privileged information for *you!* The Conservators are the intruders! They're inside of us!"

Cole lunged for the passenger, his usual smile warped into a dark scowl. The stoplight blinked green, and the AV pulled away, leaving Cole kicking at air, again and again, working himself up into such a state the passersby began to stare.

Eli, Wily, and Sage sprinted after him as he barreled toward the park's double barbed-wire fence plastered with KEEP OUT signs.

What on shaking Earth was happening?

Had the nano reform attacked and disabled Cole's Quest Bot? But he'd suffered from chronic depression. This . . . this was something different.

Please just stay away from me, Cole had shouted at Crys.

She remained where she stood.

Beside her, Nolan slipped his shawl from his shoulders, offering it to Willis to wipe the tea from his scalded hands and forearms. "You just keep finding ways to strip me from my clothes, don't you?" Crys's brows shot high. What was happening *here*? More mind games, looking to butter up her uncle, getting him to talk?

Nolan removed the string of bottle caps from his neck, tearing off his miniature microphone and attaching it below the collar of his undershirt.

"Our agreement was to allow you to embed yourself in the warehouse with us, *not* to tag along with the Exiles ad infinitum," Crys said. "Isn't it time for you to return to your little cave of a recording studio?"

"Wild horses couldn't drag me away now, my dear," Nolan answered. He was glowing, like he felt unstoppable. Energized by living an interesting story, rather than documenting someone else's.

Crys scoffed and crossed the street, heading for the park. She walked the fence line, searching for a way through the locked gates that barred them from a field of overgrown shrubs and trees. There was no sign of the gathering place of Unfortunates that Willis had heard rumor of. Why had she been stupid enough to put her trust in that man again? Hadn't he taught her the painful lesson of disappointment over and over when she was a child?

Crys caught the scent of her signature perfume and knew Willis was close behind. She turned, noticing the slight limp he'd been left with after the fire no longer bothered him. Was he still on painkillers? Or was it something else?

Willis followed at her side, staring down at her glass vial with a wavering smile. An arrogant disregard for the unsuspecting power she clasped in her hand flashed across his mold-colored eyes.

Crys shook her head, squeezing the case of her nanoweapon so tight, she risked the glass shattering. "Are you taunting me?"

"No," Willis answered quickly. "I'm admiring you. I have no idea what's in that perfume of yours, but I bet it does more than make my sorry ass smell like peonies."

He knew the top notes of her signature perfume?

Willis chuckled at her surprise. "I just appreciate that you still got some grit under all that Adsum class."

Crys laughed, humorless and sharp. She looked a long way from any definition of "class." She didn't need a mirror to know this. She also didn't need false flattery.

Storing away her vials, Crys increased her pace, outstripping Willis's hobbled gait. "I grew out of needing your validation long ago," she shouted over her shoulder. "Just leave me alone. You were a master of it for years; I think you can manage well enough now."

"Looks like someone's made a thieves' tunnel," Wily said from nearby. Crys joined the others at the spot in the gate where a hole was dug out underneath the metal bars.

"You think you might have been a touch cruel?" Eli murmured to her, nodding toward Willis. "Maybe you should cut him a break. Life has roughed him up pretty bad, like the rest of us, and he's your uncle, after all."

Family didn't always mean blood, Crys recalled. *Sometimes family was who you'd bleed for.* Jade's favorite maxim.

And Crys's uncle had never spilled a drop for her.

"Where's Cole?" she said, ignoring Eli.

"Already took off," Sage answered. "Said he had to be the first to see." She crawled through the thieves' tunnel, and Crys slipped through after her. On the other side, she slinked down an old dirt path and caught sight of a whimsical white wooden house, its deep porch sagging and gabled roof crumbling.

It was a lighthouse, Crys discerned, staring up at the tower and its rounded lantern room surrounded by paneled glass windows. She spotted a bold mark painted onto its base, a large sharp-edged *U*. *This is a safe place,* in old hobo code. A language Crys was forced to learn after Hariri appropriated it for his fear symbol.

A fitting site for the Unfortunates to gather, Crys thought, the symbolism of the structure not lost on her. Hope and security, a place to help weather the Conservators' storm.

Then Sage's fervent whisper was in her ear. "Is that the *Gravestone?*"

Crys nearly froze. The Gravestone. Wasn't he the bodyguard for the mayor of Dry River City? LA's downtown encampment, the Conservators' first target for nano reform?

And Sage and Wily's former home.

"Holy Quake, it is," Wily panted. He slapped a hand to his stomach, which had rounded out without his Quest Bot. "Do you think he'll recognize me?"

"Wily," Sage said, grabbing his hand. "It's your quick wit that wins everyone over." She placed his palm over her heart. "Not a fast metabolism."

Wily's free hand dove to his chest pocket, checking that his secret syringe was still there.

Had he found an alternative bot like Sage had, a way to try and engineer his weight and keep his lissome figure?

"Wily, Sage!" The Gravestone's roar battered against the pavement. One enormous hand blocked his eyes, the other pointed shakily at Crys. "You keep that one away from me!"

So the Gravestone still feared her. Crys smiled, though she lingered back. Eli stuck close, watchful, while the others made their way to the lighthouse entrance.

"It's all right, she's not Jade," Crys heard Wily try to explain.

"That's not the problem," Sage answered, swiftly assessing the situation for what it was. She threw a glaring glance to Nolan and his microphone before leaning close to Wily and whispering, "The Gravestone seems to have been spritzed by Crys."

Crys marched forward, waving an impatient hand toward the Gravestone, who stood still as a large chunk of concrete. "Oh, just tell the softy to close his eyes." Crys had lived with her fear bot for three tormenting years. Her sympathy for the grown man was as paltry as the river he came from. "And I wouldn't squander a spray on *him*. Wily, you remember that miserable night I was imprisoned in your mayor's tent?"

Before she'd begrudgingly aligned with Jade, before the Conservators had begun their citywide "conservation" efforts, a shadow war against the Unfortunates.

Realization dawned on Wily. "Oh, right. I threw your perfume vial out the door." The very door the Gravestone stood watch beside. Wily shrugged, sheepish, to the loutish bodyguard. "No hard feelings? I didn't know Crys was packing fear grenades."

Neither had she. Crys hadn't known it at the time, but the Gravestone was her first victim, the first person she'd made cower from her presence. A sudden powerful urge took hold of Crys, her blood quickening with a desire to add more to the collection of people who feared her.

The Gravestone grunted, his back to Crys. "Mayor's dead," he said, neck bent like he was praying. "Those guys in platinum suits took him right from his bed. They had on those stockings, but it was Hariri. I tried to fight him off, but that laughing bastard threw me to the navy suits. I was in a cell when they stripped Dry River."

"Are you infected?" Eli asked, heedless of Nolan's presence, his prying mike. Whatever Nolan learned now would not be kept quiet. But it was Eli's truth, and it was his to tell. "Because I am."

The Gravestone nodded heavily in reply. "But I'm not sick like the others in there."

"Then why are you here?" Crys asked, gazing up at the derelict lighthouse. She wondered what she'd see behind its rotted walls. What Cole would witness. Alone. *Please, stay away from me.*

Crys found her feet carrying her toward the entrance.

"I came across someone else worth protecting," she heard the Gravestone answer proudly. "I'm the bodyguard of the woman who runs this place."

Willis grabbed her by the arm.

Crys began to pull away. "I thought I told you—"

Willis cut her off. "A warning," he said, releasing her arm. "It might be bad in there."

"And you think I haven't seen bad?" Her mind fell into darkness, and she was trapped inside a pile of rubble, her mother and father entombed beside her, silent and unmoving. Crys shook her head, ridding herself of the memory before the smell came back to her.

She crossed the lighthouse entrance, distantly realizing that the lower level of the building was once an old Victorian home. Squinting as she roamed the dingy space, she hastened for the living room, where she discovered Cole's dark silhouette leaning against a splintered pillar, his body slouched and trembling like he was on the verge of a fear incursion. One look around the makeshift shelter, and Crys was shaking, too.

A dozen people lay terrified against the stained walls, their bodies stiff as wooden dolls, begging their arms and legs to move. A man and woman stood screaming at each other on the chipped staircase, their words so slurred Crys couldn't make out the subject of their quarrel. A young woman lay rocking in a bed of blankets in the corner, mumbling to herself hysterically, scared eyes scouring the air around her.

"Cole?" Crys whispered. "Are you all right?"

He stayed silent, watching the hallucinating woman. His bright hazel eyes swam with anguish. Resignation.

Something tore inside Crys's chest. She wanted to seal her own eyes closed, but she held them open. Latching on to Cole like an anchor. Softly, she padded to his side. Her hand dangled next to his. "Cole, please. Don't go quiet. Don't go dark."

He choked out a sigh. "This is what's next for me, isn't it?"

Crys thought of Eli and Willis. Of Jade. *She volunteered for this.* How could she have been so reckless? So stupid? *Because she's selfish.*

"I'm contaminated," Cole said softly. Brokenly. "I'm disgusting."

"No—" Crys cried. She squeezed her hand around his, pulling him to her, but he jerked back like her touch was lava on his skin.

"I told you to stay away from me!" He turned and ran for the stairs, barreling past the speech-impaired couple toward the lantern room.

Panic spiraled up Crys's spine. She felt herself losing all sense of control.

"*I control fear,*" she all but screamed aloud, clenching her vials tight as she raced after Cole. "*I* control fear."

On the third-floor landing, she burst through the door and gripped the wooden railing of the circular balcony. Unable to stop the rising dread that left her dizzy, she looked up and saw the line where sky met sea. A clean, unobstructed horizon in a messy, congested world.

Instantly, she felt steady.

Instantly, she thought of Yates.

For seven years at Adsum, she'd had a view of the Pacific right outside her window. *What do you see when you stare out at the unfathomable ocean blue?* Yates had asked her once. *A barrier, or a gateway?*

Possibility, she'd answered straightaway. He'd hugged her, his eyes sparkling like the waves before sunset. *A true Quester,* he'd called her, and a peacefulness had washed over her that she hadn't known since the quake.

Right now, Crys could see no gateway. She saw only the endless, impenetrable barrier that loomed before her.

The Conservators are winning, she imagined Jade's taunts on the wind. *You failed to find your pseudo-father. Admit you failed and that he's probably dead. Admit that you're scared.*

Fear does not control me, Crys hissed back. I *control fear.*

"I don't know your tread, you must be a new arrival," a woman's gruff voice said, snapping Crys's attention away from the sea. She saw Cole approach a silver-haired figure standing on the far side of the balcony, facing the sweeping cliffside. A white collapsible cane stood out against her golden-brown skin, a cape made of blankets tied around her throat, the thin cotton flowing in the breeze. Crys remembered the survival trick. *Never be caught sleeping cold.* A red-haired boy the age of an Adsum first-year cowered beneath the folds.

"How many?" Cole asked by way of greeting. "How many infected with the nano reform have come to you like this?"

"Ah, so there's an official name for these intruders," the woman said, tapping a long finger against her temple as she turned to face him. She was willowy and gaunt-cheeked, and although her misty gray eyes were blind, they shone with an intensity that struck Crys in the chest. *This woman is a fighter.*

"Right now it's fifty," the woman answered. "But every day more keep coming in from the outskirts of the cities. They can't keep roaming to stay safe like the other Unfortunates, so I had to do something." She gestured to the run-down lighthouse.

Cole lowered his head. Crys moved to stand at his side as the others burst through the lantern room's arched door onto the balcony, the Gravestone pushing past Crys to station himself protectively beside the woman and the boy. "All good here, Celene?"

"What'd I tell you about not needing any guarding?" Celene said, without heat.

"Sage, can any of those Brainious juices you drank be of use here?" Wily asked.

Frustrated, Sage rapped her sharp acrylic nails against her thighs, staring back at the door. At the people suffering below. She unleashed a tirade of curses in Korean, a language she'd uploaded to her mind with the Smart Bots.

"A pilot *and* a medic?" Willis said, confused. "That's asking too much, even if she did go to Adsum."

"Oh, the things Adsum gave us," Wily lamented under his breath, likely thinking of his Quest Bot.

"Shouldn't these people go to the hospital or something?" Eli asked Celene. Crys kept her eyes from Cole, from the thought that *he* might need to go there himself.

Celene sighed and shook her head, her tight curls falling into her eyes. "And risk seeing those diagonal slash marks and hollering their heads off? Any doctor would send them straight to a psych ward. A few of them downstairs narrowly escaped that fate."

"Unfortunates don't want to end up in that place, trust me," Willis chimed in.

Nolan cleared his throat. "I would be remiss not to ask—has a man named Damon Yates been through here?"

"Everybody only ever cares about a missing white billionaire," Celene sighed again. "But a whole community of homeless up and vanishes?" She rubbed at her sightless eyes. "The LA mayor throws a restoration parade."

"I didn't mean any offense. He's disappeared—" Nolan began.

But Celene cut him off with a bitter laugh. "Sorry to disappoint, but there's been no sighting of the great tech giant anywhere near these sad parts," she said. "Some philanthropist he turned out to be."

The boy emerged from the folds of her cape, blinking up at Crys. He swatted the air, stumbling toward her as he reached a bandaged hand to touch Crys's uncombed golden curls. "Your hair's the same color as Hicks's."

Celene kept her collapsible cane folded at her side as she moved for the boy, patiently unlatching his grasp. "He has hallucinations," she explained. "Sometimes sees things that aren't there."

Hicks. Crys closed her eyes, shouted the name in her mind. Listened to it echo off the walls of her memories.

Youthful features from an old photograph appeared in the dark. Hollow cheeks. Desolate eyes. Lips like a rigid line that never learned to smile. It was the face of Hicks.

Damon Hicks.

The forgotten memory burned through Crys, igniting her hope. Her conviction. Hicks was Damon's undisclosed surname before he'd been adopted as a Yates.

I found you.

Crys struggled to keep her voice steady as her heart battered against her ribs. "What happened to Hicks? Is he here?"

"Before I started this place up, me and the boy, Lucas, kept company with a quiet man who kept forgetting things. Kept wandering off until, finally, he never came back."

Crys's hope plummeted. Yates was still out there somewhere. Lost in his dementia.

If he was even still alive.

Suddenly Eli's whisper was in her ear, hot and urgent. "Check your phone, Jade's been blasting us with *rfa*s. She wants us back at the ranch."

Crys didn't bother to keep her voice low. "We're in the middle of our own *rfa*. If she wants us, tell her to come to me."

"Yeah, I told her you'd say that," Wily replied. "But she said it's about Hariri and something called an Exhibition. She seemed to think you'd know what that meant."

Goose bumps prickled Crys's arms, a cold sweat stinging her palms as if she'd grabbed hold of an electric fence. Yet to say she was shocked would be a lie. If there was one thing she'd learned living among billionaires, it was that they loved to posture. To flaunt their fortunes. Make a show of their power. And there was no grander stage than the exclusive Exhibition.

Hariri means to unveil his nano reform to the Fortunates of the world. Was he about to take the Conservators' invisible war against the poor global?

"We have to go," Crys implored. *"Now."*

No one put up an argument. They must have heard the *red fucking alert* in her voice.

"I'll get tickets for the next hyperloop to Austin," Sage said, thumbs working her phone.

"And us?" Celene asked. "Here I thought you folks were here to help. What am I supposed to do when the navy suits finally come peeking under the rug we've swept ourselves under?"

"We can't just leave them," Eli pressed. "If these people get put into institutions, it'll be ten times harder to find them when Hema discovers the cure."

Willis stepped forward. "Nolan, order up some vans. You won't mind these fine people watching over your mansion in the Hardihood Hills for you while you're away?"

Nolan hesitated, but only briefly. "Of course not." He glanced at Crys, his eyes narrowing. *The price for access,* they seemed to say. *Paid in full.*

A colony of seagulls soared above the lighthouse, heading inland for the mountains. Northeast, toward Los Angeles. Toward home.

The dramatic V dominating the sky above them was disproportioned, the lower half spread wide, forming a hard-edged U instead.

This is a safe place.

This is a safe place.

Soon, Crys would make it true.

TEN

Jade chucked a shovelful of mesquite onto a bed of hot coals, then slammed closed the smoker's heavy firebox door. Fireflies danced under the low branches of wide live oaks. Pinks and oranges splashed across the ranch's endless horizon, setting a picturesque scene. But Jade took none of it in.

Her mind wasn't there. Her thoughts *should* be ten steps ahead, scheming ways to infiltrate the Exhibition. Strategies and backup plans to stop Hariri and his quest to bring nano reform to market. But Hema and Rhett snatched hold of Jade's nerves. Her focus. Her panic.

"I still don't believe it," she sighed. "How could they just abandon us like that?" She whipped around to Ani, who sat on the ranch's flagstone patio beside the dining table she'd helped Jade set earlier. "No note left behind. No goodbye. *No shaking cure.*"

Ani glanced up from her sketch pad, fingers dusted with charcoal. "Guardians leave," she stated evenly. "They fail. That's what they do."

She returned to her drawing of the Adsum sibs, who were gathered around a bonfire, roasting marshmallows under the big Texas sky. Two completed sketches lay on the table beside her, nine-inch by twelve-inch windows into her mind. One was a raw, moving rendering of Khari and Zoe, the other a detailed outline of the Soaring Precious, the saber that had almost taken Ani's life.

According to Finn, the straw that had broken the rabbit's back had been their failure to nab the MIT professor. Hema was desperate for backup, the impossible burden of finding a cure to the nano reform too much for one scientist alone. But Jade feared her stunt with the bot-laced gum and subsequent barring of students from the lab didn't help the high-stress situation. But for Rhett to run away with Hema and not answer Jade's *rfas* to get the hell back to the ranch, *now*? That stung.

And it also meant that Jade was left in charge. The big problem with the new guardian role? There was a jet waiting to take Jade and Ani to Monaco, to crash the Exhibition. But was she really going to leave the lab and her Adsum sibs? Add her name to the long list of lousy protectors?

She stared out at the dark, empty driveway, wishing for signs of Rhett's truck. Or an AV, crowded with missing Exiles.

"Crys will come," Ani assured Jade, fiddling with her ruby earring. A habit, Jade had noticed, much like her own with In Extremis. Jade reached for her bullet, but it was gone. Just like Crys was gone.

I'll leave you, her sister had sworn. And Crys always made good on her promises.

"Crys won't leave her family," Ani assured her. "Besides, she might not be a billion-heir anymore, but Crys still loves her *things*." Ani nodded to Jade's zipper pocket, to the fear fragrance hidden beneath her handkerchief, then tapped a broken bit of charcoal to her drawing of the ancient saber. "Priceless items she's sure to reclaim, sooner than later."

Would Crys really only return to the ranch for the chance of stealing back Yates's saber? Would she really demand Jade offer back her nanoweapon supply?

Every strand of her DNA wanted to say no. But they were still strangers, she realized. Strangers who shared a face. How odd. How pitiful. The thought made Jade want to scream.

"Just keep busying your hands with cooking, pit master," Ani said. Jade grunted and stabbed a meat thermometer into a slab of venison—still under 140 degrees. That's exactly what she'd been doing the last few hours, since they'd returned to the Texas Hill Country—occupying her impatient hands. *Busy hands, quiet mind*—a guiding principle for life at Quest. She wondered briefly what new doctrine Palmer had imposed, now that he'd taken the keys to the Yates Empire.

Waiting for Crys's response to her *rfa*, Jade had paced the property and found a walk-in deer cooler, a rancher's ultimate trophy case, and focused her hands for five minutes while she picked its lock. When Jade saw the prized cuts of game meat hanging on large hooks, she decided she'd cook the sibs a feast. Smoking meat took hours and constant attention, a challenge that would ground her mind into the present.

Except it hadn't. She'd forgotten to dry brine the venison, too distracted by things out of her control.

"The meat's going to be tough," Jade sighed, frustrated.

"I don't think anyone was expecting something tender from Jade Moore," Ani said with a quick laugh. "It'll be fine; we'll just slather it in a lake of barbecue sauce."

Tires on pavement cut through the chorus of chirping field crickets, turning Jade's attention back to the driveway. Not Crys, but Iris, who'd stayed back at the private airfield miles from the ranch to "make some calls." The formidable woman struck Jade as the type who was even worse at standing still than she was. Her arrival probably meant it was wheels up, with or without the passengers they'd come to collect.

"Think we can hold her off with some down-home cooking?" Jade asked.

"There's no need," Ani said, nodding to a second vehicle pulling into the drive.

111

Before it even came to a stop, Eli and Cole shot out of the AV and charged for the lab, where they likely thought they'd find Hema.

"Who's going to tell them the unfortunate news?" Jade sighed.

"I'll do it." Ani gathered her sketches and rose from the table, setting off for the garage. "And you go make good with Crys."

Crys had emerged from the passenger seat, advancing for the Adsum sibs at the bonfire, not even glancing in Jade's direction. Jade had been avoiding the fire like a fear symbol, a top reason she'd chosen to station herself at the smoker. Of course Crys had chosen to hide out there.

"Something smells like it's burning," Wily said, approaching the patio with Sage.

Jade slipped her bandaged arm behind her back. Wily plucked a slab of venison from the smoker before rushing to the dinner table, downing every last glass filled with water. "But I'm not complaining," he mumbled over a mouthful of meat.

"Whatever you've been up to seems to have brought back your appetite," Jade said, raising an eyebrow at how he devoured the venison like it was his last meal. "Where exactly have you been?"

Sage grabbed a handful of asparagus from the grill rack and set it on the table next to where Wily stood. "Does it hurt?" she asked, changing the subject, pointing a long acrylic nail toward Jade's injured arm.

"A little," Jade lied.

Sage and Wily shared a look, like they knew the truth of her pain immunity. Or was it more than that?

"What are you hiding from me?" Jade asked.

Wily locked pinkies with Sage. "We're coupled up."

"You don't think I've seen you two together on Hema's bench?" Jade scoffed. "I know you're keeping more than that. Where have you been?"

"You should talk to Crys," Sage said. "Be the better woman, and go to her first."

Jade glanced at her sister. She was perched on a log beside Iris at the bonfire, no doubt getting caught up on the crew's recent escapades. Crys's run-down appearance contrasted with the sleek image Iris cut in the light of the flames. But even beneath all that grime, Crys still bore the elegance and poise of a Yates. The two billion-heirs were more alike than Jade and Crys would ever be.

"Something I've never been," Jade replied. "The better sister."

"Well, now's your chance," Wily sighed, sitting down at Ani's vacant chair. "It could be now or never, right?"

Sage jammed an elbow into Wily's arm.

All right, what on shaking Earth is going on? Jade thought.

"Toss me some of Ani's charcoal," she said to Wily.

Sage rolled her eyes. "For Savior's sake, your sister's not going to poison you."

"Right," Jade said, "but she might poison even more of *you* against *me*." She closed the lid of the smoker and stormed off toward Crys, but she froze when a familiar, raspy voice called to her from an oak tree near the patio.

"Jade Moore. Still playing with fire, even though she got burned."

Uncle Willis approached her cautiously, green eyes scanning the strips of deep red blisters poking out from her gauzed-up arm.

"Yeah, well, you should see the cake." Jade tucked her arm behind her back and studied Willis in turn. His shaved head, his beard crusted with blood. His splintered fingers, the gashes in his faded clothes that Jade recognized as knife marks. He looked like a roughed-up stray, and yet he was still, somehow, smiling. Jade didn't know if she should give him a hug, a handshake, or a left hook. Family reunions never had begun well for the Moores.

Jade settled on a scowl. "Crys brought you here?"

He nodded. "She found me in a Conservators' fighting ring. It's a wretched story. Maybe we should gather round another bonfire sometime, and I'll tell you about it."

Same sadistic humor. Same laughable promises. Willis's unease around flames was twofold compared to hers. Was he challenging her? Testing her madcap reputation?

Jade put his offer on the back burner, switching back to Crys. "So she'll talk to you but not me?" she said, temper flaring. Was Crys trying to nettle her nerves, to destabilize Jade further? Shake things up, per Willis's long-standing advice?

"Hey, Gem!" Willis yelled to Crys. Jade had to breathe and count to ten. Willis used to call Crystal "Gem" and Jade "Stone," familial nicknames for the gemstones their parents had named them after. "Can I steal you away for a second?"

Dredging up the old epithet got the precise reaction that Jade had expected: bold-as-brass rage. Crys stormed over, arms crossed, the oak-bark roots of her hair gleaming in the firelight. "Don't cause a scene," she hissed.

"Why would we cause a scene?" Willis asked. He seemed genuinely disconcerted, holding out his hands as if saying a benediction. Did he really expect Jade and Crys to take them? When they didn't, he scraped a calloused palm over the short bristle on his head. "Streets take me," he gawped. "You both are as tall as me. Stunners of course, just like Emmy."

Jade's mouth dropped open at the man's sober audacity in mentioning their mother. She took half a second to inhale for a long tirade, but Crys's tongue-lashing struck him first.

"Willis. We might share blood, a last name . . ." Jade remembered the story of their parents and uncle united in legally changing their surnames for a fresh start. They liked that Moore meant "an area of uncultivated land." And they could be the lords of it. "But that still leaves us far from a family," Crys continued. "I only let you come because I pity you. And I don't abandon people. Unlike the two of you."

Jade raised her uninjured hand. "Digging my heel into this fresh wound, but you're the one who left *me* this time."

"You made me," Crys shouted. "Do you regret your choice?"

Jade kept her burned arm hidden, her cards close to her chest. "I was trying to be a team player. Push the research forward—"

Crys laughed, sharp and bitter. "Please. You were trying to be a martyr like Maxen. Romeo and Juliet, but make it apocalypse."

It was Jade's turn to laugh. "You want to talk about you and Cole? Moores who live in glass houses shouldn't throw stones."

Something launched at Jade's chest. A silver chain. A bullet. *In Extremis.*

"You found my necklace and kept it from me?" Jade raced forward, toe-to-toe with her sister, brandishing the silver chain, the bullet swinging between them. "Why?"

"Because I thought you didn't need it. But have at it. Never let go of the time you took a bullet for me."

"It's always about *you*, isn't it?" Jade reared, shoving In Extremis into her zipper pocket with her perfume vials.

"Lay off!" Willis yelled, pushing himself between them. "If your parents could see you both now—"

"Well, they can't," Crys spat. "They're gone, and we were stranded with *you*. You deserted us, and the only reason you're crawling back now is because you need us. You're infected, and we're your ticket to the cure."

"Topple it all," Willis cursed. "Do you really think I didn't come back for you? I went to the Quest gates for a year after Damon Yates took you."

Jade and Crys locked eyes.

"I even set up tents, though Yates's damned enforcer would steal them from me anytime I left for a supply run."

Jade never saw the tents. Never thought to hope.

"Were you just looking for a payout?" Jade asked cruelly.

"I knew I didn't deserve you," Willis croaked, "but I wanted you both back. Yates offered me cash to stay away. I never accepted a penny from him, I swear it."

Jade could believe it. He looked the portrait of a bankrupt man. But his green eyes swept over them now, sparkling like the brightest gemstone.

"I suppose you told yourself we were better off without you?" Crys said, sharp as a slap.

All three of them stood silent, visualizing how things might have been if there'd been no Adsum, no Yates, no bots to have kept them apart.

Jade suddenly became aware of Iris nearby, arms crossed, a sneer curling her red lips. "Good, you've come up for air just in time. We're setting off."

"Setting off where?" Willis asked. "We just got here."

No one bothered to catch him up.

Jade looked to the smoker, the sibs, the table set for the promised feast. "Okay," she began, struggling to switch her brain back to guardian mode. "I just have to set things in order with the sibs first—"

Iris shook her head, her sleek bangs falling into her eyes. "No, not you three," she said. "The Moores were selected to stay behind."

"What do you mean 'selected'?" Crys said.

"It means that for once, Crys, you're not the chosen one," Wily said.

Jade noticed Eli hanging back, looking as cast out as she felt. Cole sat behind him like a dark shadow on the grass, picking at the clunky boot around his lacerated foot.

"Turns out the Exhibition includes four spots per invite," Sage chimed in. "While you three were busy cracking open the past, the rest of us were pitching our qualities to make the cut."

"But *I'm* the one who scored the invitation code in the first place—" Jade started, indignant.

"Jia Wu Er Zhu," Iris stated in Mandarin, her keen eyes running over Jade and Crys. "A family cannot have two heads. Your collective baggage will weigh down my jet. The Moores will remain here." She turned to Sage, Wily, and Ani. "I'll give you five."

With that, she turned and strode back to her AV, leaving Jade with a thousand questions.

"Ani, what the hell?" Jade said. "Thanks for the heads-up? You could have at least pitched for me."

Ani didn't even have the decency to blush. "It's not my jet, so it wasn't my call." Her thick brows knitted into a scowl. "Iris sees my focus, says my grief is a powerful tool, more dangerous than my knives. I'm an asset, Jade. I've given more tears, sweat, and *blood* than anyone here."

Jade kept her mouth closed, though her disgruntlement burned higher than the bonfire.

"And Nolan?" Crys said, peering around the patio. "Where's he? No way he didn't throw his mike into the ring."

"*Nolan Ortiz* is here?" Jade asked, gobsmacked.

"Iris 'doesn't negotiate with reporters,'" Wily answered. "He's been sequestered inside the ranch house, after being pressed into signing an NDA, of course, saying that Iris was never here."

"And soon she won't be," Sage said, looking at her watch. She took hold of Wily's pinky and looked to Ani. "We've got to go."

Jade could barely hear them over the pulse pounding in her ears. *It's just like you dreaded,* the scapegrace in her thought savagely. *Without your fearless bot, you're ordinary, mediocre,* useless.

"Well, be sure to bring back souvenirs," she snapped, louder than she'd intended. *Preferably in the form of platinum suitcases filled with Hariri's nano reform intended for the Exhibition.* She spun on her heel, moving for the ranch house.

"Aren't you going to wish us luck?" Ani shouted after her.

"Fortunes change," Jade whispered painfully.

She entered the doorway. No one followed her. She unwrapped her bandages, fingers hovering over her burn, then dug her nails into the oozing scabs, her skin sliding from her arm like melted wax.

She felt nothing. It was an advantage, Jade told herself. A power.

And she intended to utilize it, one way or another.

ELEVEN

Iris scanned the private rural airfield, seeking any signs of drones, police spotlights, white-tailed deer. She'd been warned by her pilot that the local hoofed pests had been cause for more than one collision this year already. The deer would often leap the high fences, scampering about the runway in a frenzy, warming themselves on the asphalt. *Or they're crazy with love,* she recalled her pilot suggesting.

I'll have nothing delay us, understand? Iris had ordered. Especially not love.

The Gulfstream jet was right where Iris had left it, the only lights shining in the small, towerless airfield. Its twin Rolls-Royce Pearl 900 engines were powered up and roaring, its tank filled with premier sustainable aviation fuel for their five-thousand-mile journey overseas.

The AV transporting Iris and her team rolled to a stop beside the jet. Iris bolted out from the front seat, anxious to separate herself, at least for the few brisk steps it took to get to the airstairs, from the suffocating gazes of Poppy's former foster children.

At the ranch, Iris had thought that seeing the students Poppy had chosen to spend her life raising would lift the weight she'd been carrying in her chest. Yet their desperate faces, their *fear,* had only added a greater pressure. She was crushed. Could barely breathe.

She used the five steps to pull herself back together. Reinflate her ego. She could fix Poppy's mistakes. Infiltrate the Exhibition. Punish

Hariri. Palmer, too, if she was lucky. *And free Maxen,* Iris promised herself, doubling down on her promise as she stared back at the three Exiles she'd selected to accompany her.

Ani, Sage, and Wily had spoken little since their departure. Ani kept clutching her ruby earring, her charcoal-stained thumb rubbing meditatively over its glittering surface. Sage and Wily hooked pinkies, glaring holes into Iris as if they expected at any moment her red suit would flip to platinum by the magic of money.

"We want the same things," Iris assured the trio. "If we are to succeed in setting right Poppy's wrongs, I need you to trust me."

"Trust is a currency," Sage said, raking back an auburn lock with her long nails.

Wily wagged a scarred brow. "And we're too broke to go spending our savings on strangers."

"I'll give you mine," Ani announced, moving toward the airstairs. "Even though I left Adsum, I still thought of Poppy as my foster mother. And she may have not been my blood . . ." She turned to Sage and Wily. "But in the end, she bled for us. Didn't she?"

Poppy had taken the Conservator's bullet, Iris knew. Had died to save the students.

A doleful grin cut across Wily's face. "Well, Iris, I guess that makes you a part of our extended family then."

"Right." Iris nodded, another weight added to her chest.

She boarded the jet first, entering the bespoke cabin, customized by Iris herself to be her home away from home during her ultra-long-range business flights. She glanced around the elegantly appointed lounge, ensuring that all was set to her specific standards. Fresh-cut flowers on the marble table, three convertible beds outfitted with luxurious bamboo sheets placed between the black leather chairs, a glass of Veuve Clicquot and a silk sleeping mask awaiting her on a silver tray in her private suite at the back of the cabin.

"Well, I think it's safe to say someone has a thing for wood," Wily said, stepping into the lounge, his neck craning to take in the *huanghuali* ceiling, floors, and walls.

Iris ran her hand over the smooth rosewood, cut from a thousand-year-old tree from the Hainan Province, a habit she took to after a folklore class at Oxford one summer, when she'd read the lore of "Tiggy Touchwood," a children's game of tag where players who touched a piece of wood were given a form of protection from their opponents. Iris had surrounded herself with immunity, and she grazed the cabin's wall every time she landed to give her an edge over her business competitors.

"It looks expensive," Sage said. She stood beside Iris with her body folded in, like she feared luxury would rub off on her if she touched the prized wood.

"Mm-hmm," Iris agreed. Class spoke for itself. No need to educate them that they walked on micro-sliced wood grain reserved for royalty in dynastic times, worth more than their weight in gold.

"Should we check to make sure Jade hasn't stashed herself in the cargo hold?" Ani said, bending her knees to stare out a circular window. "Telling her to 'stay put' is like asking the tectonic plates not to move . . ."

"I already had my pilot check," Iris answered, setting her bag down on a reclining sectional sofa.

"And yet you still had an unexpected passenger board your jet," a silvery voice jeered.

Palmer Yates emerged from the cockpit in a platinum suit, a smile playing on his lips.

Surprise bloomed across Iris's face. She had thought he would be at Hariri's side in Monaco, not getting his own hands dirty in Texas.

"Traveling without a security detail?" Palmer clicked his tongue. "Always were the bold little viper. Pity you went for Vance instead of me. I know exactly which parts of you to touch to make you go tame."

"Oh, really?" Iris said, withdrawing her stun gun. "Touch this." She lunged, striking Palmer in the chest. But the shock backfired, sending seventy billion volts of electricity up her arm and dropping her instantly to her knees.

Ani hurled a knife that went straight through Palmer and sank into the wooden wall behind him.

"It's a hologram," Sage seethed.

"A pricey trick," Wily spat, helping Iris to her feet.

Ani screamed. Iris whipped her head back to see the ruby earring dangling from the hand of the *actual* Palmer Yates, laughing from the runway, the airstairs folding closed in front of him.

"Your moves are predictable, Iris, unlike mine," Palmer boasted. His pale blue eyes shone like diamonds in the dark. "That's why I'm in charge of my family's fortune and *you're* expendable."

"You *betrayed* your way to power," Iris scolded him, hoping he'd confess to where he'd hidden his brothers and missing father.

"Prove it," Palmer teased. "Oh wait . . ."

The cabin door slammed shut. Her earlobe dripping blood, Ani rushed for the cockpit, but the compartment portals sealed, trapping them inside the lounge.

"I'll be sure to give Hariri your regards," the holographic Palmer mocked before disappearing with a laugh.

Iris pressed her palms against the rosewood wall, willing a form of protection to surround her for whatever came next. She felt the twin engines fire up, the jet suddenly rocketing them down the runway.

And just as he had with Vance, Palmer was carrying Iris out of sight.

TWELVE

Crys sat by the dying fire, gazing at Cole through the flames. He leaned against the squat trunk of a live oak, staring up through its arched branches at the pristine night sky. Was he searching the stars for Zoe's and Khari's satellites? Contemplating whether his own satellite would be added next to the constellation of the Adsum slain?

A dark and yawning dread yanked open a pit in Crys's stomach, threatening to swallow her courage whole.

No, she whispered. Vowed. I *control fear.* I *can control Cole's fate.*

She shouldn't be idling here. She should be out leading the search for Yates. He could still be alive. She could still find him. Make him answer for what his tech, his ambition, had given rise to.

Crys brushed the tattoo at her ribs, remembering Yates's favorite Latin phrase. *Semper in altioribus. Always higher,* Crys thought bitterly as she surged to her feet.

Then an object hurtled into the flames in front of her, sending sparks flying. Crys leaned closer to the embers, spotting an . . . *inhaler?*

Finn scampered from the ranch's patio toward the fire, in a hurry to flee from Jade.

"Quick," Jade shouted. "Crys, grab him!"

Crys remained unmoving. She wouldn't obey Jade's command. Besides, there was little risk of Finn running. Jade must have known this. The Hill Country air had enough of Finn's asthma triggers to make certain he wouldn't get very far if he tried.

"Topple it all, Crys," Jade yelled as she stormed over. "Are you not listening? *Grab him!* What's your problem?"

It seemed Jade was the one with the problem. Mild, amenable Finn, who Jade believed she had wrapped around her crooked little finger, appeared to have upset her.

Crys watched as he attempted to fish his inhaler out with a stick, but the wood snapped in half, pushing the melting canister deeper into the smoldering embers.

Jade arrived, practically frothing at the mouth. "Well, maybe you'll listen to *this*. Finn is an informer. He just let drop that he sold us out to Palmer Yates."

Crys's fine hairs shot up as her heart sank. So she *did* have a problem. A monumental one.

"Palmer just took over Iris's jet," Jade continued, glaring at the back of Finn's head as he tried to scoop his inhaler from the flames. "The Conservators will be here any minute. But please, just stand there, *Crystal*. I do everything myself anyway."

Cole sprinted to the pit, hovering outside the fire's fading light. He avoided Crys's eye. "I heard screaming. Did someone spot a fear symbol?"

"Palmer raided the jet," Crys told him, though she could hardly believe her own words. Her fingers slid automatically to her pouch. To her vials. "He's coming for us next."

Eli charged from the direction of the laboratory. His custom-made lab coat hugged his broad shoulders, a pile of Brainious juices slipping from his hands as he reached for Cole. "What's the matter?" he panted. "Is your nano reform progressing?"

Since learning of Hema's absence, Eli had taken over the lab, though the most he could do was raid the cache of Hema's leftover Smart Bots for anything useful. So far, no luck.

"I'm fine," Cole snapped, shrugging off Eli's touch. "It's the A Team you should be worried about. Palmer captured them." He bent back his head, hazel eyes hunting the sky. For Palmer's drone, or for more satellites? Crys wasn't sure.

Jade knelt over the fire, reaching in with her bare hands to pluck out Finn's inhaler. She didn't flinch as she held the canister out of his grasp, the unthinkably hot metal scorching her fingers a bright red. Only then did Crys notice the gauze haphazardly wrapped around her sister's forearm. The burn wounds underneath.

She's like Cole and Willis, Crys realized with a pang. Crys bet that Jade had been keeping secret her insensitivity to pain, thinking she'd gained a new kind of superpower, like her former bot-induced fearlessness. She had no idea of the true level of danger she had put herself in. How her symptoms could rapidly progress, like those of the Unfortunates at the lighthouse.

But Crys wasn't going to be the one to reveal it to her. On the hyperloop back to the ranch, Cole had made them promise to keep the distressing details of the nano reform's side effects to themselves, until they learned more. Spare those infected the terrifying knowledge of what was to come.

Eli dropped the last of the juices, balling his empty fists. "Where did that scion of scum take our sibs?"

"Exactly what I'm trying to figure out," Jade seethed, as Finn barreled into her torso, wrestling for what was left of his inhaler. Crys noted that the plastic holder had melted, but the canister containing Finn's vital medicine remained intact.

"Tell us where they are," Jade demanded. "And I'll give back your inhaler."

Willis appeared in the edges of the fire's glow. "Jade, lay off, he's just a kid."

Jade didn't look up, her laser focus directed on Finn. "None of us have been kids since the quake. Since the day our guardians left us," she said matter-of-factly. "Finn is an adult, who made a *childish* decision to go against his family."

Crys took advantage of Jade's distraction and lunged for the inhaler. Using her jacket's thick sleeve to shield her skin, she snatched the canister from Jade's iron grip and tossed it to Finn. "Talk," Crys said, backing off, giving him space to breathe.

Jade could do nothing but scoff.

"I don't know where Palmer took them, all right?" Finn whispered, his eyes darting everywhere else but at the faces he'd betrayed. He juggled the metal canister as it cooled. "I just know I can't live like this anymore. All of us want out." He gestured to the dozens of silhouetted figures by the drive, stacks of duffel bags and suitcases gathered at their feet.

"Or back *in*, you mean," Crys sighed. "What did Palmer promise you?" It shouldn't have come to this, Crys thought. She should have been more present, more of an anchor in the mayhem for the foster sibs. It was partially her fault that they'd gone adrift.

"He swore we'd get our Quest Bots back, our futures," Finn said in a rush. "He's reopening Adsum Academy—"

Jade choked out a cry. "And you believed him?"

"It's better than believing in *you* anymore," Finn huffed. "I was a track star, destined for Dartmouth. Now I can't even *walk* outdoors without worrying I'll trigger an asthma attack. I'm not going back, Jade. I refuse. So yes, I told Palmer where Poppy's niece and half the Exiles were headed. Yes, I told him about the ranch, and the lab, and where they could pinpoint you and Crys."

From the sides of Crys's vision, Nolan glided closer, holding out his microphone.

"You've got to be shaking me," Jade fumed, turning to Crys. "How could you let this guy in?"

Crys shrugged.

"What is this?" Finn stuttered, wide eyes on Nolan. "Is this the 'Adsum Atrocity' podcaster?"

"What's the matter?" Cole suddenly hissed. His face twitched, his usual easy smile grown hard. "Afraid millions of listeners are going to learn what a shit-bag of a brother you are?"

Everyone looked at Cole, staggered by his tone. Even Finn hung his head low, cowed by the rebuke from his sib, who never saw a bad day or bad person he couldn't fix. Crys tried to will Cole's gaze to her, but Eli stepped forward, blocking Cole from the group's scrutiny.

"I have a sneaking suspicion Hema and Rhett didn't really give up on us," Eli said, the veins in his temples popping with his effort to stay calm. "You offered them up on a platinum-loving platter . . ."

Finn didn't object. In some ways this felt like a relief to Crys. *Hema was kidnapped.* Hema didn't flee. They hadn't conceded defeat.

"And now there's zero chance of a cure," Eli continued, "and tens of thousands of those infected, like me, can never go home." For every step Eli took toward Finn, Finn took three back. "And after tomorrow's Exhibition, the nano reform will spread across the globe, potentially controlling millions, even billions, all so *you* can live comfortably on Adsum Peak. Did I miss something?"

Finn blanched and turned toward the driveway, but his apparent guilty conscience made him circle back. Toss them some crumbs. "Just so you know . . . before they left, I overheard Hema talking to Rhett. Hema had received a message. A poem, I think. The sender was anonymous, but they were both excited. They even kissed." His cheeks flushed red. "I don't know anything else, all right? I didn't stay to watch."

A poem? The poem that led to Yates's fabled hidden treasure? Crys was dumbstruck. *Not this again.* The last time she was persuaded to hunt for Yates's treasure, she was nearly obliterated by a hyperloop pod. Crys looked to Jade, who picked at her soiled bandages, somehow finding the decency to keep her mouth closed.

"I bet Palmer sent the message," Eli theorized. "Lured Hema off the ranch to go chasing fool's gold."

Or the possibility of a cure, Crys thought.

"You better go," Finn said, suddenly urgent. "Palmer's enforcers will be here any minute to collect his strays."

With that, he drew from his inhaler and half jogged to the drive.

Once he was out of earshot, Jade whispered, "Palmer has the MIT professor. He doesn't need Hema."

The statement hung in the air. The unsaid possibility that Hema and Rhett were captured and likely . . . Crys couldn't finish the thought.

"The Exhibition," Nolan said. "Can we still make it?"

Jade grunted at his use of "we."

"The platinum suits will be watching all flights to Monaco," Willis pointed out. A chuckle escaped his throat. "Unless someone here knows a person with an extra private jet lying around . . ."

Now all eyes were on Crys.

She knew dozens. But only one who was perfect.

"Let's get to a portal," Crys said. "We're going to New York."

They waited in an empty building on East Fifty-Seventh Street, the "luxury row" property that was to be the flagship location for Crys's premium perfume line, the launchpad for Crystal Yates's lofty ambitions, her investment in her future outside of the Quest Empire. It's what Damon Yates would have expected out of an heir. Ingenuity, independence, enterprise.

An old life and dead dreams, Crys thought, feeling no connection to the girl who'd schemed for the very top of the world.

She'd given over her bonus apartment on the Upper East Side to the thirty Adsum sibs who'd chosen to stay in exile. Their loyalty, their sacrifice of the Quest high life, their belief in Crys and what the Exiles were doing, had given Crys a second wind.

"The same trick can work twice, right?" Jade asked her, eyes glued to the gold-plated revolving door.

The plan was to lure their mark, ever the venture capitalist chasing the next hot trend, into an exclusive meeting with the designer of a luxe upcycle fashion brand about to take the industry by storm. A sample jacket was sent to his Tribeca penthouse via a white-glove service, a note tucked into its patch pocket with the place and time of a private impromptu fashion show.

"The man's an easy catch," Crys said. "The lure of growing his portfolio is too much for him to resist."

Eli, Willis, and Nolan were lined up beside Jade, while Cole rested atop an unfinished plywood counter behind them. His unfocused, glassy gaze blinked around the room, waves of his coffee-brown hair soaked in sweat, his lips curled in a grimace instead of his usual bright smile. Even if he couldn't feel it, the nano reform was wreaking havoc on his body and mind. How close was he to becoming like the Unfortunates at the lighthouse?

Crys wanted to go to his side. Comfort him. Tell him she wasn't repelled but attracted to him, like opposite poles. *Don't go dark,* she wanted to cry out. *Don't go dark.*

She knew Cole was right, that it would be easier if she stayed away. But Crys could control *fear.* Not love.

Then why was she too scared to move? To speak to him?

To be his light?

"I think we caught ourselves a live Fortunate," Jade announced, pulling Crys's focus back to the store's entrance.

Leo Benson appeared behind a glass panel of the revolving door. The wide canopy rotated as slowly as the million-heir's gait, the bold, horizontal, navy-and-white lines of his pinstripe suit making him look like a prisoner behind plexiglass.

Which was exactly what he was about to become. Crys's hostage.

He held the white box containing the shiny bait. A coat of mismatched wool and silk sleeves exquisitely patched together by Eli from four pairs of Crys's trousers he'd found in her penthouse apartment.

Eli gave himself a small grin. "The guy actually came."

"Of course he did," Crys replied, pleased with her little scheme. Eli had a talent, an originator's eye, for creating harmony between contrary fabrics and patterns that left her in awe. This space could be Eli's someday. Filled with his own designs. His own lofty ambitions.

As Benson stepped inside the barren perfumery, he leveled a glare at Crys and Jade, then dropped the box to the dusty concrete floor. His pale face flushed crimson as he scraped his red-soled dress shoes across the stylish coat. He knew he'd been scammed.

"I see I have *two* Moores trying to trick something out of me this time," Benson said, clicking his tongue. "Afraid I don't hand out favors to beggars anymore. As I've already fulfilled my charity quota for the year by supplying you the Doc's 'calling card'"—he leered at Jade—"I'll be off." He buttoned his suit jacket and spun on his heel. "And while you're in the city, do be sure to take a long walk off a short pier. Do the world a favor."

Crys took her time as she stalked toward him. There was no need for a chase. Benson was already inside her cage. Glass vial concealed in her grip, Crys was contemplating her cleanest move to strike when Jade shot out in front of her, wagging her fear fragrance between her fingers for Benson to see.

This wasn't the plan. There was to be no talking, only action. *Spray it, don't say it* was the name of their strategy. In and out, no wasted time. Yet here Jade was, draining crucial seconds. *Critical* seconds Cole might need.

"See this?" Jade asked as Benson turned back, Crys stepping shoulder to shoulder with her.

"A sample of Crystal's godawful perfume?" Benson answered, smug and unconcerned. "What of it?"

"One spray, and you'll be out of your mind with fear when you look at me. At *us*." She nodded to Crys.

"Well, it's not like your faces elicit feelings of *joy* in the first place . . ." Benson quipped.

Crys shoved Jade's arm down. "What are you doing? We don't parley with *heirs*. His father is one merger away from joining the billionaires' club, and you know what group might then recruit him into their platinum fold?"

A shadow passed across Jade's dark eyes. Crys wondered if she saw the fear symbol. Her own vulnerability. Why was she hesitant to use their greatest weapon, *now*, when they were the most desperate?

"It looks like you still haven't found your backbone," Crys threw at Jade.

Jade stiffened as Benson glared cross-eyed at the glass vial. His expression suddenly hardened, humorless and pensive. "I heard a few guys at the Say-So club whisper about making the hobos their puppets. I asked what they used as the strings, and they showed me empty hands."

"That's because they're using nanobots," Jade explained patiently. "They're practically invisible."

"I know what nanotechnology is, thank you," Benson snipped, straightening his silver sapphire cuff links. "I was a loyal customer of the Doc's Brainious juices. I knew there were some advanced . . . *ingredients* in there; I just made sure never to ask."

"Speaking of asking," Jade said, lowering her vial, holding Crys back with a firm hand. "We need you to order your father's long-range jet to be ready in an hour to take us overseas. To Monaco."

Benson laughed. "Impossible."

"Wrong answer," Crys said. Slapping aside Jade's hold, she inhaled deeply, then locked her lungs before flicking Jade a half-second warning to shut her mouth and quit breathing. *And talking.* Crys lifted the nozzle just under Benson's pointed nose and pressed the trigger.

He uttered a yelp of surprise, then his exclamations ballooned into horror. He tried to run, but Crys and Jade pinned him in, trapping him in twin terror. Benson sealed his eyes shut and curled into a ball on the concrete floor.

"If you come quietly," Crys told him, "we'll give you an attack bot."

Jade kept out of his eyeline but bent close, making sure he heard. "It's an antidote. It will stop the fear."

Benson nodded, his moans eliciting sympathetic winces from Willis and Eli.

Crys looked to Cole. Dark meeting dark.

She turned her back and strode for the door. Jade followed, close at her heels. "You didn't need to do that," she whispered as they moved into the bustling Manhattan streets. "I had him."

"Sure you did," Crys said, storing away her vial.

Willis trudged up behind them, hooking an arm around each of their shoulders. "I'm gonna tell you like it is. That performance back there was shaky. Weak. If we want to really topple the Conservators, you're gonna have to learn to band together."

Your fortune is in your bond, their mother used to tell Crys and Jade.

Crys shrugged Willis off, avoiding Jade's eyes as they sought to pull Crys back to her. She set off alone for the AV that waited curbside, refusing all the ties that tried to bind her.

THIRTEEN

The clock on Jade's phone shifted from a.m. to p.m. in a blink. The Benson family's private jet had just crossed into Central European Time.

Theoretically, Jade was going on thirty hours without sleep. She should try harder to catch a few winks and recharge like everyone else aboard the jet, but rest was not in Jade's cards. The A Team had been taken. Palmer and Hariri unequivocally knew the other half of the Exiles was on its way.

The main issue keeping Jade up this morning—*night*—was that the B Team did not have an invitation to the Exhibition. All the efforts that she, Ani, and Iris had made to get the codes were wasted. And her present plan of action wasn't bulletproof or watertight. It was riddled with giant holes.

The Conservators will see straight through your silly ruse, the scapegrace in Jade taunted.

She shook her head, hard, detaching the cynic from her thoughts. She brushed In Extremis, which she'd stored inside her jacket pocket, wrapped in her bandana with her perfume vials.

For the entire transatlantic flight, she'd been scrolling her phone, desperate to keep her speeding thoughts in check. She pulled up a decades-dead social media app she kept for emergencies just like this. It was how she did her best mental preparation. She clicked on the time capsule that was her parents' joint account. It felt like visiting their graves. They weren't good with filters, and they were terrible with captions. But the thousands of simple snapshots and unedited videos of average days in their life together never failed to make Jade smile, relax. Muse.

She scrolled and scrolled, the past flashing by her restless eyes as she mapped out schemes for her near future.

The Exhibition was at seven p.m. They'd only have half an hour to obtain proper attire and infiltrate the party, but if Crys could dust off her old street charm, Jade's scheme just might work.

Tonight, everyone who was anyone at the Grand Prix de Monaco, the most important and glamorous Formula One race in the world, would be attending the swankiest after-party of the year. Jade had never been starstruck—at Quest, she'd met Hardihood's biggest and brightest—but soon she'd be brushing shoulders with the motorsports' pinnacle drivers.

Jade's fingers itched to grab a steering wheel. She imagined adrenaline racing through her veins, guiding her, confident and euphoric, through the track's every twist and turn. The two dozen buttons, knobs, rotary dials, menus, displays, and LEDs on the sophisticated wheel did not intimidate her. Only enticed. She was a blur speeding past, an overwhelming sound, a thing you couldn't catch.

Suddenly Jade's phone vibrated in her hands, crashing her reverie. It was a notification. From *The Adsum Atrocity* podcast.

A new episode had just dropped.

Her pulse rocketing, Jade flicked her eyes around the cabin.

On the sofa opposite her, Eli stopped pinching his arm—Jade couldn't work out if he was pinching himself to stay awake or to check if he could still feel it—to snatch his lit-up phone from his lap. "That scandalmonger scum."

Cole's head rested against Eli's shoulder, his eyes closed. Good. Cole was finally sleeping.

Jade snapped her eyes to the hall of the main suite. Where was Crys? Sure enough, her sister came barreling through, long hair still damp from her recent shower. Her curls looked darker. Not the deep chestnut of Jade's, but less golden.

The sight should have made Jade happy, but it troubled her. Even more than the bomb she brandished in her fist.

"Did you know about this?" Crys yelled at Jade, a rigid finger stabbing at the episode's title: "The Severed Sisters: Who Really Was the Chosen One?"

"Nolan's here at *your* blessing," Jade answered flatly. "This time, at least, I'm blameless."

Who Really Was the Chosen One? What on shaking Earth could that mean? Jade didn't think it was the prime time to find out. She locked her phone, shoved it into her pocket. Hoped Crys would do the same.

But in what universe had they ever been the same?

Crys charged for the front row of plush leather seats and ripped the soundproof headphones from Nolan's ears. He jolted awake in a panic. "Has Palmer tracked us? Is the jet under attack?"

"Looks like we're under a different kind of assault," Crys fumed. She thrust her phone into his face.

Nolan's thick lashes flitted in shock as he read the podcast's title. "Do *not* listen to that episode."

"But you're just fine with the rest of the world listening?"

"I suspended this episode," Nolan promised. "But it appears my co-host was impatient to release new material. Keep the famished listeners fed. I told her this was empty calories. My investigations, I think you'd agree, have evolved beyond the narrative of the Severed Sisters."

Yet Crys, apparently, was nowhere *near* getting beyond it. She hit play, and dramatic intro music blared through the cabin's speakers.

"Welcome back to The Adsum Atrocity. *I'm Nolan Ortiz, and on today's episode, I'd like to discuss the scapegrace and the billion-heir."*

Jade threw up her arms. "Wonderful, a group listening party. You sure you don't want to livestream our reactions?"

"Shhh," Crys snapped, head down, consumed by Nolan's voice.

"Get out your gloves for this one, truth-seekers, because we're digging right in . . ."

No, Jade thought, livid. *Let's keep the truth nice and buried.* Savior only knew what unpleasant skeletons Nolan had uncovered.

Damon Yates's spirited voice emanated through the cabin. Everyone went still. *"Poppy, darling, I've done it."* He was breathless with excitement.

"What have you 'done' this time?" Poppy Szeto asked, her voice soft with affection.

An old phone conversation, Jade gathered, seven or so years old. Before the gilded power couple's messy divorce. Stealing private recordings? Nolan really was a sneaky sleuth.

"I took a stroll around Echo Park Lake to center the mind—" Damon continued.

Poppy tsked. *"Tell me you had your security detail with you . . ."*

"Of course not, that would be asking for attention. The point is, I found the final student for our inaugural class."

A cold shiver snaked up Jade's entire body. They were talking about Adsum.

"Did I ever tell you that before my parents chose me, I lived in a foster home by a pond?" Damon asked.

"Darling, your first ten years are a wiped hard drive . . ."

Damon tittered.

Willis emerged groggily from the media room. "The archfiend's laugh is a piss-poor alarm clock." He kept his tone light, but he gazed heavily at Jade. "Can we turn this drivel off already?"

"For once I'm on the same page as Willis," Jade said. Just as she dove for Crys's phone to cut off the podcast, Crys deftly slipped it into the pouch that stored her fear fragrances. It was a crafty move. She knew Jade wouldn't risk breaking the vials.

"At the lake there was this twig of a girl standing by the dirty water," Damon said through the speakers. *"Do you remember the wonderful lotus beds that used to bloom in the neighborhood lake before the encampment took over?"*

"Vaguely . . ."

"Well, the girl didn't forget them. She'd somehow kept safe a single lotus shoot at the edge of the lake. It was a runt, like her, but she tended to it, shielded the fragile beauty from the muck around it."

Jade watched Crys's face go pale, her eyes wide with shock.

The twig of a girl was Jade Moore.

Damon Yates was talking about *her.*

"The girl had attracted the attention of another man. A rather large one with a large knife. I watched as he plunged his grubby hands into the dirty water and cut the stem of the lotus. He took off, presumably to sell his rare bounty on the streets. I could see in the girl's eyes she wanted to stop him, fight him, but she had no weapon."

"This is a terrible story."

Yet the entire jet was listening, rapt.

"Think about what a soul like that could do if I gave her the means and the courage . . ."

The courage, Jade repeated to herself. Her Quest Bot.

After Jade had fled Adsum at fifteen, she'd tracked down the man who'd stolen her lotus flower. Found out he'd sold his illicit clipping to a nursery in Reseda, which had then started growing runners, offering them for sale.

Jade had the courage then to steal back the entire bed. Return them to where they belonged in Echo Park Lake.

"Is the girl alone?" Poppy asked, jolting Jade out of her memory.

"Her name is Jade. I heard her sister calling for her. They're twins, I think."

"Oh, Damon, you can't separate them . . ."

Jade stopped breathing. Closed her eyes to block out the stares. Everyone understood what Nolan's podcast was implying.

Crys was only chosen for Adsum because of *Jade. Jade* could have been the billion-heir. The daughter. The one with the famous last name.

She opened her eyes, but Crys's back was turned to her. *In the end, you were the chosen one,* Jade wanted to shout at her sister. But a terror-stricken wail tore from Cole as he shot to his feet, taking a swing at Eli. He missed, eyes wild with hate. With vengeance. He swung again. Missed. Did he really think he could land one on the Knockout?

Cole's words were garbled, nonsensical, but Jade understood one word clearly. *Yates.*

He took another swing at Eli, who he was somehow mistaking for Yates, and this time, Eli let Cole's fist connect with his chin.

By the time Jade and Willis pulled Cole away from him, Cole's hard face had slackened with remorse. Confusion. He sank down onto the floor at Eli's feet, clutching his sweaty forehead. Crys and Eli shared a quick, grim look.

"Crys?" Jade asked, eyes narrowing. She *knew* they'd been keeping something from her. "What the hell is happening to him?"

Crys's gaze lowered to Jade's burned arm before dropping back to Cole, avoiding Jade's eye.

The Severed Sisters, Jade thought miserably. She wondered if Crys would ever speak to her again.

Her stomach dipped as the jet started its descent and the pilot's voice took over the speakers. "We're approaching our destination. Everyone please buckle up; it's going to be a bumpy landing."

"Ha!" Willis grumbled from the sofa. "Even bumpier than the ride?"

I'm fine. Cole's fine. Crys will be fine.

"We're all fine," Jade shouted to the cabin.

No one answered.

In Extremis felt heavy in her pocket, her fear vials a weight that made her hunch as she marched to the main suite at the back of the private jet. Jade needed something to ground her. To steady her nerves. To steal a bit of counterfeit courage.

Benson was passed out on the full-sized bed, a silk mask shielding his eyes from the overhead lights. From Jade's scowling face.

His Rolex sat on the nightstand, gleaming, begging to be taken.

Jade snapped it around the wrist of her burned arm, the last piece of her plan secured.

Everything will be fine.

She might not feel the scrape of gold against her blistered skin, but she could feel *that* in her gut.

Everything will be more *than fine.*

Jade tramped down the world-famous Place du Casino, the beating heart of Monte Carlo, where the Maritime Alps slinked into the French Riviera. Everywhere she looked reflected such casual, obscene wealth that Jade found it hard not to spit. Scuff up some of the extravagance.

Willis read her mind, hawking his contempt onto the gleaming walls of Chanel, one of the countless high-end retail shops that lined the quarter. The same store he'd pitched his tent against back in Beverly Hills, the same kind of glitzy street that had sent her uncle running from the Conservators' fear symbols.

But here, Jade had no fear she'd stumble on the carefully disguised slash marks. The tiny city-state had no need to employ them—Monaco was so affluent that homelessness essentially didn't exist. The poverty rate was an eye-popping zero. It was a place for playboys and princesses, a Disneyland for billionaires and home to more millionaires per capita than anywhere else in the world.

The ideal location for Hariri to host his Exhibition. *And the perfect timing,* Jade thought as an F1 star drove his car around a tight corner at impossible speed toward the marina, more than likely about to lord it up on a superyacht. The Grand Prix, a two-mile hairpin street circuit laid out around the harbor of Monte Carlo, was run under the patronage of Monaco's royal family, which meant the presence of world diplomats and a who's who of influential richlings. The Conservators would have little difficulty blending right in.

"This principality has a countrywide twenty-four-hour surveillance system," Crys rebuked Willis, "and one police officer for every one hundred residents. *Try* and keep your hands and *spit* to yourself."

Crys still hadn't spoken a word to Jade since the "podcast heard round the jet." She was being dramatic. Selfish. Tonight wasn't about the scapegrace and the billion-heir. So what if Yates had once favored—*chosen*—Jade? In the end it was Crys, wasn't it?

Jade wanted to scream at Crys to get over it, accept a ceasefire. But Crys had kept her distance since landing at the private airport in Nice, France, only consorting with Eli, who was now at her side. Jade had designated Nolan to stay behind to watch over Cole and Benson on the jet. The threat of her fear fragrance had put an end to any arguments or ideas about posting any more podcasts while they were away.

Now Jade and Willis turned into the lavish courtyard that led up to the Casino de Monte-Carlo, the grandest and most exclusive gambling den on Earth, where a barrage of Ferraris, Bentleys, and Rolls-Royces were pulling into the valet, a sight that would have triggered a former adrenaline junkie like Jade into a relapse. Keeping her head low, Jade was able to walk right past the luxury vehicles without the itch to hijack them, instead following the others to the back of the Beaux Arts–style building.

Jade counted four footmen in red tuxedo jackets, huddled around an ornate pilaster, smoking Gauloises cigarettes. She'd been hoping for fewer potential roadblocks, but she had to take the gamble. With her old scapegrace swagger, she shot forward, pushing ahead of Crys and Eli on the stone pathway to the casino.

She ringed her finger around the watch's diamond dial for luck. Not for herself. For the four footmen, if they didn't take her bribe. Crys was edgy, trigger-happy. More than ready to douse anyone who stood in her way with fear.

But the idea of causing another terrorized cry made Jade's skin crawl. She'd only been threatening Nolan on the jet, utilizing the perfume's intimidation factor, though in truth, she'd heard enough screaming to last a lifetime.

Jade forged a smile as she approached the men, slipping Benson's obscenely gaudy Rolex from her wrist. The timepiece made her think of Maxen, and for a moment her mind was back in California, wondering where and how he was. If he felt like she'd abandoned him. Jade clenched her jaw and kept walking.

She hadn't admitted it to the others, but she was taking a move out of Maxen's playbook. She'd seen him buy silence from others countless times. It was a Yates men's trait. Trinkets for privacy.

What, are you playing Jade Yates *now?* she could almost hear Crys hiss.

Jade shook off the unsavory thought as she held up the Rolex, ready to make a trade for their secret entry into the high-security casino.

"*Bonsoir,*" she greeted the footmen in their native French, each of them striking enough to be a runway model. Fingers crossed, good looks weren't a prerequisite for *all* the casino's workers, or Willis would be a dead giveaway that subterfuge was afoot.

The one with the chiseled cheekbones held up his hand. "This is not an entrance," he said in accented English.

Was her French *that* poor?

No matter, money would speak for her.

She offered Cheekbones the watch, nodding toward the arched stone door.

He glanced at his three companions, all of them eyeing the Rolex with interest.

"*Fouille-les*," said the footman with the golden eyes. *Search them.*

"Frisk away," Jade said, holding out her arms. They'd known better than to try and waltz into a high-security place like this while packing weapons. Visible ones, at least.

Jade felt Crys stiffen beside her when Cheekbones rifled through the pouch at her waist. He smirked, holding up a palmful of her perfume vials.

"Do you stink that badly to need so many?" He laughed and motioned to Willis. "Or are they for that grizzled creature?"

Crys snatched the vials back without comment, but Jade could see her trigger finger twitch, yearning to fire a cloud of bot-induced terror that would tear the sneer off the man's pretty face.

"We good?" Eli asked, stepping between Crys and the footman.

But the one with the golden eyes paused when he felt the bullet-shaped object in Jade's pocket. He pulled out her necklace, shaking his head. "No ammunition on the casino grounds."

"But it's already been fired, look, it's dented—"

"The watch and the bullet or you walk," he insisted.

Jade moved to rip In Extremis from the man's unworthy grasp, desperate to reclaim the bullet that lent her courage, when she stopped. Let her hand drop.

Let it go, Crys had told her at the ranch.

She looked at Crys now, took a deep, grounding breath, and did just that.

The assholes took the watch and her necklace, and Jade and her crew took their way in.

The small break room had auxiliary staff uniforms hanging on a rack in the corner, just as Jade had wagered. Hariri most likely estimated that Jade's plan would be to barge in with all her tricks. But her strategy was simple. Classic. No-frills. There were hundreds of workers at the casino, but the Fortunates' noses were held too high to spot those they deemed below them. *No one ever notices the help.*

Jade and the others quickly stripped and threw on servers' tuxedo uniforms. The disguises were almost perfect, if you didn't gaze too hard and notice that Eli couldn't button his too-tight jacket and Jade and Crys had to cuff their trousers.

"I'm not wearing those," Willis objected, shaking his head at the white gloves Crys held out for him. "The blowhards can take their champagne from my bare hands."

Crys shrugged. "Then you'll stay behind."

"Listen," Jade pressed, "if I can give up my lucky memento, you can put on a pair of server's gloves for half an hour . . ."

"Just spit in their drinks," Eli told Willis, helping him shove on his gloves. "It's what my sister used to do at our parents' restaurant when a customer got too uppity."

Jade had to squeeze her eyes shut to keep from staring at Crys. To keep from reaching for her missing necklace. The quake had stolen Eli's sister. Jade's was right here. They were side by side, but severed. Of their own damn choosing.

Jade opened her eyes. Nodded at Eli. "Perfect concession. An easy way to equalize the power structure." She tugged on a pair of the gloves, adjusted her bow tie, and slinked out of the servants' rooms and into the lively Salles Touzet.

The showy, almost operatic atmosphere made Jade feel like she'd just stepped into a scene from a movie. The walls were decorated with masterful, life-size paintings. A stained-glass ceiling and diamond-patterned carpets surrounded the high rollers gathered around mahogany gaming tables, playing for nearly a million euros, judging by the amount of chips stacked on the roulette layout.

An empty martini glass was shoved into Jade's chest, reminding her of her current role as an extra, not the star. "Two more, extra dirty," a haughty voice ordered.

Jade's cheeks burned hot. She managed a deferential nod, perform-ing her expected line. *"Bien sûr, monsieur."*

"Anything?" Eli whispered to Jade. He'd somehow managed to nab a silver tray and was gathering empty cocktail glasses as Jade scanned the swanky gamblers for signs of the Conservators. This gilded salon was mem-bers-only, but even that wasn't exclusive enough for the history-making event Hariri was hosting. No doubt there was another level of privilege in this private world with all its codes and particularities. They just had to keep sniffing around.

Jade shook her head. "No platinum suits here. Let's keep moving."

She glanced at every face they passed, paranoid that at any moment a security detail masquerading as millionaires would get wise to her deception. Nab her and toss her out, before they could find the Exhibition.

From a table away, she saw Crys nudge Willis's shoulder. He was bowing over a woman in a jeweled-encrusted couture gown. He handed her a craft cocktail, a white bubbly layer that was most *definitely* not fancy foam floating just above its rim.

Willis smirked as he limped after Crys toward the Salle Médecin.

Jade and Eli followed, staggering their entrances into the grand ballroom. A hundred-person winner's banquet was in full swing, giddy revelers seated at two long cloth-draped tables under sparkling chande-liers. A fleet of footmen were lined up behind the high-backed dining chairs, gripping confetti cannons in their white gloves.

The Grand Prix champion raced about the room, hoisting his ster-ling silver trophy over his head and screaming exultantly. The confetti cannons exploded, thousands of diamond-flecked bits of paper raining down like precious snow.

A flash of platinum at the center of the merry madness captured Jade's attention. The entire room's attention. Her gut knew before her eyes did that it was Hariri.

He hadn't changed. *How Fortunate for him.* Same sharkskin suit, same pompous airs, like nothing, no one, could cut him down. His long black-and-silver mane hung as loose as his high mood, his dark beard framing an oppressive, too-white smile.

He leapt onto the banquet table, drawing the Soaring Precious from its leather sheath at his back. An ornate marble vase was tucked beneath his arm. *Not a vase,* Jade realized with a pang. *An urn.*

Hariri set the mounted urn onto the table, patting the bronze lid like the head of a well-behaved dog. He picked up a bottle of Cristal, and the crowd gasped as he flourished the gemstone saber and used the blade to slice open the bottle's neck.

Jade envisioned Ani's blood pouring freely in place of champagne.

"Look what we've achieved, Poppy," Hariri laughed, then bent to set an overflowing glass before the urn.

A shocked scream died in Jade's throat, only to echo behind her.

Crys had gripped her arm, hard enough to bruise. Jade couldn't feel it, but she felt the pain inside her chest. The terrible ache of fury and betrayal. Not from the sight of Hariri, or the urn of their late foster mother and dean, but for the golden-haired man who sat, tranquil and smiling, at the table between them.

Damon Yates.

They had found him.

And his pale blue eyes were looking straight at Crys.

FOURTEEN

Damon hadn't the slightest idea why, but he craved a plate of dried chiles. He wondered if he could ask the server with light brown curls, who was glaring in his direction, whether she could fetch some for him.

He never got the chance to signal her. She disappeared in the rainbow storm of confetti before he could even lift a hand.

But *there*. Beside a pillar. The young woman had reappeared. But no, surely not? The hair was chestnut. Russet eyes more alarmed than fearsome, like on the similar face he'd seen before. He raised a hand, but she vanished a second time.

Damon shifted in his chair. Several blue and magenta streamers spun in the air above him, like out-of-control space divers without chutes, a handful dropping into Damon's lap. One at a time, he picked up a streamer and began ripping the thin paper into further shreds, settling his mind.

"Damon!" an unfamiliar voice shouted. A man in a shiny silver suit came stumbling toward the head of the table, raising his glass to Damon. "It's good to have you back playing with us again," the man blustered. "Where'd you hide yourself this time? Off on one of your wellness retreats, 'renovating your chakras' in Thailand?" The man laughed.

Damon pretended to smile. Was that where he'd been? In his mind's eye, he dove into the halls of his memory, only to find locked doors.

A woman in a pewter-colored column gown perched on the empty seat to Damon's left. "I'm devastated to hear about your ex-wife . . ." Damon swung his eyes to Palmer, who sat to his right. His son stared fixedly at him as he polished off his foie gras. "Not *my* mother," he said wearily, as if Damon had already embarrassed himself with this mix-up once before.

Closing his eyes, Damon grabbed a door handle. He visualized a tension wrench, a hook pick, then a bum key, until finally, the lock clicked and the memory cracked open.

The woman was referring to Damon's second wife. Poppy. She was dead. Something about a fatal attempted robbery on a HyperQuest pod.

He'd forgotten.

The woman glanced tragically at the urn. "Good of Hariri to bring Poppy to the Exhibition. She would have liked the gesture."

Was this true? Damon pounded against another door in his mind, but the memory stayed sealed.

"Text me if you need any comfort . . ." the woman whispered, handing over a long piece of confetti, a cell number scrawled in black eyeliner on one side.

Damon took it. Ripped up that one, too.

Hariri vaulted from the top of the banquet table and sheathed the gem-encrusted saber. As Damon stared, unblinking, at the white-jade hilt, Hariri's voice echoed up from the past. Decades, years, days foregone? *That saber is invaluable. The embodiment of power. The Soaring Precious is mine.*

Damon wondered when Hariri had gained possession of it. He reached for the memory, his mind stretching back to before he'd arrived in Monte Carlo with his club of Conservators, a crude, ill-healed scar on his upper arm . . . but he grasped at nothing. Lately his mind had felt like a massive star that had exploded, creating a black hole around certain timelines of his life.

Hariri beckoned for him, his jeweled fingers cupping two gold-rimmed champagne flutes. Damon smiled, hiding his confusion, and went to Hariri's side, accepting the second glass.

They clinked rims, the cheerful sound drowned out by Hariri's mirthful laugh.

"Here's to us, friend." There was a twinkle in his eye when he spoke the word "friend" that discomfited Damon. Like the word was a sleight of hand that Damon's mind was too slow to catch.

An old toast from their days at Princeton flared from the dark corners of Damon's mind. "To us," he blurted. "Masters of our own fates."

Another twinkle in Hariri's amber eyes. His grin dropped open into a howling fit like Damon had said something funny. "Right you are, friend," he agreed, wiping tears from the deep furrows of his laugh lines. "And tonight, you will watch as I become a true pathfinder. Witness as *I* reset the rules of the whole world."

He turned for the ballroom door, beckoning for Damon to follow. "Come, the global stage awaits."

Damon placed his untouched flute beside the urn. Something felt wrong. Terribly and violently wrong.

He just couldn't, for the life of him, remember what.

Palmer fell in beside Damon as Hariri led them away from the banquet and into a sumptuous salon that was equal parts Vegas and Versailles.

Why had the names of those cities suddenly come to him? In this moment, Damon couldn't place either on a map.

The promenade took them past a winding mosaic bar and exclusive gaming tables that were works of art beneath the warm glow of chandeliers. In front of him, Damon watched as Hariri drank in the elaborate ambience, touching the wide wings of every angel sculpture he passed.

A pair of stout men in black tuxedos manned the entrance to a private balcony near the end of the salon. Damon wasn't surprised when their party was instantly waved through. A single footman greeted them, bowing his head as he held out a silver tray. The man wasn't serving more champagne or hors d'oeuvres, but hosiery. Two threaded with white gold, a third set with an immense ruby.

Hariri and Palmer each took a beige stocking from the tray, slipping the nylon over their eyes and noses, distorting their faces. The sight made Damon hesitate. Brush the scar on his arm.

"It's fine, Father," Palmer assured him, exasperated. "The masks were your idea, remember? 'To foster our guests' sense of anonymity'?"

"Now, now, Palmer, show your betters some respect," Hariri said, smiling. "The man has many important things swirling around that great brain of his. He can't be expected to remember the petty details of party attire."

Anger rolled through Damon. He knew he was being mocked. *Great brain?* How had he lost so much control? Of himself? Of his place in the world? He tried to master his emotions but found he didn't have the tools.

He wrung his hands again and again, until he recalled the confetti in the pocket of his platinum suit. He tore up little bits, watching them fall to the floor like breadcrumbs. He wondered, if he came across them later, would he remember? Might they lead him back to himself?

"Shall we?" Hariri said, the continued glint in his eye letting Damon know that he was being toyed with, although he didn't know why.

Damon's anger swelled, but he nodded and slipped the hosiery over his head, covering his eyes and nose. Off balance, he moved after Hariri through the terrace doors.

"I decided to host the Exhibition outside this year," Hariri mused aloud. "Under the stars, no roof to limit the possibilities of the evening's festivities."

Damon nodded, only half listening. The moment he stepped out onto the grandiose terrace, he felt the sea breeze hit the lower half of his face. He breathed deep and looked past the elegantly dressed guests—important people, he assumed, though all strangers to him—to the expansive dark blue of the Mediterranean.

A vibrational sound burbled in his throat. A word, meaningless to him. *Shirim.*

Somehow that helped Damon transcend his anger, focus his mind, if not clear it.

Shirim, he hummed, drawing out the *M.*

He gazed at the platinum suits and gowns scattered across the balcony with their masks of precious stones, and thought of an armory of sabers with gilded hilts. He rested his eyes on the Soaring Precious sheathed at Hariri's back. He guessed *his friend* was general of the night.

"Show us your goods!" a voice thick with a lilting accent heckled from the crowd.

Damon couldn't see the spectators' expressions, but he noticed their arms crossed with uncertainty, their feet shuffling with impatience.

Good. This wasn't simply one of Damon's normal confusions. This was an Exhibition, but where were the upmarket displays of art and innovation? There was just Hariri, on a simple stage, his magnetism and infectious smile the only things on display.

"I hope everyone has enjoyed the complimentary champagne," Hariri toasted, receiving a boisterous cheer from his audience. He lifted his arm, though he held no flute of his own.

Suddenly a realization exploded in Damon's mind with the force of a supernova. *Hariri laced their champagne. This* was the wrong. The terrible and violent wrong.

Terror-stricken screams erupted across the terrace. Half the crowd cowered, and the other half sprinted for the sealed doors.

The opaque wall behind Hariri had snapped clear. It wasn't a room behind the glass wall, but a . . . tank? Damon had to rub at his eyes to make sure he was thinking correctly. *Seeing* correctly. A lone, docile manatee floated innocently in the shallow water. The sight of the endangered gentle giant of the sea brought pure, cold terror to the most powerful humans on Earth.

Damon had to give it to Hariri for his showmanship. *This* was wealth. *This* was power. The two united, supreme.

And just as he had with his saber, Damon had handed it right to him.

Memories, one after another, flashed across the pitch-blackness of his mind. He couldn't escape their burn.

This was all Damon's work. The work of his Quest Bots. *He* had been the pathfinder, the Savior, dead set on changing the world.

But he'd fled.

He'd fled.

Damon watched now as diplomats from the globe's mightiest countries, founders from the most influential tech companies, billionaires who'd bought up the world but desired to own more, all shrank before Hariri's display.

This was the work of his fear bot. Damon's most valuable innovation. His most dangerous.

"We have to get out!" a woman shrieked.

I must get out, too, Damon thought.

But when he closed his eyes, he saw the memory of slash marks flash behind his eyelids. He muffled a cry. There was a face beyond the symbol. Silhouetted, unformed. He'd given her the first-generation bot. What was her name? *What was her name?*

Damon started when a figure cozied up beside him. Damon remembered *his* name. *Palmer.* His son rolled up his mask, revealing his eyes. There was an unbearable coldness in them that made Damon feel adrift. Frightfully isolated and alone. He shivered.

"I'm only telling you this because you will forget it by the end of the hour," Palmer professed, in a whisper Damon had to lean into to hear over the screams and Hariri's laughter. "I know you didn't think me worthy of your fortune. But I want you to know how much I will enjoy taking everything that took you away from me. Your empire, your tech, your students, and your Gens."

My Gens.

His Questers used to call Damon's family Gen 1 and 2. *Vance and Maxen.* His chest twisted in pain. Loss. Where were his children?

Then the face behind the fear symbol returned, searing into his vision. A name, like a planet he could never reach, floated somewhere in the dark of his memory.

He stretched his mind, grasping for the name to pair with the faint, abstruse features.

The screams had stopped, and the terrace had gone quiet as a church. The glass wall was opaque again.

"You have experienced a mere taste of what I have to offer," Hariri preached. "My nano reform is even more potent . . . destined to be the newest high-market craze . . ." The crowd's heads tilted upward, as if they'd just witnessed something divine.

My nano reform is even more potent. The meaning behind that threat shot its way to the surface of Damon's mind. Hariri had warped, amplified, Damon's fear bot, turned it into an unstoppable weapon of war.

Celene and the boy who helped Damon after he fled his campus.

They were infected.

They needed his help.

"You're Hariri's little pet now," Palmer whispered to Damon. "His jester, kept close to amuse him at his bidding." Palmer lowered his mask. "I won't save you, but I will save Quest. Goodbye, Father." He didn't depart, merely stood there, gripping Damon's arm.

He's waiting for my memory to desert me, Damon realized. He whispered feverishly to himself. *Remember, remember. Save yourself. Save yourself.*

A copper-haired man, the only maskless face on the balcony, approached on Palmer's right. He wore a dull platinum suit and a sophisticated prosthetic in lieu of his forefinger.

"Where's your stocking?" Palmer hissed, tugging at his ear. "If anyone recognizes you—" Palmer stopped his reprimand short. He sniffed the air as the Conservator drew closer.

"We have a few uninvited guests," the Conservator whispered.

A perfume wafted off the man, hints of amber and cedar. Damon knew that scent.

Crystal. His daughter. Gen 3. She was *here.*

Another name sparked bright from his memory.

Jade. She was here, too. Damon had seen them both at the winner's banquet.

Their names triggered a wormhole within his mind, shooting seven years' worth of memories to the surface. His knees buckled with the shock of it. The shame.

He closed his eyes, desperate for a retreat. He had to get out. He had to flee.

His mind stuttered, thoughts disappearing like he'd just missed a step on a ladder. He fell back into darkness.

When he opened his eyes again, he felt a brutal despair.

But for the life of him, Damon couldn't remember why.

FIFTEEN

Crys stood at the center of the electrified crowd on the terrace. Without the prop of a silver tray, her server's tuxedo mingled seamlessly with the platinum guests' finery.

She'd stolen a black nylon stocking off the head of an unsuspecting Conservator, the man with the prosthetic finger who'd shot Poppy and tried to strangle Crys at Quest. One spray of her fragrance put a quick end to his attempt to lay another finger on her. Donning the mask made Crys's skin crawl, but she was grateful for the anonymity. A gratitude, she was certain, felt by every influential spectator who was "present" but "never officially here."

Crys was even more thankful that the mask concealed her teary eyes. She didn't want Jade to see. Her sister hovered by her side, trembling, nearly toppling, as if she sought to crumple in Crys's arms.

Pull yourself upright, Crys wanted to snap at her. Was it really so startling to find Damon Yates in league with the Conservators, a billionaires' club *he himself* had cofounded?

The naked truth was *yes.* Crys had believed Yates dead, or off starving, suffering, wandering the outskirts of LA like a broken, wretched exile. Yet here he was, platinum clad and standing tall behind Hariri. The image shot more terror, more pain into Crys's system than any fear bot ever could.

The way Yates looked at her at the winner's table . . . like she was nothing, *no one*, to him. Had he already forgotten her? In a mere few weeks, had Yates's Adsum family disappeared from his diseased mind? Or had he struck a deal with Hariri? A new Quest Bot to keep his memories in exchange for realigning with the Conservators? Either possibility was gut-wrenching.

Crys shook her head, homing her focus back onto the terrace. She was certain Hariri and Yates had laced their guests' champagne with the Quest fear bots, not Hariri's own novel nano reform. He wouldn't dare infect the world's richest and most powerful.

It would be bad for business, she thought bitterly.

Crys snarled at the stench around her, the stink of greed. The desperate need to *own* fear.

Like you, Jade's gravelly voice tittered in her mind.

No, Crys hissed back. *We're not the same. I'm nothing like them. Or you. Or Yates.*

Then who are you?

All at once, sleek bidding paddles shot up around Crys, alighting like monstrous fireflies across the terrace. Extravagantly high numbers were called out at hyperloop speed. One billion, five. A breathtaking twenty billion euros. Thirty-five.

Jade leaned in close, her whisper hot with panic. "This Exhibition is a shaking *auction.*"

Hariri had managed to keep his disruptive technology in stealth mode, Crys realized—no PR, no big NDAs—and still incite an international arms race, a frenzy to secure first-mover advantage.

At center stage, half of the auctioneer's face was concealed by jewel-encrusted hosiery, but Crys would know that knife's-edge smile anywhere. And that silver leather handbag, packed tight with rags soaked with nano reform. *The Conservator who'd infected Cole.*

In an instant, a vial was in Crys's hand. She moved toward the stage, her trigger finger on the nozzle, but Jade gripped her elbow.

"Palmer's here," Jade hissed, nodding in the direction of the bar. "And he's got Ani's ruby." The gemstone set between Palmer's eyes glinted like a pool of blood in the paddles' lights as he hunted the crowd.

Crys almost wanted Palmer to find her. To *see* her.

Jade's fingers dove for the vials in her jacket pocket, but there was no need. Palmer was already the prize of Crys's burgeoning collection of people who cowered before her.

Take off your mask, a vicious thing in Crys urged. *Take back the gem.* She stored away her vials, her fingers moving for the gold-threaded hem of her nylon stocking. *Make your former brother confront what terrified him more than anything else in the world.*

You.

A lighted paddle rocketed into the air beside Crys. Jade had just placed a bid for forty billion euros.

With whose fortune? Crys wondered.

Jade placed another bid at twice the price, driving the sale to impossible heights, switching on these Fortunates' ruthless need to compete, to win. To own it all.

"You may have been the intended billion-heir, but you're out of your depth," Crys snipped. "Your street tricks won't work here." She grabbed the paddle and pushed it down.

Jade raised it again.

Crys snatched it from her, their scuffle turning heads, when the ornate sconces along the marble walls started blinking. A siren chimed over the speakers.

Willis and Eli had triggered the fire alarm. *The contingency plan.*

But it was too late.

Crys seized the paddle from Jade just as the auctioneer struck her gavel, closing the bidding at one hundred billion. The sale was a done deal.

"Shake it all to hell," Jade cursed. "This is *not* good."

Crys scoured the crowd for the highest bidder. There were no signs of celebration. The guests were already shuffling out, guided toward the emergency exits by security guards.

"Did you see who got it?" Jade whispered. "If we don't catch whoever won the nano reform—"

Jade's panic was a cancer. Crys couldn't let it spread.

I control fear.

A gemstone glittered against the flashing lights of the fire alarm, catching Crys's attention. She turned and saw a man in a beige mask with a tremendous emerald faceted over his nose. He dipped his chin in a nod toward the stage.

Was it a greeting? An assent? An understanding?

Crys whipped her head toward Hariri, who nodded back to the mystery man. Crys could hear Hariri's laugh over the bustle of his guests' retreat.

Fool, Crys wanted to scream. Did Hariri really think he could control the nano reform once it was in someone else's hands? Had Yates's fate taught Hariri *nothing*?

Or is that his endgame? Crys calculated. *To become the ultimate disrupter? To shake up the world?* The thought sent chills down her spine.

Back on the stage, Hariri smiled and patted Yates's arm. Yates returned a full grin.

Old chums. Thick as thieves. Stealing the future from millions. Potentially billions. Crys's gut twisted like she'd received a brutal jab from the Soaring Precious.

Hariri turned, and Yates followed, marching for the exit near the wall that held the manatee tank. With great effort, Crys turned her back on Hariri, on his saber and *his Yates*, snapping her attention to the man with the emerald nose. He was halfway to the double doors by the balcony. Straightaway, Crys went after him. Who was he? And more importantly, what did he want with the nano reform?

"Wait," Jade urged, an annoying shadow that trailed her. "We have to go after Yates. Without Hema, he's our only shot at finding the cure."

"It's better if we split up," Crys argued, increasing her speed. Palmer was only a few feet away now. She had to stop herself from whistling him over. "I'll take the mystery buyer, you take Yates."

Jade shook her head. "We should swap targets. You were his daughter, the last thing he said to you was 'I'll never let you go.' Tell him he doesn't have to if he comes with you."

But the catch was Crys had spent the last month letting Damon Yates go. When she left the ranch, she thought she'd been ready to find him. To see her former father once again. Yet now that he'd betrayed them a *second* time, everything inside of her wanted to avoid Yates like a megaquake. She locked her trembling hands in front of her to hide her rising panic.

"You really can't bag Yates alone?" she goaded, projecting her emotions onto Jade. "Or are you too scared that your nerve will break?"

Jade huffed. "Meet me at the car," she fumed, turning for the terrace doors.

"Meet *me* at the car," Crys answered, a bit too loud. "Because I'll be there first."

She fell into the crowd, moving through the opulent Salle Blanche toward the exit, keeping her eye on the back of the buyer's head. She noted the details: trim, average height, olive skin, judging by his exposed hands and clean-shaven chin. He wore a black suit, well cut but plain, understated. This man could be anyone from anywhere.

Inside the salon, the alarm cut off, replaced with an announcement in French and English for the guests to proceed to the VIP stairwell. But the buyer walked straight past the emergency exit and back into the casino.

Did he have his own way out, a rooftop helipad? Or was he going to meet Hariri to discuss the details of their deal, unbothered by the prospect of a fire inside the building?

Crys followed the buyer into the half-empty grand ballroom. Then in her peripheral vision, she clocked a man in a dark suit and nylon mask tracking *her*. The buyer's enforcer? Or Conservator muscle, sent after her by Palmer?

She lifted her fear vial as the stocky man lunged forward, a pistol clutched in his long-fingered hand.

Crys held her breath and sprayed.

The man shuddered back, his confusion turning into terror when Crys peeled up her mask to expose her face.

She left the man screaming, incapacitated with fear. Searching for the buyer, she spotted him slipping into the gambling rooms and moved to follow when an elbow locked around her throat.

"Do not pursue this man again," an icy voice threatened in her ear.

The auctioneer, Crys realized. *The Conservator with the knife-edged smile.* The woman squeezed, an exclamation point to her throat.

Distantly, reluctantly, Crys understood why threats had always made Jade smile.

She slammed her chin onto the woman's forearm, then rammed both elbows into her ribs. The woman stumbled backward but didn't let go. Undeterred, Crys pivoted her body and rotated into a forward roll, using her momentum to throw the woman over her head and onto the banquet table littered with champagne glasses. The woman gasped, the wind knocked out of her, rage scribbled across the lower half of her hard, oval face. She reached for her handbag, for a rag she'd doused with the nano reform.

Crys dove on top of her, pinning her to the table with her knees. She drew her own fear fragrance and slammed down the nozzle. A torrent of perfume hit the woman full in her gaping mouth. She cried out, kicking and screaming to flee from the sight of Crys's face.

The woman began to choke on her fear, and still Crys kept spraying.

Her eyes went to the rag laced with the nano reform. She should press it to the woman's mouth. Infect her, like she had mercilessly done to Cole and countless Unfortunates.

Give her a taste of her own medicine.

A buoyant laugh called Crys out of her spell. She turned to the emergency stairwell and almost started choking herself on her sudden fury.

Hariri stood at its entrance, holding up one of Crys's perfume vials. He wagged it in front of him, toying with her, challenging her to come and take it.

The vial she'd dropped in the fighting ring.

Crys's vision tunneled, all thoughts of the buyer and the woman pinned beneath her escaping her mind. She cursed, pulled her mask back down, and barreled after Hariri only to find an empty stairwell. She threw her upper body over the railing, desperate to find Hariri. Hear his laughter slapping against the marble walls.

But there was no one.

Then a door across the landing burst open. Wild chestnut curls emerged from beneath elastic hosiery as Jade ripped off her mask. Chest heaving, she bent forward, hands on her knees.

At Crys's approach, Jade stood erect, her feet in a fighter's stance, fear fragrance now drawn and at the ready. Her eyes were wide and feral, like a caught stray. *This* was the one Yates had chosen to give courage to over Crys?

Imagine what a soul like that could do.

Crys yanked off her nylon mask. "Calm down, it's just me."

"Yeah, I can see it's *just* you," Jade mocked, covering her false alarm. "Where's the buyer?"

"Taking the VIP elevator to the ground floor," Crys lied, turning to bound down the steps. "I'm going to beat him to the bottom."

Jade sprinted after her. She wasn't as quick, her body racked with injuries and side effects from the nano reform. Still, that didn't make Crys slack her pace. "Did you lose Damon?" she spat over her shoulder.

"*Lose* is a strong word," Jade huffed, a few steps behind. "I've *misplaced* him."

Crys had a stitch in her side. For a single moment, she slowed. Only a twin would notice it.

"You need to take a break?" Jade goaded, catching up.

Crys took a shuddering breath and charged ahead. "You've always said *I* had an heiress's airs, but you've always been the smug one. I don't know how the three of us even *fit* inside this stairwell—"

Winded but keeping pace, Jade looked up, feigning a search for a third person.

"Topple it all, you know I'm talking about your *ego*," Crys snapped. "I bet you replay that *Atrocity* episode in your mind like it's your new *theme song*."

"You've got it all wrong, as always," Jade insisted.

"I was wrong to think you needed me. That anyone needed me." The words tumbled out before Crys could stop them. "I was just a tagalong stray that Yates made room for. *You're* the one who changed our fortune."

Jade grabbed Crys's arm as they reached the ground floor. "*Gem*, the only fortune I want is the one Mom always promised us."

Your fortune is in your bond.

There were days in Crys's childhood when she'd had to scour dumpsters or starve. But she'd never felt poorer than at this very moment. Not that she'd ever admit it to Jade. Not now.

"Yates separated us once," Jade said earnestly. "Don't let him do it again."

Just as Crys was about to shoulder open the stairwell's fire exit, she paused. "Say that you're sorry."

"I'm sorry?" Jade said. "Meaning . . . come again?"

I'm. Sorry. Two words Jade rarely spoke in tandem. In their eighteen years, Crys had only ever heard her sister say them once. Jade didn't give apologies, only took them.

"Say you screwed up," Crys prodded, "that you shouldn't have taken the nano reform without talking to me first."

Jade bit at her lip. "You wouldn't understand," she spat. "You could never understand what I had. What I lost."

"I've lost out on every one of my dreams, and a last name worth billions, but go on—"

"My Quest Bot *made* me, Crys!" Jade yelled, her anger bouncing off the walls. "I was fearlessness incarnate. You heard Yates on the recording! I could have taken on the world; now look at me. I'm *breaking*, literally and figuratively, and I'm scared shitless with every damn breath I take."

You're going to change the world, Yates had once said to Crys. But really, he'd chosen Jade for that.

"You never did anything good with it anyway," Crys whispered, unrelenting. She might have been handed the worst of the Quest Bots, but Crys had made do with what she was given. She always had. Gripping her vials, she moved for the emergency door.

"And that's what we're doing with your bot?" Jade asked by her side. "Something good?"

"Now *that's* something the former scapegrace should understand," Crys answered. "I'm tired of being *good*."

Something dropped to the ground beside them.

"Is that . . ." Crys faltered.

A wooden top spun round and round, an exact replica of their childhood trompo.

Then a voice, sharp and boisterous as a drunken brawl, sounded from above. "When it stops turning . . . *boom*."

It was the same threat Jade had promised Hariri when she'd used the trompo to escape the Conservators during their last encounter. Crys jerked her head up the stairwell to see Hariri throw back his head and let out a deep, howling laughter. It echoed throughout the stairwell, and then he was gone.

Jade managed a shrug. "Maybe it's just an empty threat, like mine—"

The trompo burst open, a cloud of smoke choking Jade's words. They covered their noses and mouths with their jackets and went for the door. It was locked.

Crys's eyes stung, her throat burned. *This isn't an ordinary smoke bomb,* she thought in a fury. She could feel in her bones that it was laced with something much more vengeful.

Until next time, Hariri had promised them.

Together, Crys and Jade threw their bodies into the steel door, smashing their full weight into the crash bar. Once, twice . . . on the third collision, the door burst open, and they fell face-first to the pavement. Crys gagged on smoke, struggling to swallow deep breaths of the fresh sea air.

Their limbs shaking, Crys and Jade leaned on each other for balance as they elbowed their way through the throng of high rollers scattered outside the casino.

A woman in a black sheath gown pointed toward the door they'd just exited, smoke pouring from the stairwell. "Fire!" the woman cried, just as a large custom Rolls-Royce pulled into the drive.

A white-gloved hand beckoned Crys and Jade from the vintage car's front passenger window. *Eli.*

Crys and Jade piled into the back seats, and Willis, dressed in a valet's uniform, slammed down the accelerator.

"Stop!" Eli suddenly exclaimed.

The tires screeched, and the headlights illuminated a golden-haired figure in a platinum suit stumbling down the drive, a bronze-and-marble urn clasped protectively to his chest.

Crys's heart skipped a beat, then fell to the floorboards.

"It's Yates," Jade yelled. She turned to Crys with the first genuine smile she had seen her sister wear in weeks. "We found him."

Crys opened the car door and staggered toward Yates. His pale blue eyes locked on to her face, searching her features. Did he remember her? Even if he did, he wouldn't recognize her with the gold stripped from her hair and the ocean blue of her eyes returned to the dark color of earth.

Crys nearly went for her vials, but then a name rattled from Yates's throat.

"Crystal . . . Is that you?"

"No," she answered evenly. "I'm Crys Moore." She nodded to the car, so similar to the Quest AV that Yates had appeared in that day in Echo Park to pluck her and Jade from the Unfortunate streets before whisking them off to a dreamland. *A nightmare,* Crys amended.

"Get in," she commanded Yates, spinning on her heel to turn her back on him. "I won't let you go."

Sixteen

The tears on Rhett's cheeks had long since dried. His corneas were swollen, burning so bad he could scream. But he'd done so much of that already, his throat was stripped raw.

His eyes had been wide open for hours. Too terrified to close them, too panic-stricken to even blink. If he did either, he'd see the fear symbol Palmer's drone had seared onto the back of his eyelids.

They'd cuffed his arms behind his back, preventing him from shielding his eyes and blacking out the three diagonal lines of red light that signaled straight to Rhett's brain: this was *definitely* not a safe place.

There was nowhere to run and not a damn place to hide. He was trapped in a glass cage. Locked on a rooftop balcony at the top of a timber tower of the Forest, twenty stories high, overlooking Quest Campus. The transparent floor and railings triggered his acrophobia into overdrive. Just as Palmer had known they would.

Everywhere Rhett looked sent his head spinning, his stomach heaving.

He didn't know which was more torturous: closing his eyes and seeing the fear symbol or forcing them to stay open and taking in the dizzying heights.

Rhett rolled over on his side, adding to his piles of bile.

Palmer is one depraved richling. His thoughts came slow and painful. *He would've made a better enforcer for his pops than I ever was.*

So, Rhett theorized, it hadn't been Damon that sent the anonymous message to Hema, steering them in the direction of Yates's hidden treasure. What Hema had guessed might lead to the cure. Had it been Palmer all along? Luring one of the best scientists in the world out of their lab and into his trap?

The bastard better not have even thought *about touching Hema.*

Anger throbbed in Rhett like a heartbeat, and he saw red.

And blinked.

Three diagonal slash marks flashed behind his eyelids. Fear roared through his mind, a rasping scream tearing up his throat.

He fought to swallow the cry, and tore open his eyes.

A fresh stream of tears ran down his raw cheeks. His shuddering body drenched in sweat as he struggled not to obey his mind's pleas to *flee.*

He wasn't sure how much more of this he could take.

Bam.

A pounding against the heat-strengthened wall. Or was the sound just inside his head, which ached and pounded and felt like it was about to break?

Bam. Bam.

Rhett latched on to Hema's voice, determined to endure.

I know why no one has found Yates's treasure . . . Hema had said on their bench outside the ranch. *It's not on campus.*

It's above it.

That still sounded like a puzzle to Rhett. But he wanted to believe it. To hold on to the hope it still could have been Damon who'd sent them the message. The clue.

Grinding his jaw, he made himself look out the transparent balcony wall. Quest Campus had seventeen mountain peaks and countless highrises. Was that what the blasted poem had meant? That the treasure was stashed at the top of one of those places?

Rhett's head began to swim, his vertigo sending him onto his back, eyes glued to the tip of his nose.

The intrepid billionaire *did* have a thing for heights. Rhett ran over the other possibilities in his mind, distracting his focus.

Damon's home, Castle in the Air. No, that had been blown up by the Conservators.

Damon's world-class theater, Summit Auditorium. It wasn't all that tall, but was the "Summit" in the building's name a clue?

Damon's favorite mantra, *always higher*. His daughter had the Latin phrase as a tattoo. Was the treasure somehow *inside* Crys?

Rhett only registered that the banging had stopped when an ear-splitting crash sounded from the balcony's wall.

He rolled his head toward the noise, straining to keep his eyelids open.

He needed to blink. He must be hallucinating.

There was a gaping hole in the shatterproof glass wall, and Hema Devi was charging through it.

Hema plopped to their knees at Rhett's side. Something dropped from their hand. Clattered on the ground in front of his desert-dry eyes. A steel leg from a chair rigged with a fat cone-shaped diamond at its tip.

"I created my own window-breaking hammer," Hema explained, cutting the zip ties that bound his hands.

Of course they had.

Rhett stared at the diamond hammerhead, recalling that very sparkler hanging around the neck of the MIT professor they'd failed to nab. A thank-you gift from his gemstone-loving bosses?

"Professor Snyder has joined the platinum side," Hema said, nostrils flaring. "He's the scientist behind the nano reform."

"That stupid son of a—" Rhett's tirade was cut off by his own stifled moan. He'd blinked, the fear symbol flashing behind his lids.

A soft hand soothed his sweaty brow.

"What did they do to you?" Hema asked, breathless. Rhett felt a cooling breeze when Hema ripped open his shirt, steady hands sliding across his bare chest and stomach. "Tell me where it hurts."

Rhett must have been half mad, because he had half a mind to hold his tongue and let Hema's hands keep searching.

Then his eyes blinked involuntarily, and he barely kept himself from screaming the answer. "That yacht-snot scratched the damn symbol behind my lids."

"Palmer?" Hema asked, keeping their eyes locked on Rhett's. "He's here, on campus?"

The billion-heir hadn't kidnapped Rhett and Hema himself, of course. He'd sent his own new breed of enforcers for that, ambushing their AV outside of the Hollywood HyperQuest portal.

Rhett shook his head. "His drone branded me."

Palmer's voice had taunted Rhett during the short procedure, threatening him as only a Yates would know how.

The next time you see me, Frankenstein, you'll be paralyzed with fear.

Rhett writhed on the ground in agony. "Hema, I've never wanted anything more than to tear off my own eyelids right now," he groaned, desperate to blink, to find even a morsel of relief.

Hema foraged a hidden pocket in the inseam of their jacket. Their hand came away with a single glass vial.

"That one of your attack bots?" Rhett asked, gasping, tears rolling down his face.

Hema nodded, the blunt ends of their bangs falling into their steadfast eyes. "From the final test batch I took with me from the lab."

"I can't risk it," Rhett insisted. "If it disables my Quest Bot . . ." All the muscles in his body suddenly stiffened in protest. Revolted at the prospect of Palmer's threats coming to life.

You'll be paralyzed with fear, he'd all but promised.

Had Palmer gotten wind of Hema's attack bots from one of the Adsum students? Had he orchestrated this exact moment for Rhett as revenge? Punishing a nobody orphan from Kansas for rising so high? For being told by Palmer's pops that he was the son he'd never had?

Choose, Rhett could almost hear Palmer ask through the robotic hiss of his drone. A broken body? Or a broken mind?

Hema sensed the impossible battle he struggled against. They held up the vial containing the attack bot. "This new formula was inspired by the reckless stunt Jade pulled in my lab. I infused elements of her old Quest Bot, thinking the engineered fearlessness could counteract the nano reform's assault on the fear region of the brain."

"Will it stop the prion disease from spreading?" Rhett asked, hopeful.

Hema's face fell. "No. I still haven't found the cure."

"But it's something."

A hell of a something. If it worked, it meant no more running. No more fear controlling the Unfortunates, locking them out of the cities. If the prion disease would eventually kill them, at least they could die at home. In a safe place.

And that was a risk worth taking, even if it meant disabling his Quest Bot, the only thing keeping him together. He reached for the back of his neck, rubbing his fingers along the knobs of his spine as Hema uncorked the stopper, holding the vial over his mouth.

"Wait, what about you?" Rhett said, staying Hema's hand. It was long-boned and soft-skinned, with a grip that felt like it would never let go. "There's no chance Palmer had you spared from the nano reform. If this works, it's you who should be free of the symbol."

Hema shrugged. "Right now, you're more important."

Tears of laughter sprang from Rhett's eyes. Right now, there was no one in the world more important than Hema Devi.

"I'm serious," Hema pressed, lowering the vial to Rhett's lips. "I can't let you tear off your own eyelids, now can I?"

Hema smiled, and that was that.

169

"Fine," Rhett said, "I'll be your test rabbit." He smiled back, though it twisted into a grimace, and opened his mouth.

The liquid slid down his hoarse throat, and his lids spasmed closed. Only for a nanosecond, but enough to make him moan. *This isn't a safe place, this isn't a safe place.* But how could he escape his own body? His own mind?

When he tore open his lids, Hema was right there. Still gripping his hand.

"It may take some time to see a conclusive result," Hema assured him. But a certain tilt of Hema's head, a shrewdness in their gaze, reminded Rhett of his pops when he used to check the farm's wheat for stripe rust.

You'll be paralyzed the next time you see me.

Rhett lay there. Waiting for the diagnosis.

"They brought you in to replace me, haven't they?"

Hema crushed Rhett's hand at the sound of Professor Snyder's unhinged voice. A few of Rhett's knuckles cracked, but he didn't mind. It meant he could still feel. His Quest Bot was still working.

"You're here to steal all the credit, wipe my name off my Nobel Prize–winning discovery." The man loomed over Hema's shoulder, his low ponytail wild like he'd almost ripped his hair out at the thought. His red-rimmed eyes were clouded with jealousy. With spite.

"The last time I checked, they weren't giving out Nobel Prizes for bioterrorism," Hema said cuttingly. "You warped the biotech I created into a weapon of mass destruction. You're a butcher, not a scientist."

Snyder let loose a maniacal laugh. The smooth, whimsical professor who chased after coeds was gone, replaced by a mad scientist desperate to hang on to his shot at fame and glory.

To kill for it, Rhett thought. He didn't like the way the professor was looking at Hema. Not at all.

"Get away from Hema," Rhett growled, lifting himself up. But the professor shone a palm-sized mirror into Rhett's eyes, and the reflected sunlight forced Rhett's lids closed.

The fear symbol sent a shock of terror across his mind.

Through his screams he heard Hema threaten to tell the world what Snyder had helped the Conservators unleash. How they didn't care if they were brought down with him for their part in inventing the nano reform. That there was a prison cell waiting for him, not a Nobel Prize.

Then Hema's hand was ripped from Rhett's grip. Their cry blended with his screams.

His lids burst open to see Snyder banging Hema's head against the balcony's railing. On the third hit, blood streamed down the glass. He wasn't going to stop until he broke Hema's skull wide open.

"No—" Rhett roared, hurtling toward them.

He faltered. His head spun. His acrophobia sent him to his hands and knees.

But you can still move, he yelled at himself. *Your bot is still working. Swallow your fear and stand the hell up.*

The diamond hammerhead lay on the glass floor in front of him. The light rebounding off the gemstone blinded him.

Not again, he thought as his eyes sealed shut.

But this time when he saw the fear symbol burned behind his lids, it wasn't terror surging through his blood. It was fearlessness. A reckless adrenaline that rocketed him to his feet.

Hema's attack bot worked.

Now unafraid of the towering heights, Rhett raced for Hema. He blinked once, twice, three times in rapid-fire, a kind of power surging through him. When Snyder saw him coming, he tossed Hema aside and locked his wild eyes on Rhett. He charged and wrapped his mitts around Rhett's throat, pushing him backward against the railing.

Rhett's upper body dangled, twenty stories high, his view straight up into the sky. And a jolt of recognition hit him right between the eyes. He didn't scream. *He laughed.*

Yates's treasure wasn't on any mountain peak or rooftop.

It was in the sky. Above the clouds. Past the atmosphere, orbiting at the edge of space.

Semper in altioribus. Always higher, the eccentric magnate's favorite phrase.

The professor pushed Rhett farther over the balcony, and still he laughed, exhilarated by the dizzying height, by the discovery.

A discovery he wouldn't get to tell Hema.

Then the hands around Rhett's neck went slack. The professor's weight collapsed on him, and he saw the diamond lodged in the back of the man's skull.

Rhett pushed the dead man off and ran to Hema, who swayed against the glass railing in a daze. "I just murdered someone," Hema muttered.

"No," Rhett corrected, "you saved my life—"

"Not just any someone," Hema pressed, "but the only person who might have known the cure."

"Hema," Rhett stammered, "I know where Yates hid his treasure—"

But Hema had collapsed in a pool of their own blood.

SEVENTEEN

A sixteenth-century Gothic church wasn't all that different from Husk Row, Jade mused, hunched on a rock-hard wooden pew. At this late hour, the Cimiez Monastery was abandoned and quiet, lit by candles and decorated with works of art.

Jade stared up at the church's ribbed, vaulted ceiling, its beautifully intricate wall paintings making her think of Ani and her mural of the City of Angels back on their old hideout's cracked concrete floor. She'd depicted Yates as a black-winged archangel in white, standing high on a mountaintop as the world went to hell for the wingless mortals below him.

Oh, how the mighty fall, Jade thought, her gaze dropping to the man in the flesh.

Yates sat hunched on the floor in a far corner of the chancel, hands moving restlessly in his lap. His golden hair was disheveled, a furtive look in his pale blue eyes verging on confused panic. The serene calm that had always emanated from him with such force, the peace that came with power, with *control*, was gone.

Hariri had stripped Yates of his empire, his family, his Quest Bot. *His mind.* Held him hostage as some kind of twisted plaything, a pet to amuse him, taking advantage of his dementia and publicly humiliating him on the world stage. Wasn't this what Jade had always wanted?

Wasn't this justice for all that he'd done to her? To the Exiles? To her and Crys?

For years Jade had thought the only thing separating them was Damon Yates. Now she knew better. They kept *themselves* apart.

Crys leaned against the baroque altarpiece at the front of the sanctuary, intricate stained-glass windows as her majestic backdrop. Jade didn't think Crys was praying, but her brow was furrowed in heavy contemplation, most likely pondering what nanoscopic weapon Hariri had laced inside his smoke bomb. What new bot was swimming through their blood vessels.

What new engineered terror lay in wait for them.

Jade was sure it contained the nano reform, infecting Crys, doubling down on Jade's exposure.

She had done her best to shove it out of her mind during the half-hour drive to Nice. To focus on regrouping and recouping, on stashing the luxury getaway car by the marina, throwing off their scent by staging their escape on one of the hundreds of superyachts. But really, they were now holed away in a medieval monastery, on a high hill above the seaport city, where they'd reunited with Cole, Nolan, and Benson.

On their back-alley escape from the casino, they'd grilled Yates with questions. He'd withered under the heat. *I don't remember, I don't remember,* he'd muttered again and again.

Eli didn't believe him. Jade noticed he'd stopped pinching his arm and upgraded to a blade to test his pain levels, running the sharp tip along his forearm to make sure he could still feel. When he never flinched, Jade's gut twisted, realizing his nano reform had progressed like hers. *If it turns out Yates is pretending not to remember, to get out of punishment . . .* he'd hissed to Jade as they'd entered the sanctuary.

We won't let him, Jade had promised. *We'll find the answers.*

Here, only ten feet away, was the man who had the solution stored inside him. Somewhere deep in his mind, he knew how to stop the spread. He had the knowledge, the answers, he just couldn't access them. What would it take to trigger the hidden memories? And how much time would be lost? Jade glanced at the old wooden pew across the aisle, where Cole lay splayed, alarmingly still.

The sound of a heavy door opening broke the hallowed silence. Willis, who steered clear of churches as much as he did fire, was finally entering the sanctuary, after loitering in the narthex since their arrival. By the tread of his footfall, it seemed he had something urgent to say.

He stood in the front aisle between Jade and Crys, on the verge of a speech, but he faltered when he spotted the ornate urn next to Jade on the pew.

Jade shrugged, offering no explanation. She wasn't going to leave Poppy's ashes in Yates's care. He didn't deserve them. He couldn't be trusted. So she'd taken possession, keeping them safe for Maxen. For Iris, who, chances were, had no idea Hariri had raided her family crypt in San Francisco. Flown them to Monaco to be another plaything in his sick game.

Willis scrubbed a rough hand over the stubble on the crown of his head. "Now, I'm not usually a stickler for rules, per se—"

Crys and Jade grunted in unison.

Willis waved a stern finger at them. "But I'm gonna make some anyway."

This should be rich, Jade thought, leaning back against her creaky pew, ready to hear the new commandments she wouldn't be following.

"Rule one," Willis said. "While we're in this sanctuary, we're done rehashing the past. That's what bit us in the ass at the ranch, and old grudges are gonna chew our heads off whole if we keep it up." He snapped his chin to Yates, whose platinum suit made him look like a lightning rod Willis couldn't help but strike. "Rule two. *You* don't even *glance* at my nieces. *My* family."

Yates didn't acknowledge Willis's command, his attention trained instead on Cole. If Jade thought *she* was on the verge of cracking, Cole had already ruptured.

She ran her eyes over the scuffed boot wrapped around his injured foot and the soiled bandage on his head, his knuckles bruised from slugging Eli, his best sib, after deliriously thinking he was Yates. Now, his mumbled ramblings were directed at a different guardian. Not one of the twenty-six lousy foster homes he'd cycled through when he was in the system, but the one he'd never met. His birth mom. Cole was having a full-blown conversation with the woman as if she were beside him on the pew.

Jade threw Crys a glance. How was she so unmoved? So stubbornly stoic and distant? Crys might be unrecognizable to Jade, but one thing that hadn't changed was that Crys would be the last person in this room to shed a public tear. Did she think that made her strong? Fearless? It only made Jade feel pity.

Crys was focused on her phone, scouring the internet for clues to the mystery buyer: paparazzi photos from the race, video of guests entering the casino party, headshots from a renowned list of the richest men alive. There had to be a trace of the man *somewhere*.

Willis whistled, a surprisingly effective move. Cole even rolled on his side to listen.

"Rule three. Everyone, when I say so, will let out a collective scream."

There was a collective sigh.

"And wake up the monks?" Eli asked. He unfastened his bow tie and wrapped it tightly around the cut on his forearm.

"No monks," Nolan corrected, holding up his phone. His voice was warm honey, sweet and languid, as he grinned up at Willis. "Google says the Franciscan monastery is purely a museum now. I always say screaming to the heavens can be therapeutic."

Willis blinked in surprise at Nolan's open support. He cleared his throat, then looked at each of the ragged Exiles in turn. "We gotta shake things up. Shift the mood. We'll let go of our losses together with a good, long holler."

Yates the tranquil meditator, Jade thought, comparing the two men, *Willis the rowdy agitator.* How odd it felt to be in the same room together, let alone in the sanctity of a church.

Benson emerged from behind one of the thick, ornamental columns. He wore the trendsetting coat Eli had magicked from Crys's wools and silks. Jade had let him have it. For now. "Is this like an Unfortunates' war cry or something?" Benson scoffed. "Scream at no one listening, and just hope things will change?"

"Rule four . . ."

Benson made a rookie mistake and turned toward the source of the voice. Crys. He let out a muffled cry at her features and slammed his eyes closed.

"If you open your trap again," Crys threatened, "I'll pour your attack bot into the Mediterranean."

Benson crossed his arms, staring down at his naked wrist, sulking about his lost Rolex.

Not sorry, Jade thought, getting to her feet. On the occasions when she screamed at the world, Jade liked to stand. It was better for the rib cage; she could suck in more air, release more power. She balled her fists, bent her knees.

Willis shrugged. "All right," he heralded, "have at it."

Jade let go.

Everyone did. Their elongated cries jumbled in an odd harmony, like an eight-person hellion choir.

Yates's scream, a deep, indignant roar, lasted a few heartbeats after the others' cries had died out. Purged of all the fury, frustrations, and pain she'd held inside, Jade had to admit that, for now at least, Willis's primal-therapy tactic had worked.

The silence pounded in Jade's ears. On instinct, she almost laughed to fill it, but instead she broke the quiet with a sigh. Laughter belonged to someone else. It seemed like Hariri owned the sound. "Damon—"

She faltered. Even Crys noticed the shift. Jade had not been on a first-name basis with their benefactor and betrayer since she'd run from the academy. A first name was too personal, too cozy. Yet it had slipped right out. *He's not worthy of your pity*, the scapegrace warned Jade. Yet staring at this shell of a man shot empathy straight into her crooked heart. Damon was just as lost and out of control as she was. As they all were.

Crys sheathed her phone. Popped up from the altar. "What's next, Jade? Are you going to call him *Father*?"

The word snapped Damon awake. He was standing now, blue eyes clear and open as windows that Jade wished she could sneak into and rob every last memory that was fast disappearing behind them.

Damon tilted his head, the muscles in his fine-boned face tightening. "Crystal?" He stumbled toward her, his brows bumping together in a frown, as if reaching to remember took all his concentration. "What are we doing here? Where's Rhett? Tell him we'd like to leave now. I'd like to go home."

"Well, you can't go home," Crys told him.

"Why?" Damon answered. He stopped short, rocking back and forth on his heels, his pupils dilated in confusion.

Slowly, Crys approached him. Outstretched her hand. Damon reached to take it, but Crys's fingers plunged into the front pocket of his platinum jacket and came away with a Conservator's shiny pin.

She held the red slashes so Damon could see. Instantly, he covered his eyes with his palms. Fell to his knees. Let loose a soul-shattering cry that outlasted any fear incursion.

Jade noticed Crys's closed eyes, her clenched jaw, and knew. Crys was infected. Jade wanted to join in Damon's screams.

"None of us can go home because of your nanobots," Crys pressed. "Because of your quest to play God. You always praised your 'no locks' policy on campus. Only open doors. Well, you let a monster through, and now there's nowhere to shaking hide."

"I don't remember," Damon whispered.

"It's all right, you can open your eyes now," Crys lied.

He lifted his head with sheer childlike trust. Again, Crys thrust the fear symbol to cover his vision. Again he cried out.

"*You* might have chosen to flee after the Conservators attacked Quest," Crys shouted. "Chosen to give up and forget. But *we* haven't." Damon tore at his golden curls. "I don't remember!"

"Tell us Hariri's endgame. Tell us how to find the cure."

"I don't remember . . ."

"Tell us who the mystery buyer was at the Exhibition. What did Palmer do to Hema and the rest of the Exiles?"

Damon shook his head. He rocked side to side, his silver-clad torso juddering like a skyscraper in a quake. "I'm sorry. I'm sorry," he stammered. His words were quiet, a voice trapped beneath rubble. "I don't remember."

Eli grimaced. "All right, Crys, that's enough. It's clear he has dementia. He doesn't know."

Crys didn't pull away. She towered over the man who had terrorized her with both her own reflection and her own twin's face for three lonely years. Jade feared Crys would take this torment too far. She moved to her sister, surprised when Crys let her swipe the pin from her trembling hand.

Damon stopped his rocking, his eyes finding Jade, then Crys. They were unfocused with tears, but there was a clarity in them that shone like a spotlight through cobalt glass. "I might be unable to recall the worst and lowest things I've done . . ." *And a good thing,* Jade thought. They'd be here all night if he could. "But right now, I do remember my highest achievement. And that was bringing all of the Adsum sibs together."

"So you could use us?" Crys snapped.

"Please, just let me get this out while I still can," Damon pleaded. He rose to his feet and placed his hands on the altar. "I brought you together so you could utilize *each other*," he said, his voice ringing with confidence. "Since I was eleven, I'd always dreamed of changing the world. And for a while there, I thought I had. But now I understand it was never meant to be *me*. But each of you."

"Tell us how we can change it then," Jade pressed, seizing on his moment of lucidity. "How can we find the cure for the nano—"

Cole released a heart-stopping cry, and the moment was gone. The windows slammed shut behind Damon's eyes.

"I can't see!" Cole screamed, banging his palms against his eye sockets. "I can't see!"

Eli jumped to his feet, pinning Cole's arms against his sides.

Crys pounced on Damon. "What's happening to him?"

Damon cowered, shaking his head. "I don't know, I don't know, I don't know."

"Come on," Willis exploded. "You've been around those bastard intruders for weeks. You had to overhear *something* useful."

"Like the word 'prion'?" Eli asked, as Jade moved to help him guide a now eerily calm Cole back down onto the pew. "I've got a working list of all the symptoms I've observed from the infected, including Cole, Jade, me, and the Unfortunates at the lighthouse," Eli continued, a shaky hand pulling out his phone. "Personality changes, hallucinations, dementia, loss of motor functions, difficulty speaking . . . blindness." He stared down at Cole, who looked up with eyes like dark caves, penetrating nothing. "It all adds up to prion disease. The whole painlessness thing, that's a novel symptom, which shows us prions are some scary shit and wreak absolute havoc on the brain—"

"Prion . . ." Damon mumbled, and everybody's head snapped to him. He'd switched back on, his face aglow. "Yes, that's it!"

"Tell us everything you remember, *fast*," Nolan said, his investigative prowess kicking in. "No one interrupt."

Damon took in a deep breath. "The Conservators used Creutzfeldt-Jakob disease as their foundation, lacing my nanobots with their own genetically engineered prions," he said rapidly. "They unleashed the brain-wasting disease with the plan to scatter the Unfortunates around the outskirts of the cities, the nano reform killing them off slowly and sporadically. I thought Hema would have more time with the message I sent." He tilted his head at Cole. "The disease wasn't supposed to progress this quickly. Cole must be one of the unfortunate cases."

"Wait, what do you mean 'kill off?'" Jade asked.

But the light in Damon's eyes had gone out.

Jade turned to Eli. Just a few months ago, Eli was handing out punches, not a world-changing diagnosis. "Well?"

Eli's large shoulders sagged, the weight of his knowledge too much to bear. "All prion diseases are one hundred percent fatal."

"But Hema could still find the cure—" Crys protested.

"There *is* no chance of a cure," Eli said with finality.

Jade ached for the reassuring weight of In Extremis at her neck. She had to stop herself from reaching for the bullet, her morbid memento, the last thing she had to reassure her she could still conquer fear. *Death.*

Crys suddenly rushed over to Cole, placing a soothing hand on his cheek. "We have to take him to a hospital."

"No effective treatment exists," Eli said heavily, handing Crys his phone to show her his research. "It says here the only thing we can do for Cole is offer palliative care . . . make him feel safe and comfortable with sedatives or pain medications."

"Painkillers," Willis repeated, lumbering down the church's main aisle. "I'm on it." He hurried out from the sanctuary. Jade thought of his legs, racked with old burn scars from the Greater LA Fire. He'd spent over a decade seeking out any and every underhanded way to relieve his pain.

"He'll find some," Crys assured Cole. "Don't worry, we'll find the cure. We're all going to make it through this."

Wavy strands of Cole's coffee-brown hair caught on his long lashes, dancing as he stared up at Crys, unseeing. "Is that Crys Moore," he whispered weakly, "looking at the bright side?"

He leaned into her touch, and Crys smiled. "Don't tell anyone," she whispered back.

"Don't worry," he said, mustering a faint smile. "I probably won't remember."

Crys let her tears fall free. "Don't go dark, promise? Let me be your light."

Everyone looked away. Down at their hands. Or up to the moon's silver rays slicing through the stained glass.

Jade focused on her bandaged burn, wondering how long she had until she'd forget how she'd earned it. She took a deep breath and set her jaw, refusing to indulge in self-pity. She wasn't giving up just yet.

While Crys was occupied with Cole, Jade slid up to Damon's side. "Where's the treasure?" she asked quietly, clean and to the point. "Was that why you messaged Hema? To lead them toward the cure?" She'd held the questions in as long as her curiosity would allow. Jade didn't even know if she still believed in the treasure anymore, but apparently Hema did. And Rhett. But Jade needed to know if it was real while she could still remember. While Damon might still remember.

He stared back at her, desperate to give her what she wanted, but it was clear he didn't know how.

Jade surprised herself and took Damon's hand. She squeezed. "It's all right, Damon. Forget it." And she let it stay buried. For the time being, at least.

Nolan cleared his throat, gliding to the center aisle. "Now for the billion-dollar question." He held a long pause, as if he hoped someone would fill it. "The nano reform cannot be cured, but what will you do to stop the spread?"

He wasn't addressing Yates. Instead, his challenging stare moved steadily from Eli to Cole, then to Crys and Jade.

Intruders

"I think we've kept this 'Atrocity' a private, family affair long enough," Crys answered on a sigh.

No locked doors. It had been Yates's downfall, but it could help the Unfortunates rise.

Jade marched to Nolan, tearing away the microphone affixed to his shirt collar. "What do you say we finally let a few people in?" She pinched the mike between her thumb and middle finger, a smile crawling up her cheeks. "Do a little spreading of our own?"

"The viral kind?" Eli said, standing.

Cole nodded, still gazing up at Crys, gripping her hand. "A conspiracy of *un*silence."

If the authorities wouldn't listen, the public might. With a single podcast, they could lift the stocking masks right off the Conservators' secrets. Tens of millions could help them identify the mystery buyer.

This wasn't over.

Jade nodded to Nolan. "Let's make some noise."

183

EIGHTEEN

Maxen had always known that the sun was a star, he'd just never truly felt it before. Loafing on the bow's helipad, his prison jumpsuit tucked under his head, he understood the difference between knowing and feeling. After a month in a concrete cell, the unfiltered sunlight felt heavenly on his bare skin.

For a night and two days, Maxen had sat lookout at this spot, a shard of glass he'd broken from the bathroom mirror clasped in his hand, and the word "HELP" spelled out in plush lounge cushions at his feet, the only makeshift distress signals he could manage after ransacking the superyacht from bow to stern.

Not that there was anyone to signal *to*. The only thing Maxen had seen in his careful watch were flocks of seagulls. Which at least told him he was no more than a hundred miles out to sea. But *which* sea? The Earth was 71 percent ocean. The possibilities were endlessly maddening.

Maxen began to doze, contemplating which body of water Palmer hated the most. Certainly the yacht was nowhere near Palmer's favored Seychelles islands or French Polynesia . . .

A deep, steady thrumming seeped into Maxen's half sleep. He'd always loved the sound of engines at full throttle, the high-speed vessels they propelled, on land or water, his version of the Quietude, his father's meditation haven. But out here, in the vast drink, an engine meant rescue. Maxen jolted awake. He sat up, looked to the starboard side, and found he wasn't dreaming.

A bright blue speedboat cut through the water at a heart-pumping eighty knots, its course set directly toward the superyacht. Maxen raced across the deck to the railing, waving his prison jumpsuit in the air with one hand, signaling with the glass shard with the other.

The speedboat reduced its power to idle, swerved ninety degrees, and slammed to a stop in front of him. His cry for help died in his throat, all hope sinking, when he saw the name on the shiny hull: *In Deep Ship.*

In different circumstances, Maxen would have enjoyed the pun. But he knew Palmer wasn't joking in the slightest.

Palmer's predatory drone emerged, circling the four hooded figures huddled on the boat's flat deck, arms bound behind their backs. A platinum-suited man Maxen didn't recognize stepped away from the joystick controls, unsheathing a knife.

Was he about to witness an execution? Maxen recoiled from the railing. He refused to be a spectator to more of his family's atrocities.

A sharp cry, then a heavy *splash*, followed by a second. *They're being thrown overboard.*

Maxen hurtled back to the railing, tossing a life buoy at the flailing figures, who helped each other rip off the hoods that clung to their faces. *The knife was to unbind their hands*, Maxen realized.

Splash, splash, the other two figures hit the waves, followed by two hard-case boxes.

The boat's four outboard engines cranked up, accelerating the vessel to sixty knots in a matter of seconds, leaving its jettisoned passengers bobbing in its wake.

"Swim to the stern!" Maxen shouted, tossing a second life buoy into the water before charging to the rear of the yacht.

On the aft deck, Maxen scurried across the pine flooring to activate the wide swimming stairs. One by one, fifteen wooden steps unfolded like a welcoming hand, stretching down to the ocean. A figure stumbled up. Dark clothes hung off her wiry frame, heavy from the water. She stumbled, landing with a splash onto her knees. It couldn't be . . .

Maxen didn't bother with the steps, but jumped toward her, and as she lifted her head, clumsily scraping away the wet mop of inky hair plastered to her face, Maxen swallowed his disappointment with a gasp. It wasn't Jade.

But . . .

"Ani?"

She's alive.

"How in quaking hell did *you* end up here?" he sputtered. He helped her stand, his hands steering clear of the saber slash on her stomach that must still be healing.

"Same question to you," Ani answered, coughing the sea from her lungs.

When Maxen had last seen Ani at the hyperloop portal, he'd thought she was fading fast, not long for this world. Last night, he'd slept in the open beneath the night sky, gazing up at the Zoe and Khari memorial satellites, thankful there were still only two. It wouldn't be like Palmer to keep up the public display of mourning. Nevertheless, Maxen liked to think the other sibs were watching the sky, too. It comforted him. Made him feel he knew where he was, even if he was lost.

To his utter astonishment, Ani pulled him into a hug. "It's good to see you well, sib."

Then a familiar voice echoed off the water. "A little help here?"

Wily. And Sage was beside him, both lumbering up the steps with bulky hard cases. Breathing heavily, Wily dropped his case and bent over, exhausted. *That's strange,* Maxen thought. Wily had been the strongest swimmer at the academy, with a seemingly endless supply of energy. And yet the short swim from the speedboat had worn him out?

Maxen rushed to help Ani. They each took an end of a hefty container, probably filled with provisions, judging by similar boxes he'd found in the galley. *How thoughtful of Palmer.*

They'd only just made it up the stairs when Maxen turned, remembering the fourth person in the water. Iris was standing on a center step, waves lapping around the hems of her red suit.

"Is that salt stinging your eyes . . ." Iris asked, "or are you just happy to see me?"

"Cousin," Maxen breathed. He could barely move from the shock.

Barefoot, Iris mounted the stairs. She took hold of both his hands, clasping tight as if to make certain he was real. "Who knew all I had to do to find you was get myself kidnapped?"

A cry came from the upper deck. *Two* cries.

Maxen glanced to Wily and Sage, realizing Ani was missing.

"She found Vance," Maxen said, sprinting up a staircase to the second-tier deck.

"As in Vance *Yates*?" Wily spat.

"I call first swing," Sage roared, hard on his heels.

Maxen accelerated his pace. How in Savior's name was he to keep them off his brother? *Half* brother. Was he really going to *protect* him? Fight for him? *With* him?

Vance liked to think himself the champion fencer of the family, though that title unquestionably belonged to Crys. All of Vance's victories had been paid off and rigged. Not by their egalitarian father, but by Gen 1's status-climbing mother, Liliane.

Maxen could hold his own. He was far more *under*worldly than his half brothers. Still, four against two? Jade would've liked the odds.

Maxen bounded up another set of stairs to the stern's third tier. The last he'd seen of Vance, he'd been "acclimating" in the Jacuzzi. He wondered if Ani already had him half-drowned by now. He turned a corner, straight into an eyeful of freezing white gas.

"Stay back!" Vance yelled from behind the cone-shaped horn of a fire extinguisher. "Let's all calm down and be rational."

Wily and Sage parted, moving for either side of Ani, pinning Vance further against the railing.

Another cloud of gas shot out in a wide arc, keeping the Exiles at bay.

"I don't know about y'all, but I'm calm," Wily said, his chin tucked low, scarred brow upraised, sharp as a knifepoint.

"I'm rational," Sage assured him, raking back the auburn locks plastered to her sunburned cheeks. "That CO_2 won't last long, and you don't have a gun to hide behind this time."

That's right. Vance had shot at them during their campus break-in, at the wildflower fields at Splendor Park.

Oh brother. Vance was really on his own now.

Something flashed in Ani's hand. A blade she'd somehow snuck past a Conservator's thorough search.

Iris appeared on deck. Red as the fire extinguisher, she shuffled toward Vance. Stopped three paces behind Ani. Through the thinning cloud of gas, Vance caught sight of her. He lowered the discharge nozzle. Maxen swore he saw him smile—*smile*—at another Szeto aboard a Yates ship. But his grin was fleeting. Ani, Sage, and Wily had swarmed in. Ani kicked away the tank. Sage and Wily gripped Vance roughly beneath his arms.

They're going to toss him overboard.

If Vance even made it past the lower deck. What was Palmer's twisted version of their father's favorite idiom? *You can't make a soufflé without a few broken legs.*

"I myself don't like littering," Ani said, helping to lift Vance as he thrashed. "But just this once won't hurt."

Vance let out a lurching cry. But it wasn't directed at the three who held him, ready to hurl him over the railing. It was directed at Iris. "Please! Stop them. *Tell* them."

Iris remained silent. Unmoving.

Maxen bolted toward her. "Tell us what?"

"He claims to have told Iris about a scientist working for the Conservators," Ani muttered, unimpressed.

"And I smuggled in Maxen's Quest Bot for him!" Vance bellowed.

"Two good deeds do not a Savior make," Sage jeered.

Wily started the countdown to launch. "One!" Together the three rocked Vance's weight back and forth to gain momentum. "Two!"

"Iris!" Vance shouted. He was more irate than scared. "You asked me to side with you. I did. Now side with *me*!"

"Three!"

Iris jolted forward, catching Vance by his ankles. She yanked back with a grunt. The sudden shift in weight sent everyone crashing to the deck.

"Why . . ." Sage panted, clutching at the side of her head, which had banged against the deck.

"Would you do that?" Wily finished for her.

Iris got to her knees. Vance fumbled to his. Their foreheads met, lips brushing as she proclaimed, "Because this traitorous fool is with me."

Maxen's mind struggled to make sense of what his eyes were witnessing. He'd overheard phone arguments between his mother and his uncle Hoi years ago, hatching plans to "end Iris's youthful and foolhardy escapade." Had they been speaking of *Vance*? Maxen didn't know whether to be repulsed or envious.

Iris had strayed from her father's wishes. Had refused to marry, spurned an exceedingly wealthy family, inciting a potential scandal to the Szetos' honor. Maxen now saw why, though he didn't understand it. Iris was heir to the Quartet Line. One of the wealthiest, most desirable women in the world. And she wanted . . . Vance *Yates*?

As he held his tongue with his teeth, Jade's raspy voice overtook his thoughts. He imagined her whispering the old Latin proverb: *Love is rich with honey and venom.*

The Exiles stared wide-eyed as Iris and Vance stood, hand in hand. Only Ani hadn't released her clenched fists. "Some of us might be itching to get off this love boat more than others," she said.

"Well, I certainly am," Maxen interjected. "Do any of you have any big ideas on how to get out of here?" *A way to break free of the flames, the wildfire.* Maxen was done acclimating.

"I'm assuming you've already tried every means of escape?" Ani asked Maxen. "Or you wouldn't still be stranded here."

Maxen nodded. "The control system's locked, and I checked the engine room, we're completely out of gas."

Ani turned to Sage. "Any of those Brainious juices telling you something that could help hijack us out of here?"

Sage scrunched her eyes, frowning in what looked like painful concentration. Jaw clenched, head quivering, as if trying to *will* the information to appear in her mind's eye. Maxen recalled that she had once possessed a photographic memory with the power of her Quest Bot, and now, it seemed, she'd ingested Hema's Smart Bots. But he didn't think this was how the mind upgrade was supposed to work.

Wily twinned pinkies with Sage. *When did they link up?* Maxen thought absently. "You don't need any bots for this one," Wily assured Sage, a light finger stroking her temple. "You made solar-powered batteries at Dry River, remember? You're a *natural* engineer."

Sage bit her lip and glanced away, her face relaxing. Allowing her knowledge to rise to the surface of her mind. "Okay . . . the engine is most likely diesel. I could convert it to use a mix of methanol and vegetable oil. Or . . ." She peered up at the sun, ideas flowing through her like water. "If I could rig a large enough mirror and a small reactor, I could transform captured CO_2 into a biofuel . . ." Wily beamed proudly at her as she paced over to Maxen, one hand on her curvy hip. "How much corn is in the galley? If there's enough, I could make ethanol."

"Your imagination is impressive," Iris conceded. "But none of that will be necessary." She peeled out of her soaked blazer, carefully draping it across the balcony railing to dry.

Sage scoffed. "Tell me that's not some high-class way of throwing in the towel?"

Iris's red lips parted in a sly grin. "Oh, believe me, I've only just begun." She pressed two fingers into the soft flesh of her underarm in a precise pattern.

A code, Maxen realized. *Of course.* After his uncle Hoi was kidnapped for ransom in his own academy days, it became a family tradition for all Szetos to be implanted with anti-abduction microchips. Poppy had insisted that Maxen and Crys carry on the precautionary custom.

"You had that damn thing in you *this whole time?*" Wily barked.

"Palmer didn't find your chip?" Maxen pressed. "Surely he had his drone scan you."

"Please," Iris retorted. "His little toy was no match for the sensor blocker shielding my chip." She disrobed to her undergarments and sauntered into the Jacuzzi, Vance close at her side. "I think we all know exactly what Palmer's drone is making up for. And yes, Wily, I bided my time. If a Yates went through all that trouble to kidnap me, I thought I ought to see where he takes me." She eased into the heated water, leaned against the headrest, and closed her eyes. "Sit back, relax. My family will be here shortly."

But Maxen couldn't relax. He was almost too ashamed to say it, but it seemed he didn't have to. Ani was already moving toward him with her thin blade. "The government embedded you with a tracking chip, I'm guessing?"

Maxen nearly asked for the blade to be sanitized, but he'd been through much worse. He shook off his hazy prison memories and held out his forearm.

He was going to be free.

Still a convict, yes. But free to prove his innocence.

And return to the fight.

Nineteen

Over the bustle of New York City, Crys heard her own voice.

She leaned her head against the open window of the AV that was shuttling her and the others down Park Avenue, back toward her old apartment, where their Adsum sibs waited.

Crys's voice—and Jade's and Eli's and Cole's—emanated from the speakers of every yellow cab, AV, and pedestrian they passed. The world was listening, reacting. *Believing.* "The Unbanished Truth" had rocketed straight to number one on the podcast charts. Hundreds of millions were now learning about the Conservators' conspiracy. The nano reform, the Unfortunates' fate. Hariri and his atrocious ambition. It was all out there, their story, and it was spreading.

The search for the mystery Buyer of Monaco was catching across the globe.

Crys wished Sage were here to witness what her brilliant idea had catalyzed. She was the one who'd studied Nolan's podcast, brought him into the Exiles' fold. *I hope she's listening with Wily and Ani somehow,* Crys thought. She hoped Hema and Rhett could hear, too. And Maxen, wherever he was. She wanted them to know the rest of the Exiles were still fighting. And that now, they weren't alone.

Crys unlocked her phone and pulled up the Grove, the front page of the internet. The world's most popular message forum had countless sub-discussion boards featuring theories about the mystery buyer's identity. The public was spearheading the investigation, not the navy suits or the mainstream media. The Exiles hadn't heard a peep from either institution, and Crys wasn't holding her breath.

But the sheer volume of intelligence coming in from their listeners took her breath away.

u/_Lone_Wolf_0

Versus Samaras, Greek shipping magnate, known for his hardline anti-refugee stance. Would use the nano reform to block Syrian migrants from crossing into Greece.

u/_YinHe88

Zang Ma, an associate of top Chinese government official Sun Xing. Would use nano reform to eradicate the Uyghurs and other ethnic minorities from China. We must stop him.

u/_UnfinishedSentenc

This baddie sounds like cartel henchman Juan Salinas Velasco. Imagine what Mexico's most brutal cartel would do with the power to instill even more fear?

Crys sighed, frustrated, as she stared at the photos attached to each post. Any one of the faces could've been the man hidden underneath the emerald-nosed mask.

It had been fourteen hours since the auction gavel had struck. Fourteen hours for the mystery buyer to lay down plans.

And when he does make his move, Crys thought bitterly, *what can we even do?* They were powerless—all they could do was wait and react. Crys loathed fighting defense. She preferred to lunge, not parry.

She shifted her gaze to the sunroof that Yates was peering through, his wide eyes taking in the tops of the soaring skyscrapers. Did he remember how high he had always sought to climb? How he had inspired her to do the same?

She studied her former father's face, pale and smooth and perfect, as it had always been. But was Damon Yates really inside there? Without his memories, who was he? A new being? Living perpetually in the present, like his meditations had always taught? His dementia created for him his own private Quietude. A sanctuary, rather than a prison.

The Exiles had given Yates another form of sanctuary. "The Unbanished Truth" was clear of any admissions about his experimental academy. They needed to keep all eyes and ears on the Conservators.

Cole's head rested in Crys's lap, her hands a supportive pillow. Gently, she slipped an arm free. The sedatives Willis had found for Cole were still in effect, and she didn't want to wake him. Beneath her ratty sweatshirt, so no one could see, she twisted the soft skin of her wrist. Once, it was a habit of hers to pinch herself each time she crossed Adsum's threshold. *Still here,* she'd whisper. Now, she pinched herself to see if she could even *feel* the sting. She could. *Still here.*

But for how long? The bitter taste of Hariri's smoke bomb lingered at the back of her throat.

"I'd say people heard us," Jade said beside her, readjusting Poppy's urn beneath her arm before pointing out her window. A crowd had gathered outside a wealthy high-rise, home to countless tech magnates and affluent politicians.

Leo Benson had a gaggle of his own watchdogs surveilling his apartment building when they'd dropped him off, Hema's attack bot already in his system, as promised.

"I counted fifty-eight sub-boards tracking Hariri alone," Eli announced from the front seat. "Twenty for Palmer, but so far they're both just stashed away at Quest. We'll know when they make a move." Crys smiled. Their own army of amateur detectives, keeping tabs on the Fortunates of the world.

She was thankful her secret penthouse apartment was known only to her. No listeners or Conservators would think to trace the Exiles there. Even so, she'd directed the AV to pass by the front entrance and turn instead into the private parking garage.

From the passenger seat, Eli reached out to the passcode stand just outside the gate. "The code?"

If it weren't for Cole, Crys would have crossed the cabin and punched in the numbers herself. Her brief hesitation earned a gruff sigh from her uncle. "What? Are you worried I'll try and squat in your fine palace once this is all over?"

"No," Crys said in defense. As things stood, it was highly probable Crys and those infected with the prion disease wouldn't make it out of "this" alive. For the past year, she'd hoarded the apartment as a selfish status symbol. Now all she cared about was the symbol of fear. And how to rid the world of it. She cleared her throat. "Zero seven two five four six." She hoped no one thought to recognize the numbers as a date.

The automatic gate parted, and the AV rolled forward. Crys kept her eyes lifted to the sunroof, feigning an inordinate interest in the unremarkable concrete ceiling.

"Seven, twenty-five, forty-six," Jade whispered heatedly. "Topple it all, Crys, that's the date I got shot!"

Crys flicked her eyes down to her feet, avoiding her sister's cutting glare. Across from her, Yates's restive hands picked at tissues he'd found rummaging through the side door's storage compartment. The torn shreds dropped to the floor, gathering near the tips of Crys's boots. *Not a sanctuary,* she amended. *But a life in tatters.*

The AV finally came to a stop beside the penthouse's elevator. Crys carefully lifted Cole from her lap.

"I'll help you carry him up," Yates offered, sliding out from his leather seat.

"That's all right, Ben, I got him." Eli leaned forward to scoop Cole into his sturdy arms.

"Ben?" Yates questioned, his voice tight. "Is that my name?"

"Shit," Eli said, shaking his head. "That's my bad, Damon. I used to call you Ben when I was at the academy. You know, short for *ben*efactor."

"Right," Yates mumbled. "I knew that."

Everyone exited the AV and squeezed into the cramped elevator. Crys ended up shoulder to shoulder with Jade. She swore she could hear the *clink* of Jade's missing bullet against its chain with every furious inhale. *July 25, 2046.* It had been Crys's passcode for the entire seven months she'd owned the place. *Why didn't you think to update it?* she scolded herself.

"You told me I didn't need *my* morbid memento," Jade whispered bitterly, "yet here you are with yours."

"You're wrong, as always," Crys whispered back.

They turned to face each other. Toe-to-toe. Glare-for-glare.

"Did everyone enjoy attending my academy?" Yates asked suddenly. It would have been almost funny if it wasn't so tragic.

The metal doors slid open, revealing a flurry of movement. The living room couches and tables had been pushed against the walls, and the younger Adsum students were divided into groups of four, with balloons, scissors, string, a straw, and tape set out in front of each.

"The rocket experiment." Yates beamed. He remembered the game he had always assigned the first-years their first day on the science classfloor.

My next great Quest astronaut must start somewhere, he would announce to the new arrivals. *Here, you can and will reach for the stars.*

He stepped into the apartment, and the game stopped. The chatter and laughter went quiet, and all the young, hungry eyes turned on their former Savior, unsure what to make of his sudden return.

"Please," he spluttered, bowing his head. "Do not stop innovating on my account." He staggered for the terrace that overlooked Central Park and leaned against the railing, his gaze cast down at his feet.

Crys had worried that Yates's mind would become overwhelmed when he saw the sibs, rattled by the past, by what he'd done. But instead he'd had a moment of clarity. He knew his Adsum fosters were better off without him now.

"What's the matter with Cole?" a third-year squeaked as he spotted Cole, his face sallow and slack against Eli's shoulder. "Is he dying, like Finn said we all would without our bots?"

"No," Crys answered, hoping to lighten the mood with an unwavering smile. The way Cole would. "Your sib is just very tired. How about we all play a game of possum and see how quiet we can be while he rests?"

Possum. The game their parents would play with Crys and Jade in their one-room RV, trying to get them to quiet their late-night laughter and get to sleep. Crys sought to catch Jade's eyes, to share in the memory, but Jade had turned, resting the bronze-and-marble urn safely on a side table before heading for the spiral staircase.

Crys guided Eli down the hall and into her bedroom, where they lowered Cole onto her king-sized bed. She brushed the waves of his hair from his temples and pressed her lips along his lashes, longing for his eyes to open, his bright hazel gaze to shine up at her in recognition.

"You never stopped caring for him, did you?" Eli said, nodding to the framed photo of Crys and Cole riding horseback along her favorite Quest summit trail.

She'd forgotten it was still there. Her cheeks flushed, but she didn't try to cool the burn. It was true. "He's my light," she said, interlocking her fingers with Cole's. "And I'm his."

Crys didn't realize she was crying until she tasted the tears. Salty like the ocean. Like home. Like the first kiss they'd shared that day up in the Quest mountains.

Willis cleared his throat, and Crys turned to find him in the doorway beside Nolan. He held his Medal of Valor awkwardly, his eyes and cheeks damp. She'd never seen her uncle cry before. He'd usually run off by now, never sticking around for any hard moment in Crys's life. She gave a slight nod, and Willis entered, bending low over Cole to place the medal around his neck.

"Thank you for going back for Crys in the factory," Willis rasped into Cole's ear. "You're a better man than me. I won't forget it, son. Just hold on. Keep fighting. Keep living."

Keep fighting, Crys whispered to herself as she left the bedroom to descend the short staircase to find her sister.

Jade was sitting beside the indoor pool, knees tucked to her side, one hand skimming the surface of the water, breaking the mirrorlike calm. Crys couldn't help but see patterns in the glass tiles that surrounded Jade, dozens of hard-edged *U*s declaring, *This is a safe place.*

Crys padded to the pool. Jade stilled when Crys sat beside her and slipped her pouch from her waist, setting her fear vials on the tiled ledge between them.

"Why does it *matter* that Damon saw me first?" Jade asked, her voice coarse as gravel. "You have *so* much!" She threw up her hands, gesturing around the extravagant room, the floor-to-ceiling windows, the gloating, sky-high view of the streets below. "Why do you *always* have to have it all?"

When they were born, Jade weighed six pounds, two ounces. Crys a weak and underdeveloped four and a half. Willis used to tease that when they were wombmates, Jade stole the majority of the nutrients and oxygen. Crys had always been trying to catch up, to *equalize* to Jade.

Her eyes landed on the knotted scar on Jade's shoulder. It was an angry pink, positioned *just so* to look like a brooch. A badge of honor. "For a long time, I was jealous you took that bullet for me, Jade," she said. "You thought—*everyone* thought—that I was still the weak one. The one who needed shielding."

"I didn't do it to be called a hero, Crys."

"I know," Crys answered. "But you proved Yates right, didn't you? You jumped in front of a bullet before you were given your Quest Bot. You found courage even before you were made fearless."

Jade paused, seeming to let the idea sink in. "Yet I never did anything *near* as worthy when I did have my bot. I only ever found *myself* in trouble. Never did I save others from it . . ." Her words trailed off, but she didn't reach for her absent In Extremis. She reached for Crys's hand. "Why that date, though? To remind yourself of the moment you were *this close* to getting rid of me?"

It had been subconscious, buried deep in Crys's core, but the true reason came roaring suddenly to the surface. "It was to remember how I knew I wouldn't lose you," Crys admitted, gazing straight into the face she had let become a stranger. "We survived a quake together. Then the streets and that bullet. Yates almost managed to separate us . . . but even as a hostage to my Quest Bot, I guess I always wanted to believe we'd find our way back to each other."

"I'll find you, I'll find you." Jade grinned. "We always have." She gripped tight to Crys's hand. "And we're going to survive this nano reform, too."

Before Crys even understood what was happening, a great tremor of panic exploded in her mind, and she let loose a terrible scream.

"What's wrong?" Jade yelled over her cries. "What did I say—"

Distantly, Crys realized that Jade had started screaming, too. Uncontrollably, almost feral. She looked down and saw that one of her fear fragrance vials had escaped the pouch and rolled against their linked hands. Crys recoiled, her panic doubling.

"Get them away from me!" Jade screamed, again and again, her body trembling, her bare hands digging in her zipper pocket to free herself of her own vials. She launched them to the ground, signaling for Crys to hold her breath.

Crys locked her lungs. Her cries now muffled, she emptied her pouch, and together, in a feverous frenzy, they crushed every last bottle beneath the soles of their shoes. Jade grasped her shoulders, and Crys was airborne. Then falling. They slammed into the water. Sank to the bottom of the pool to hide from the scent. When at last they broke the surface, the air had cleared. The fear incursion washed away, Crys's mind had settled.

And she finally understood exactly what Hariri had done.

He'd made them fear the touch and sight of their vials. Sent an urgent signal to their brains that they *must* destroy their entire cache of fear fragrance. *Destroy or die.*

He'd stripped them of their greatest weapon. Made Crys terrified of the thing that gave her power, *control*. The thing that made others fear *her*.

Crys struggled to the opposite end of the pool, arms shaking as she pulled herself clumsily onto the ledge. Anger thrummed through her veins. Anger at what she'd lost, at how Hariri kept winning. At how she was now going to die, powerless and afraid.

"You don't need the vials," Jade panted, hauling up onto the ledge beside her. "Just like I didn't need my Quest Bot." Chest heaving, she raked her wet hair from her eyes and slung her arm around Crys's shoulder. "Like you said, Gem, we have each other again."

Your fortune is in your bond, their mother had promised.

Crys leaned her head against Jade's shoulder and felt all her former desire to control, to command fear, fade away. In its place bloomed a fragile, bright hope.

They weren't going to let Hariri win. They were going to survive this.

Together, they would find a way to change the world's fortune.

TWENTY

Jade was up before the sun. She slipped out from the queen-sized bed she'd been sharing with a handful of her second-year sibs and tiptoed, quiet as a pickpocket, toward the guest bedroom's half-opened door.

There was no need to change. She'd slept in the clean T-shirt and jeans she'd found rifling through one of Crys's many closets. Though the clothes were too "new" for her own taste—Jade preferred vintage, and *holes*—she was thankful that she and her sister were still the same size.

And, apparently, of the same mind. Crys was waiting in the darkness of the hall beside the elevator. "You were always the early bird," she whispered as Jade padded over. Crys had Jade's scuffed-up boots tucked beneath both arms. "Or were you thinking of taking flight?"

Crys was fully dressed. High-top sneakers on, plain ball cap tucked over her light brown curls and famous features. *Good,* Jade sighed to herself. She thought she'd have to make her final return to Hardihood alone. And she didn't know if she had the strength.

The short walk from the bed to the elevator left her winded. Her symptoms had been rapidly accelerating after the smoke bomb. She hoped Crys didn't notice. Wouldn't tell her she needed to rest. That she couldn't leave.

Instead, Crys plopped Jade's boots down. "We're going after the cure, right?"

They both knew there *was* no cure. They knew their inevitable fate. But since when had poor odds ever stopped the Moores?

"Right," Jade echoed, "we're going after the cure."

And that meant breaking into Quest Campus.

If Hema was still alive, they were likely locked away in Palmer's stolen empire along with Rhett. Kept safe from the Exiles, the only possibility left for the infected Unfortunates' survival. Maybe Ani, Wily, and Sage were there, too. Iris had picked a clever, tenacious team. *They're still alive,* Jade told herself. *Still fighting.*

"We have countless eyes searching for the mystery buyer," Crys whispered, heedful not to wake their sleeping sibs on the couches. "But what *we* need is to find what can stop the spread for good."

It wasn't lost on Jade that Crys had said *what*, not *who*.

"The treasure," Jade stated. It wasn't a question.

Crys nodded hurriedly. "Yates sent Hema that message about the Quest treasure for a reason." She shrugged, stabbing a golden button along the wall to call the elevator carriage. "We have to try something. It might be a long shot, but I believe it's verging on suicide not to turn over every stone."

Jade slipped on her boots and plucked at the gauze around her wounded arm. Chances were high that she and Crys would be caught or fully eradicated the instant they stepped *foot* back in LA. But Jade had sworn she'd do everything in her ability—utilize her pain immunity, claim it as her superpower—until her body gave up and she was forced to tap out.

Jade Moore would go down swinging.

"Well," she said, grinning as she stepped into the elevator, "I'd say the weight of what we're after makes it more of a *boulder* than a stone . . ."

Crys smiled. "At least there's two of us to try to lift it."

The way down was too silent. Crys started to hum, providing her own elevator music. It was the tune of Jade's old theme song. Jade began to sing, poorly, a new set of lyrics. Poetry, actually. The original clues Yates had shared with every Quester: where to find the treasure trove. *And if you are bold, you will find riches greater than gold.*

When the doors opened onto the private garage, Eli, Willis, and Nolan were there to greet them. With three quick steps, Eli's arms were around their shoulders. "Don't worry about us while you're gone. I'll be our family's guardian. I promise no Conservators will touch our sibs." Jade had never doubted it. He'd always been the rightful leader of the Exiles. "And I'll carry Cole's light for you, Crys," he whispered. "I won't let it go out."

"I want to be there for you," Willis said as they pulled away. "*With* you."

Jade and Crys caught eyes, and they nodded. Three Moores against a club of Conservators, plus a potential sixty thousand Questers, made for higher odds.

As they moved for the AV, Jade heard Nolan clear his throat. "Try not to get hurt, all right?" The request was aimed at Willis.

"I don't get hurt anymore, remember?" Willis joked back, patting a few of his pain-resistant wounds.

"Yes," Nolan replied, his voice thin, an octave higher than normal. "But *I* would if you did."

"Oh," Willis mumbled, his neck flushed red. His beard barely hid his smile. "All right. I promise I'll try."

"Fortunes change!" Eli cried out to them, his words booming across the concrete lot.

"Fortunes change," Jade called back. And if fate wouldn't change their fortune, the Exiles would give it one hell of a shake-up themselves.

A throng of early-morning commuters jammed the HyperQuest portal's tunnels. Jade, Crys, and Willis locked arms, inching forward in a tight line. "Is it always this crowded?" Willis complained. "It's like a fire hazard down here!"

He was right. The mayhem of rush hour felt fevered, mad with a convulsive energy that fought to tug them away from the vast platform and toward the wide tier of escalators mobbed by passengers. They were going to miss their hyperloop pod.

Jade noticed that a sea of phones gleamed in the air, desperate hands stretching wildly to record a commotion at the top of the center escalator.

Were these people from the Grove discussion board? Amateur detectives out hunting for the Buyer of Monaco? Beneath the low folds of her bucket hat, Jade scanned the portal for platinum suits.

But it was something gold that caught Jade's attention.

She froze. Latched tighter on to Crys's wrist.

Standing atop the railing of the center escalator was Damon Yates.

Holy. Quake. He must have somehow strayed from the apartment, wandered off, and found his way here.

"I want to go home!" he bellowed over the chaos. "How do I get home?"

Jade's stomach twisted. News of the missing tech giant roaming New York City was bound to set the internet on fire. A smoke signal for Hariri, Palmer, and the navy suits that the MIA mogul had returned to the States. That he'd been caught waiting to catch a hyperloop pod back to Los Angeles. Back home.

"Where have you been?" a woman called out to Damon.

"Are you a Conservator?" a man roared.

Thankfully, Damon had ditched his platinum suit, though that hadn't made him stand out any less. He wore an incongruous pairing of a plaid button-down and purple striped sweats. He looked as if he'd dressed himself in the dark.

All at once, a hundred phones buzzed around Jade like a swarm of hostile bees. Shouts rang out. A few at first, hesitant and uncertain, then in a spiraling uproar that overtook Damon's screams.

"He's mine!"

"I saw him first!"

Before Jade could even curse, Crys held out her phone for Jade to see. It was a post to the main sub-board on the Grove. *The entire city of New York just received the same anonymous message. There's a $500 million finder's fee for whoever brings Damon Yates to the nearest officer.*

"This is Hariri's doing," Crys spat.

"I bet you think we need to save him?" Willis sighed, nodding up to Damon.

Jade and Crys separated, shoving their way closer to the escalator.

Damon started kicking at hands that sought desperately to grab him. "Officer! Officers! Get them away from me!"

Topple it all. A navy suit was barreling up the steps, only a few feet from Damon. It would be a hell of a lot easier extracting him if they had their fear fragrance, Jade knew. But they didn't need it. *We don't need it,* she repeated again and again.

Jade worked best on the fly. On pure, natural instinct. The stunt would come to her.

She was out of breath, at the bottom step, her strength seeping away with every painless movement, when a sudden inspiration brought her to a dead stop. "Wait," she whispered, motioning for Crys and Willis to stay back.

Two navy suits had reached Damon. They were tugging him down as a cacophony of chaos erupted around them.

"*I* brought Yates to you!"

"No, it was me; *he's mine!*"

"I saw him first!"

"Give me *my* millions!"

Damon's face had warped in terror and confusion as the navy suits escorted him through the crowd.

"We can't just let him go," Crys insisted.

"We're not," Jade said. "We're just letting the navy suits do the hard part for us."

Willis patted Jade's shoulder. "Street smarts," he said, chuckling, realizing her plan. Knowing it would work.

The quickest and simplest way to Los Angeles was by hyperloop. Jade bet the navy suits would take their bounty to the very pod that Jade, Crys, and Willis had tickets for.

With the show over, the mob finally cleared. And as the two navy suits led a calm but babbling Damon toward the departure platforms, Jade laughed, clear and unrestrained. They'd just won big.

"Well, that certainly saved us a lot of trouble." Crys smiled as they stepped into the podcar that would usher them back to Hardihood at a whisper shy of the speed of sound.

Jade glanced out the pod's slotted windows. Farmland had given way to pavement and steel. One minute to arrival. They'd had over two hours to get their plan in order. They'd have only twenty seconds to implement it.

"Hands on your triggers?" Willis grunted.

Jade and Crys nodded, their thumbs hovering over their phone screens.

"Pull." Willis jerked open the luxe private cabin door. Jade and Crys stabbed their record buttons.

At the front row, the two navy suits ignored the intrusion until Damon sat bolt upright in his seat between them. "Willis! Willis, where are they taking me?"

Jade and Crys kept their faces covered behind their phones. So far, the Conservators were clueless as to their whereabouts, and Jade hoped to keep it that way. *Here's to wishing.*

"Evening, *fellas*," Willis greeted the uniformed men. "Can't call either of you 'officers,' seeing as we've crossed into the Golden State and you're out of your jurisdiction."

And out of shaking luck.

"Get lost," one of the suits said, dismissive.

"Say hello to the world, *fellas*," Willis rasped, nodding to the twin phones aimed their way.

The two navy suits stiffened, no doubt interpreting "the world" to mean that Jade and Crys were livestreaming this unlawful encounter. But they weren't. Not yet. Posting their recording was only a backup plan. The last thing they needed were *more* fortune seekers.

"Tell me," Willis pressed, knowing they had about ten more seconds to get Damon in *their* custody before arrival. "Have you gone rogue for a chance to win the lottery by handing over a lost billionaire to the Conservators? Or has this man been placed under arrest?"

Neither of the navy suits answered.

"I didn't think so," Willis growled. He held out his hand. "Damon, would you like to come with me? I'll take you home."

Damon's face bloomed in a vibrant smile. He stood. "I'd like that very much."

The two navy suits sat on their hands.

Damon snapped his head up when the speakers suddenly played his own serene voice. "Welcome to Los Angeles, the tenacious City of Angels, where dreams remain unshakable."

The pod doors beeped open. A trio of Conservators was waiting on the platform. *Guess not all dreams come true,* Jade thought wryly.

"Damon, darling, we've been so worried about you," the Conservator with the handbag and knife-edged smile purred. She lifted her arms to Damon, looking above his head, avoiding Jade's and Crys's faces. "Come back with us, your old friends. Where you belong."

Rattled by so much attention, Damon hesitated.

Jade did not. "Run," she said, grabbing Damon and making a break for it through the crowd. As they pushed their way up the escalator into the ribbed-timber lobby, Jade sent out an *rfa* to the Grove.

u/_fortunes_change

Exiles in trouble. If you're at the Hollywood HyperQuest, stop the platinum suits. Beware the one with the handbag. She wields fear.

More Conservators weaved toward them in the lobby. They weren't going to make it to the exit doors in time. But then a group of civilian sleuths ambushed the platinum suits, umbrellas stretched out in front of them like shields. The canopies blocked the woman's fear inhalant as they pushed the Conservators back into the portal's tunnels. Trapping them inside.

"Where to now?" Crys panted when they burst through the doors onto Hollywood Boulevard.

The streets were Jade's domain. But they'd changed since she'd been away. The makeshift shelters were gone, the portable toilets removed. The quake survivors with their panhandling signs had disappeared. Instead, three diagonal slash marks had been tagged on streetlights and bus-stop benches, splashed across giant movie billboards, slapped on the windows of AVs clogging the boulevard. No longer subtle, the assault on the Unfortunates was bold and obvious. Jade bet it was a Conservator tactic to make it seem like the fear symbol was just a hoax, merely a stunt spread by Nolan's cult of listeners.

Jade fought to swallow her scream. Her body vibrated with heat, with the inescapable desire to flee. She slammed her eyes closed and heard the strangled moans of Crys, Willis, and Damon, all fighting their own fear incursions.

"The rideshare queue," Jade rasped, opening her eyes and staring down at her boots. "We have to get to one of our hideouts and rethink our strategy. Palmer knows we're coming now."

"Look, it's Damon Yates," a young man shouted. "Grab him!"

"Hands *off*," Willis growled.

Jade looked up to see her uncle take down two would-be kidnappers with his fists.

Willis Moore defending Damon Yates. Not for love or fortune would Jade *ever* have predicted this.

Then a ground-shaking whir pulled Jade's focus to the sky.

"Palmer's pet drone," Crys seethed.

Jade didn't cower. She jutted out her chin, balling her fists. "Are you too scared to face us on your own?" she screamed at the hefty raptorial drone.

The drone's steel arms extended from its armored body and latched around Damon's wrists. In slow motion, Jade watched the drone lift Damon's arms above his head and pull him up into the air.

"No!" she screamed.

She leapt, wrapping her fingers around the steel arm in a death grip. The drone rose, but Crys jumped and latched on to Jade's waist. They were lifted, their feet dangling over the HyperQuest portal. Willis and the bystanders holding up their phones became indistinguishable faces below them.

When they were high enough for a body to break at the fall, a thinner, sharper arm detached from the belly of the drone, its fingerlike clamps sharp as talons. They stabbed at Jade's hand, her wrist, breaking skin, scraping bone. Trying to force Jade to let go.

Had Palmer not realized Jade was a painless being?

She laughed as the drone took off over Hollywood, Beverly Hills, then into the vast Quest mountains. They were a hundred feet in the air, Jade's hot blood trickling into her eyes from yet another wound that she couldn't feel.

But she *could* feel that she was close to *In Extremis*, at the point of death.

And she wasn't afraid.

They flew into a cold coastal fog, shrouding them from view. *No one gets to see what happens in Yates's mountains.* The gilded rule of privilege that had been in place for decades. *But today the world will hear about it,* Jade thought.

With her free hand, she readjusted the silver chain that held Nolan's microphone. Her new necklace.

Blood dripped down her face, seeping into her satisfied smile.

TWENTY-ONE

Hema regained consciousness and sat bolt upright, choking on a scream. They pulled the two prongs of their oxygen tube from their nose, trying not to panic.

It took a few rattled breaths to regain their bearings. Their head hurt, but their blurred vision slowly cleared, revealing a stark room in the Sophia Ray Medical Center, beeping monitors, IV drips.

Where was Rhett?

Most likely dead, Hema's practical mind told them. They would have found Snyder's body by now. Blamed Rhett, Damon's former enforcer, for the hit. Kept Hema alive to be the Conservators' resident scientist. To replace the one Hema had killed.

Hema's heart lurched, then their stomach followed suit. They swallowed the bile, the rising guilt. But they couldn't stop the hurt that tore through their chest at having saved Rhett only for him to die. Hema hoped he'd had his eyes closed. Focused on the slash marks behind his lids. Gone out with courage, instead of fear.

Hema pulled the IVs from their arms and stalked to the door. Guards stood outside the window. The entire floor was probably locked down. Protecting their weapons engineer. Their new master of mass destruction.

But how long would Hema last? Years or mere months, suffering alone in the labs? The progression of the nano reform's symptoms varied widely, but the prion disease was inescapably fatal.

Hema had to get out of this room. They refused to become the Conservators' puppet of war, to be their prisoner. Hema Devi refused to die.

Not after they'd puzzled it out. *It begins in the peaks, and ends where it began . . . It is wise to time your plan.* When Hema had come to, the answer to the clue, the elusive *X* on Damon's cryptic treasure map, had flashed into their mind, clear and maddeningly urgent.

If they didn't get out of this room soon, it would be too late.

Hema rolled one of the medical monitors to the door and propped it underneath the handle. Locking the guards out. Hema needed time to think without interruption. Perching on the edge of the bed, they balled the starched white sheets in their fists and tried not to scream.

At their heartache.

At the time they were wasting.

At their desperate need to get to the cure.

At the man who suddenly rappelled from the roof and slammed against the room's floor-to-ceiling window. Was that *Hema's* diamond hammerhead in his hand?

The window exploded. Hema tucked their head between their knees to shield against the shattered glass. A sudden cool breeze lifted the soft hairs on their arms. Or was it the low, midwestern grumble above the sound of boots on broken glass?

"Care to get the hell outta Dodge?"

Hema jolted to their feet.

Rhett.

He was alive. He was okay. *More* than okay. He was a man terrified of heights, yet smiling after scaling a ten-story high-rise.

Rhett's eyelids fluttered, administering an instant shot of engineered courage with every blink.

They both spoke at the same time.

"We have to get to Questbase—"

"The treasure's buried in the sky—"

They had figured it out together, it seemed.

A pounding on the barricaded door spurred Rhett to the bed, arms open. "Afraid I'm going to have to be your harness."

Hema wrapped their body around his, and felt the gun at his waist. Hema closed their eyes, hoping some of Rhett's fearlessness would seep into them by proximity. He carried a barefoot Hema over the glass and leaned back into the sky.

"Hold on, and try and enjoy the ride," he said. "I know I will."

He jumped, and they rappelled straight down, ten stories, the wind and Rhett's exhilarated cry overpowering Hema's jittery yelp.

When they hit solid ground, Hema lingered in Rhett's arms, a few heartbeats longer than necessary. "Sorry, it's the head injury," Hema said, rubbing the gauze wrapped around their skull. "It's making me react a little slowly."

"Nothing to be sorry for," Rhett said with a grin, the scars that ringed his eyes crinkling.

Hema peeled away and headed west toward the monorail. "Questbase is Damon's only launch facility on campus. There are larger test sites and factories off the gulf in Texas, of course, but here is where Damon launched small satellites, and most importantly, his Ultra-Long Duration Balloon."

"Which I'm guessing is carrying our high-tech treasure chest?" Rhett asked, wrapping his denim jacket around Hema's shoulders to cover the hospital gown.

The world-class super-pressure balloons were for scientific investigations. But maybe Damon had found a more imaginative purpose for one, packing its payload with a treasure so out of this world that it had to be retrieved from the very edge of space.

"It begins in the peaks," Hema recited the poem, breathless. "We know now that's Questbase on the far mountain."

"And ends where it all began," Rhett quoted. "I'm guessing that means the stars?"

Hema rolled their eyes. "The whole thing sounds grandiose enough for Damon."

"Damn right it does," Rhett said. "Nothing was ever simple with that man."

Hema hoped the cure was, at least. They'd managed to undo the fear element of the Conservators' nano reform with Rhett, tricking the swarm of attack bots in his system by masking the engineered proteins in their own attack bot to appear as naturally occurring proteins in his body. But Hema hadn't solved the fatal prion disease. They didn't know if anyone could. They'd tested everything and anything they could think of.

And now I need assistance from a higher power, Hema thought, staring up at the pink early-morning sky.

But they weren't going to find the balloon by just looking. They needed to call it down to Earth.

And the only way to achieve that was from inside the highly secure Questbase.

All the way across campus.

"So you worked out that Palmer didn't send that message, too?" Rhett asked Hema inside the podcar. The monorail track cut through Quest's one thousand acres in six stops. Theirs would be the last, on the fringes of campus, where the launch facility huddled inside an isolated valley.

Hema's legs bounced with anticipation. Rhett must be asking questions to distract them.

"My theory is that Palmer must have known Damon sent the message," Hema said, "which triggered him to go after me before I went after the treasure."

Five stops to go.

"That first-class scoundrel," Rhett grumbled. "I just remembered Palmer went spacediving at Coachella. He was probably hunting for it himself, using the concert as cover to search a Quest spacecraft."

Four stops.

Hema had cracked every one of their knuckles by the time their podcar reached the next stop: the HyperQuest portal. Rhett placed his hand in Hema's lap, silently offering his own knuckles. Hema popped away, staring at the podcar door, willing it to close before any other passengers could board. Even with Rhett's jacket on, Hema's head wound would draw unwanted attention. They could feel the blood soaking through the gauze.

The monorail beeped, and a woman Hema recognized popped through the entrance before the doors closed. Liliane Yates: Palmer and Vance's mother, Damon's *first* ex-wife. Given the fabricated affair the public believed got Hema booted from Quest and led to Damon's subsequent divorce from Poppy, Liliane knew Hema uncomfortably well. She'd shared her take on the scandal with every gossip site in the world.

Liliane turned their way. Hema acted on impulse. Their hair was too short to hide behind, so they hid against Rhett, pulling him close and pressing their face to his. If he was confused by Hema's forward move, he didn't let it show. His roving lips and hands sought different kinds of answers that made Hema's cheeks burn.

"Honestly," Liliane tsked, "public transport is not a private bedroom. Questers are supposed to show more dignity than this."

Hema wished they could tell Liliane a thing or two about her *son's* dignity.

The woman stomped toward the front of the podcar, putting distance between the offending couple and herself. Still, neither Hema nor Rhett pulled away until the monorail's final stop, where Rhett helped Hema to their feet, blinking rapidly.

"Do you have something in your eye?" Hema asked.

Rhett flashed a lopsided grin. "I'm trying to blink up the courage to tell you that I think you're incredible, and that if we don't end up finding the cure, I'm going to die a happy man with your kiss on my lips." Hema stared up at him, speechless. The monorail's beeping stirred them out of each other's eyes and back to the task before them.

Hema and Rhett raced out the podcar before the doors slid shut and barreled down the empty station's metal stairs. They stuck to the edge of the wide walkway that led to the remote launch facility, passing only a handful of Questers at this early hour. All were walking *away* from the base, Hema noted.

Rhett slowed to eavesdrop on a chatty pair of uniformed engineers hurrying past. "Sounds like there's some kind of mandatory Quest-wide summit happening," he muttered.

"That explains the arrival of Palmer's mother," Hema said. "Here to witness what she's been dreaming of since the scion was born: *her* son, ruling the empire."

"Should be good for us," Rhett assured. "The eyes of campus will be on the auditorium."

Then why did Hema suddenly feel a presence at their back? They turned to see a tall man in a shining platinum suit, a curved saber in his hand like a sinister knight in armor.

"Now, now," Hariri laughed, "what would bring Damon Yates's little protégé and traitorous enforcer to Questbase? Looking for something you're not supposed to find?"

Hema saw the fear symbol attached to his lapel and covered their eyes, screaming into the sleeves of Rhett's denim jacket. They felt Rhett's hand, trying to comfort, but Hema shook him off. "Blink!" Hema shouted at him.

He didn't need to be told twice. Eyelids fluttering, he pulled Hema back around, cocked his gun, and started firing over his shoulder as they ran for the front door. It was open, miraculously, with no visible security.

Once inside the sweeping lobby, Hema went straight for the building directory. They were in luck again. The flight-control room was on the ground floor. They sprinted down the expansive hallway, the sun casting natural pools of light through the lofty glass ceiling.

And yet no one seemed to be watching them.

As if Hariri had *wanted* them to go for the super-pressure balloon. Hema couldn't think about that now. The window to recover the payload was closing. "There was a launch exactly twenty-eight days ago," they whispered to Rhett.

He nodded at a passing custodian. "All right," he replied neutrally. Hema realized he was likely pretending to understand, unsure whether or not this was positive news.

"This is very fortunate," Hema assured him. "Damon's balloons can circumnavigate the globe in two weeks."

A full grin rose between Rhett's stubbled cheeks. "It's been four weeks," he worked out. "Which means the balloon is now above Los Angeles."

"Exactly."

When Hema was a young, naive Quester, they had kept track of all Quest's rocket and balloon launches. It had been a point of pride, knowing they worked for a company that sought to reach for the stars. Later, as a hermit, and then an exile, Hema had monitored the launches out of pure habit, a ritual to mark the homogenous days while comparing their own failures to such noble quests. "We just have to send a radio command, then it will take roughly half an hour for the balloon to reach Earth's surface."

The massive, pumpkin-shaped balloon should be floating over campus this very minute. It was silly, but Hema tilted their head, gazing up through the skylight, squinting into the daylight. The balloon was twenty-six miles up. There was nothing but empty sky. *You hid it well, Damon,* Hema conceded. But like Hariri and his nano reform, Hema was about to bring it down.

Hema charged into the control room, calling the balloon and its treasure-filled payload to land. "Given the wind and environmental conditions, the landing site could be anywhere on campus," they said hastily, turning to Rhett. "And once it's spotted, we won't be the only recovery team going after it. But we *must* get there first."

"Good thing we have an advantage," Rhett said, heading for the hallway, his gun drawn. "I know Quest's terrain like the back of my—"

The control room door slammed closed. Then a lock clicked. And another.

Hariri had barricaded them inside. He was going to steal the treasure himself.

"Shit," Hema cursed. *Shit, shit, shit.*

Hema ran for the emergency exit, the deadbolt sliding into place just as they launched their body against the crash bar.

Across the room, Rhett fired on the door handle, attempting to shoot their way out. But as Hema slid down the sealed exit to the cold floor, their hope collapsed. Hariri would get to the payload first.

The cure had never felt more out of their reach.

TWENTY-TWO

Iris leaned against the Little Beach Club's patio bar, sipping a Virgin Sunrise and staring at the copper-haired Warren Briggs over the tops of her Wayfarer sunglasses. The man who murdered Iris's aunt was out for an early Malibu brunch, a gaggle of the high-society set tittering around an oceanside table grazing on bluefin tuna and lobster-tail.

The Conservator who murdered Poppy was not in uniform, forgoing his platinum suit for a linen ensemble, a pair of gloves over both hands to hide his telltale finger prosthetic.

He meant to lie low. To camouflage himself from the public scrutiny the Exiles had unleashed against the Fortunates with their podcast.

"The Unbanished Secrets" had revealed nothing of Poppy's true passing. But the man who'd shot her aunt, and left her to die, would never be able to hide from Iris Szeto.

Iris thumbed the cold enamel pin she kept safe and ready in her palm, spurring her thoughts onward. She was the heir apparent now, the next head of the Szeto fortune. And she was more than willing to prove her worth.

She unbuttoned the jacket of her vivid orange suit, the color of golden poppies, and tucked her sleek, chin-length bob behind her ear. With her back straight as a stem, she glided across the patio deck, in careful view of the murderer. Just as she'd planned, Warren Briggs turned pale. One of his companions jested that it looked like he had just seen a ghost.

And he had.

Iris had transformed herself into a carbon copy of Poppy. Briggs's old friend, his *victim*, had returned to haunt him, to remind him of the very unpleasant thing he'd so pleasantly gotten away with. Unpunished, until now.

Iris strolled down the club's beach stairs, tucked between rolling, picturesque bluffs. Pounding waves broke across the shoreline, concealing the hurried footsteps she knew were following her. She didn't turn around, but ambled along the white sands of Silicon Beach toward Savior Pier.

A thousand-foot glass bridge jutted into the Pacific, designed to generate a feeling of walking on water. *Perfect for Damon's saint complex,* Iris thought, glaring down at the calm blue surface below. She remembered that Poppy had been at Damon's side for the pier's ribbon-cutting ceremony, four years before their divorce, wearing a suit just like the one Iris had on now, striking as a field of wild gold.

Iris reached the end of the pier, a circular concrete deck with a red-roofed aquarium at its center. A spattering of fishermen cast lines from the steel railing, but otherwise, Savior Pier was blessedly quiet. She snaked around behind the building, waiting for the lone Conservator to follow the decoy.

With her back turned, she heard heavy footsteps and quick, nervous breathing.

"Tell me who you are—"

Iris spun around, her features set in a hardened mask. "You know what makes a delicious dipping sauce for lobster-tail?"

The man grimaced. Looked green around the gills.

From her jacket, Iris slipped out a bot-laced package of butterscotch candy she'd acquired at an Unfortunate shelter. "I had the chef melt these down especially for you. Infused with a little garlic and lemon and nano reform, and voilà! A five-star recipe for revenge."

The Conservator began to heave.

Iris shook her head. "Oh, we both know the bots are already in your bloodstream."

"You just gave me a death sentence!" Briggs cried.

"Is that an admission?" Iris asked, tapping the contaminated candy. "You better hope one of those scientists that Hariri abducted can find a cure."

"Hariri will come after you," Briggs threatened. "The Conservators won't let you have me."

Iris's red lips twisted in a scowl. "You think you're the first club member I've taken?"

She attached a Conservator's enamel pin, still flecked with his club-mate's blood, onto her suit's lapel. She leaned forward, tipping Briggs's shivering chin up to the symbol. He threw his gloved hands over his eyes and stumbled back against the railing. Iris pounced, binding his wrists with zip ties.

She grabbed a fistful of his copper hair and ripped his head back again, forcing him to look at the three bold slashes. "Who is the emerald-nosed buyer?"

"I don't know," Briggs panted between cries. Iris released her grip, letting him fall, his forehead slamming against the concrete. She believed him.

Briggs slid to his knees, eyes closed, mouth open in a wide smile. "What I do know . . . Hariri has Poppy's ashes." He must have sensed Iris flinch, and he laughed. "Three guesses what he plans on doing with them."

Iris grabbed his lapel and pitched him up and over the pier's railing. His deep, satisfied laughter distorted into a high-pitched scream.

Instead of a splash, there was a hollow *thud*, followed by a satisfying *crack*.

222

Iris peered over the railing. Vance, in a bespoke, ocean-blue patterned suit, stared up at her from the steering wheel of a stylish V-shaped powerboat. "I think you broke his leg."

"That's the best news I've heard all day," Iris said, alighting from the pier into the boat.

They sped across the northern curve of the bay in what felt like a matter of seconds. It was still high tide, and the sea-foam lapped the concrete pillars of the Szeto family's extravagant oceanfront mansion. A few yards from the deck, Vance cut the engine and rolled the wheel to port, docking the powerboat with precision. The Szetos' enforcers were already waiting. One saw to the mooring lines while the other opened an extendable steel ramp, a thin footbridge connecting the boat to the deck.

Iris shoved Briggs onto the ramp, making him catch his full weight on his shattered tibia. "Walk the plank," she commanded.

Briggs gazed at the enforcers ready to greet him on the deck, then back to Iris and Vance. Presumably determining that the brawny men with guns were the lesser of two evils, he limped forward.

"It appears my brother has been up to things this morning," Vance sighed, crossing the bridge.

He nudged Iris, who was staring up at Maxen on the third-story balcony. He glared down at the man who had stolen his mother from him. Though it was imperative that Maxen stay hidden—they hadn't yet cleared his name—she was glad he'd emerged to see this, the Szetos laying justice at their own feet.

The right man will soon be in prison, Iris thought, pleased. *My gift to you, cousin.*

Iris tore her eyes from Maxen to the phone screen Vance held in front of her. The sight gave her pause.

Damon Yates, Jade, and Crys dangled from Palmer's drone, high in the sky, looking for all the world like a disturbing version of a child's lost balloon drifting among the clouds.

"The video was posted ten minutes ago on a Grove discussion board, the course set for Quest Campus," Vance said.

Iris acknowledged him with a nod and turned to the enforcers escorting the Conservator behind her. "Bring him to the dining room and call for my father," she instructed. "Tell him I have an offering."

The tall one leaned in and whispered, "Your father is . . . currently engaged."

What could be more engaging than Iris's presentation of his sister's captured killer?

Shouting broke out above them. Iris looked up to the balcony window, but Maxen was no longer there. He must have just seen Jade's little ride in the sky. She charged into the foyer and up the stairs, Vance trailing at her side.

In the game room, Sage and Wily sat insolently on the fine white felt of the bubinga-wood pool table, worth more than a Quest engineer's salary. Their necks bent over their phone screens. Maxen and Ani paced the table's length, slender pool cues clutched in their hands like fighting sticks.

Iris had to force herself not to uncross her arms, reach out, and brush her hands along the table's precious wood for luck. "Maxen, be reasonable," she pressed. "I know Damon is your father, and you care for Jade and Crys. But you cannot go after them. You're still a prisoner."

"*Whose* prisoner?" Maxen seethed. He launched his pool cue like a spear into the pearl-framed magazine cover that hung on the wall beside Vance's head.

It was an early print of *Time* magazine's Person of the Year. The glass shattered across her father's face: the short onyx hair, the dark eyes, the infamous shrouded nose that tens of thousands had been vainly searching for.

Maxen fished inside the breast pocket of his loose-fitting blazer. He tossed a shiny object with the dimensions of a cue chalk onto the felt of the pool table.

The emerald.

He found the gemstone from the Buyer of Monaco's mask.

"It looks like our fathers have more in common than just *me*," Maxen shouted. "They're both deceivers. I found the emerald in Uncle Hoi's luggage."

Ani watched Iris with the intensity of a lie-detector drone. "You knew all along, didn't you?" she asked accusingly, snapping the wooden pool cue across her thigh. She lifted the two sticks, their serrated tips sharp as spears, in lieu of her confiscated knives.

Iris sighed. She'd thought Sage, with all that engineered brainpower, would have been the one to have found her out. "In actual fact," Iris corrected, "it was all *my* design."

Maxen reeled. He seized the emerald, bounding for an open window, where he yanked back his arm and hurled the precious stone with every ounce of his might and ferocity into the sea.

Sage and Wily leapt from the pool table, joining Ani as she stalked toward Iris. From the devilish look in Wily's eye, Iris was thankful her father's enforcers had stripped Wily, too, of his weapons of choice. But whatever united inquisition the trio had in mind was interrupted when Wily stumbled back against the table and onto the carpeted floor.

"I'm fine," Wily assured, though he struggled to rise.

Sage and Ani stooped to help him back to his feet.

"Wily, are you infected?" Sage asked, her voice tight with worry.

"No, I don't have the nano reform. I just forgot to take my insulin," Wily admitted. He pulled a syringe from his pocket, and Sage's face twisted with confusion. Betrayal. "Turns out my Quest Bot wasn't just giving me a killer figure," he explained sheepishly. "It cured my type 2 diabetes. Without my bot, Hema had to put me on insulin at the ranch to help control my symptoms, but I just . . . I keep telling myself I don't need it."

"Wily—" Sage exclaimed.

"Hey, I think *she's* the one with the bigger secret to reveal here," he said, injecting the syringe into his stomach as he nodded toward Iris.

Everyone's focus redirected to her.

"How exactly was it your *design* to get caught by Palmer?" Maxen said, moving to stand beside the scrappy gang of Exiles.

"Explain yourself," Vance demanded. Iris was stunned to see a thick shard of broken glass in his fist. "Am I in danger in a house full of Szetos?"

Iris held up her empty palms. "Of course not," she assured him. "You're with me." She flicked her steady gaze around her chosen team, Maxen last and foremost. "Our attendance was crucial at the Exhibition. It was imperative for our family to get our hands on the nano reform. But I also had intel that you had been moved to an off-site prison at Palmer's orders. I leaked the location of my jet to his enforcers, knowing Palmer would only see the bait, and not the steel trap. He took us right to you." Her red mouth curved into a smile. "And Hariri never saw our family coming."

"You risked giving away our Adsum sibs for your *own* family's ventures?" Sage yelled.

"I never revealed the location of the ranch," Iris urged. "I never endangered Poppy's students. And I gave the Moores and the others their fair shot to put an end to Hariri at the Exhibition. I had high hopes they would succeed."

"So," Ani interjected, spinning the wooden spears deftly in her hands, "did you just 'select' us to be on your team at the ranch because you thought we were easy marks?"

"On the contrary," Iris said. She gestured to Sage and Wily, who sat on the table again, pinkies hooked. "You two have keen business minds. Your Dry River City tours were lucrative and resourceful." She raised a brow to the impromptu weapons in Ani's hands. "And I thought you might make an interesting enforcer. You're not exactly servile, but your intuition's sharper than your blades of choice."

"And was this by design, too?" Maxen asked, disgusted. He'd picked up the phone Wily had dropped and showed the others a video that contained such piercing screams that the phone's speakers clipped.

"You think any of us are going to get into business with you after what you just pulled at Hariri's pharma company?" Wily scoffed. "You're as bad as the Conservators."

Iris tilted her head, at a loss.

"Oh please, you were so smug about all your other schemes," Sage said, unbelieving.

For a second time this hour, a phone screen was held in front of Iris's face: another video recently uploaded to the Grove discussion boards.

Mobs of workers inside a pharmaceutical warehouse owned by Hariri were running over each other, faces locked in utter terror, desperate to flee. Was it a fear symbol causing the chaos? Then a faction of the screaming mob rushed for the distribution shelves, pilfering the endless supply boxes before descending on a group of suited executives. Iris gasped as the workers began shoving handfuls of medicinal pills down their throats.

The mob was choosing fight over flight.

No, this was something different, Iris thought. *Something more.*

A whole new kind of fear.

"He kept me in the dark," Iris seethed. She spun on her stiletto heel, marching for the staircase.

"Iris," Vance exclaimed, "your father's guaranteed to go after Quest next. You realize this, don't you? Hariri's hidden behind its gates." He grabbed her arm, halting her on the bottom step. "I can't let it happen. *My* father's in there. And the Questers are innocent; they don't deserve to suffer for our family's feud."

Iris bit back a growl. "I didn't want this . . . I should have known my father wouldn't fully let me in."

She turned, moving for the living room that was guarded by her father's tall enforcer. Snarling down at Vance, he stepped in Iris's path.

"Let. Me. *In*," she hissed, reaching for her stun gun. It wasn't there.

Before she could even rally, the electric blue of seventy billion volts hovered at the tall man's neck. "We aren't asking," Ani snarled, the missing stun gun in her easy grip.

The enforcer shuffled aside, and Iris threw apart the double sliding doors, tearing into the living room.

"Iris, *not now!*" her father snipped at her.

Hoi Szeto sat alone at a work desk, poised, imperturbable, head sloped down, seeming more concerned about the morning newspaper's crossword than his own daughter's fury. Iris wished they hadn't already tossed away the emerald. She ached for another stone to throw. Preferably square at her father's nose.

"You lied to me," she said evenly. "You took billions from our family's empire to become a player in bioterrorism? You promised we'd be more magnanimous with the use of the nano reform. That we acquired it as a precaution. As a defense."

Hoi glared at her, disappointed. Impatient. "Iris, I'm a businessman, not a Savior."

"Our business, as you say," Iris prodded, "is meant to foster global harmony. It's everything the Quartet Line exemplifies."

Her father buttoned his suit jacket, a deep navy, not the buyer's black, though it had the same common notch lapel, the same tailored sleeves. "Do you really think I'd sit and do nothing," he said, "while Hariri and the Yateses combined forces to hoard and sell their nanotech, becoming more powerful than God? Big business is a weapons race now, and I had to strike first. Besides, Hariri always loved a good show, and I'm giving him one."

"What does that mean?" Vance demanded, but then Maxen barreled into the room.

"Uncle, please. There are other ways to take them down—"

Hoi cut him off with a raised hand. "It's already done."

"What's done?" Maxen pressed. "Have you ordered a nano attack on Quest?" He looked to Ani, then Wily and Sage, who'd come charging in after him. They glanced up from their phones, their heads shaking.

"I'm not seeing anything on the boards," Wily said.

Iris turned for the door. "That means we still have time."

"You and Maxen will *not* be going to campus," Hoi commanded. Her father's enforcers blocked their path.

"This is who you've chosen to align yourself with?" Hoi said. He snarled at Vance and the Exiles. "A middleman and a pack of glorified orphans?"

"You underestimate them, Father," Iris said, turning to face him. "Vance had the resolve to go rogue. And these were Poppy's foster children, after all. They've battled far worse than an old man and his two mercenary soldiers."

Ani tossed Iris her stun gun, then brandished the two pool cues, handing one to Sage. Wily wielded his empty syringe as Vance dove for the fireplace poker, lifting it into a fencer's stance. Maxen raised his bare fists and stood at Iris's side.

"And you underestimated *me*," Iris said, grinning as she flicked off the safety switch. She charged toward her father, a cry cracking from her red lips. "A family cannot have two heads."

Twenty-Three

Crys had a hawk's-eye view of Quest Campus, the same lofty perspective she'd had when she first arrived on Yates's auto-copter after being plucked from the Unfortunate streets. The vast city within a city, tucked in the private Santa Monica Mountains, still took Crys's breath away.

"Home," Damon's awed voice said from above.

Crys's arms ached from holding tight to Jade's waist. She distracted herself from the thought of falling by mapping out the empire that she, too, had once thought of as home.

There was Beelzebub Rock, the fire station, the stunning timber towers of the Forest, and the surrounding retail shops that held her first perfumery. The idyllic housing communities and the statuesque water tower, the hospital and Splendor Park. She spotted the ruins of the Castle in the Air, Yates's mansion suspended from a mountaintop, and the secret lab underneath. Cranes, bulldozers, and cement mixers surrounded the property, already laying down the foundations of a new mansion.

Palmer's been busy, Crys thought. The prince now a king, building his own castle on the ashes of his predecessor's.

Was the drone taking them there?

"Crys, you see that?" Jade said. "Ten o'clock."

Crys looked to the outlying canyons, where Yates's diverse manufacturing plants and warehouses were located. A fleet of sleek silver semitrucks were docked at the largest plant, the logo on the sides of the trailers displaying the profile of a howling wolf.

Hariri.

He was using the might of Quest to mass-produce his nano reform. It made sense, Crys knew. But the idea that Hariri was building his bioweapons on the campus she once dreamed of ruling made a fresh swell of anger rise in Crys.

The drone dropped their altitude, flying low over Adsum Peak. The sibs came running out of the academy, pointing up at them, horrified at their new benefactor's display of power.

If you go against me, Palmer was saying with this stunt, *this will be your fate.*

Finn covered his mouth and turned away as the drone banked, speeding its human cargo toward Summit Auditorium.

The roof came up fast. Damon grunted as he was unceremoniously dropped onto a glass overlook. Crys finally let go her tremulous grip on her sister as Jade released the drone. Weak-kneed, they both collapsed onto their stomachs.

Crys's skull smacked against reinforced glass. She saw stars behind her eyes. She waited for a blast of pain, but it never came. She was immune to it now, like Jade. Crys looked to her sister, who'd stumbled to her feet. If the prion disease was ravaging through Crys at this rate, it was a miracle Jade was still standing with her double infection.

Galvanized by Jade's strength, Crys shot to her feet in a blink. Dazed, she watched Palmer's drone zoom away, disappearing into the gaping hole of the auditorium's enormous retractable roof.

"Do you think Palmer called for a Quest assembly?" Crys yelled over the gusting wind.

"Yeah," Jade answered, her voice thin, stripped of its usual gravelly bite. "And let's hope we aren't the show."

Jade stalked along the overlook's railings, searching for emergency ladders or any feasible path that might lead them to a window or a foothold—*any* route out other than the wide hatch door that stood open for them like a steel jaw.

"Swallow the Earth whole!" Jade cursed.

Damon was already clambering through it.

Jade lunged to follow, but Crys grabbed her before she made it halfway down the short stairs. "Wait. You're losing too much blood."

"Oh, right," Jade muttered, seeming shocked to see the cuts and puncture wounds along her hands and arms. Crys fished through her sister's pockets and hooked her fingers around a skull-patterned hand-kerchief. Quickly, she wiped the blood from Jade's eyes and wrapped the skull-patterned cloth around the deepest gash.

"You know . . ." Jade muttered as they stole, heavy-footed, down the stairs and through an empty sunlit hall. *Where is Damon? Where are the Conservators?* "I always wore black to be like Mom. And you'd never catch me without my *calavera* bandana. I wanted to stay close to Dad."

Why is Jade speaking in past tense?

Crys felt a jolting stab inside her chest. Jade's face was pale. Her eyes, brown like solid oak trees, were growing distant.

"You're close enough to both of them here, with me," Crys told Jade, gripping her sister's arm, bearing her weight. "Stay with me, all right?"

Jade's footsteps were slowing. She kept tripping over her feet, swat-ting at the air in front of her. The floor sloped down, down, down as they rounded curved corners, until at last they spotted Damon hovering inside a balcony suite's doorway.

As they shuffled closer, Palmer's silvery voice cut through the audi-torium. "Our fearless Savior is sick . . ." Damon's face was on the jumbo screens around the stage, an unseen camera pointed in their direction.

Crys pulled Jade flat against the wall.

". . . and though his dementia has weakened his mind . . . Damon Yates will continue to live strong in our memories . . ."

Damon's open-mouthed stare wasn't aimed at his blown-up image or at Palmer, who stood center stage, his pet drone now at his feet. Damon's piercing blue eyes were instead targeted on something off-screen.

". . . I have brought him home again . . ." Palmer continued, ". . . and I know each of his beloved Questers will help him welcome the peaceful retirement he has so dutifully earned . . ."

The screen cut away from Damon's confused face when he shuffled into the luxury box suite, hands balled into fists. Crys and Jade chased after him, spotting a black-and-silver mane jutting out from behind a plush velvet seat.

"Old *friend*," Damon spat.

"Hariri," Crys gasped. The Soaring Precious rested on the chair next to Hariri, unsheathed, calling to her.

Even with her wavering strength, Jade held Crys to her side. "No," she whispered. "Right now, the treasure is more important than Hariri."

Hariri rose, his shoulders shaking with laughter. "Yates's fabled treasure." He turned his smile to Damon, running his jeweled fingers along the saber blade. "You cunning, farsighted son of a nobody. This explains why I found you flitting about campus the night of my take-over. I should have *known* your former self would not have surrendered without a few grenades for me to stumble upon." He clapped his hands, pleased, as if Damon had just presented him a gift. "You discovered my restoration plans, didn't you? And swapped the precious prize of your treasure chest before you fled. Oh, you do still know how to have a bit of fun, my friend."

Crys and Jade locked eyes. Hariri believed in the treasure? Was searching for it, too?

"Of course, I found your hidden grenade," Hariri tittered as Palmer continued to prattle on from the stage, assuring his Questers of his noble leadership. "I've discovered the treasure."

"Liar," Crys spat.

"All right, you caught me," Hariri said. He flicked his eyes lazily away from an expressionless Damon, his smile dipping, as if bored without the *full* Damon Yates here to witness his triumph. "It was Hema and Rhett who solved the poem." He brandished a hand toward the sky. "But it will be *me* who takes it."

On cue, an immense pumpkin-shaped balloon appeared above the retractable roof. Carried on the high winds, it was gone before Crys could even believe what her eyes had seen.

"That's one of Damon's super-pressure balloons," she whispered to Jade. "It's carrying a payload." And it held clues for the cure, Crys could *feel* it. *Look high, seek low,* the poem had directed. "Jade, we have to be there when it lands."

There was a flash of red across the cavernous auditorium, then an ominous *click*. Water began to shoot down from the sides of the domed ceiling, an artificial rain drenching the auditorium in seconds.

What had set off the fire sprinklers?

"I don't smell smoke," Jade panted, cupping a weak hand to her burned arm. "But I sure as hell sense a fire coming."

Crys's head shot up. Their box's sprinkler heads hadn't been activated. They were the only dry spectators in the house. Palmer was untouched, too. He stood center stage, his speech dead in his throat.

Dread twisted Crys's gut.

This was no accident. They were all kept dry for a reason.

"What game are you playing now?" Jade shouted at Hariri over the rising din of panic. The doors of the auditorium were locked, the Questers trapped inside.

A voice answered over the speakers, low and distorted.

"Good afternoon, Questers. Listen carefully to what I say."

The auditorium erupted into full-blown pandemonium. Outbursts of violence, screams, shrill cries to make the voice stop. The captive Questers cowered to the floor, their hands pressed frantically over their ears.

"They're terrified of the voice," Crys gasped.

"The water in the sprinklers must have been spiked with an alternative nano reform," Jade reasoned out. "One with a fear bot activated by *sound* instead of sight."

Had they gotten to the water tower, too, spreading the infection campus-wide?

"This is your new quest," the voice continued, "the voice, the fear, will stop when Hariri and every Yates on campus is dead."

The voice was deep and robotic. The identity of the speaker undetectable. It was the Buyer of Monaco, Crys was certain.

"This is your new quest: the voice, the fear, will stop when Hariri and every Yates on campus is dead," the message repeated. By the third replay, thousands of terrorized eyes in the auditorium had found the voice's targets, hovering in the luxury box seats.

Hariri, Damon. *Me*, Crys realized.

Though she no longer looked like Crystal—no golden hair, no perfect, pristine image—it was clear that the Questers still very much saw her as a Yates. Crys couldn't feel herself trembling, but she looked down to see every last hair on her arms standing on end.

Jade stepped in front of her. Shielding her. But over a thousand Questers' minds had been hijacked with engineered fear. Nothing would stop them, *stop the voice*, until she was slain alongside Damon and Hariri.

A strangled cry from the front of the auditorium broke Crys out of her terror.

On stage, Palmer's drone was battling to protect him, stabbing with its claws at the mob come to kill its master. But there were too many of them. The hijacked Questers yanked it to the ground, tearing off its rotors and charging after Palmer, who'd tried to escape backstage. But he didn't make it far. He careened face-first to the floor, four rotor blades sunk deep into his back.

Crys looked away. If Damon understood that he had just witnessed the murder of his son, he didn't show it.

"This is your new quest: the voice, the fear, will stop when Hariri and every Yates on campus is dead."

"I'll take the privilege of cutting down the next Yates for myself," Hariri jeered.

Crys turned just as Hariri slashed at Damon with the ancient saber.

Damon ducked, and when Hariri drew the blade back again, he paused at the rumble of pounding footsteps from down the hall that led to their balcony suite.

The mob was coming fast, calling for Hariri and the Yateses by name. Terror surged through Crys at the strength of their cries.

Hariri abandoned his attack on Damon and hurtled out of the suite's exit.

"He's going after the treasure," Jade seethed.

Now Hariri needed it just as much as they did. It was the key to the cure, the only way to permanently free the Questers from the murderous voice inside their heads.

But how many of the Buyer of Monaco's targets would leave campus still breathing?

Crys and Jade *had* to get their hands on the treasure first. They couldn't let Hariri beat them. He would use the cure only to save himself. But the Exiles—the *Intruders*, Crys thought with a small grin—*they* needed to save thousands.

Crys stole through Quest, ready to rob the Conservators blind.

Twenty-Four

Willis was glad that his bad back and busted knees couldn't feel their current mistreatment.

"Streets take me," he cursed, his growl echoing off the corrugated steel of the *just* wide enough storm drain he was slithering through. "How much longer can this thing be?"

He had hazarded a guess that the Quest gates would be flooded with Conservators and civilian sleuths. So he ventured the rainwater runoff pipes that led from the mountains to the bay.

Back in the months when he'd squatted outside the campus gates, wretched and desperate to see his nieces, he'd stumbled upon an opening in the drainpipe outside the western barrier near the base of Adsum Peak. He'd never worked up enough courage to make the suffocating journey. Once he started, there would be no way back. He would have to worm his way forward, in the dark, hoping to reach a small hole of light.

Willis squinted. Where the hell was the damn light?

Sweat dripped into his eyes. Claustrophobia was setting in. He could really use a drink. No ice, straight from the bottle. Willis gritted his teeth.

No, he scolded himself. He was through with all that.

Now, he was a man who wasn't afraid to snake through storm drains. An uncle who didn't abandon his nieces in need.

He finally spotted slatted sunlight twenty yards ahead.

"There you are," he grunted.

He crouched when he reached the iron grate, shoving his fingers through. He took a deep breath, and pushed.

"Son of a Savior, that's heavy," he cursed.

He pressed his shoulder to the grate and drove up with the full weight of his body. The cover slid just far enough for him to crawl out, and he emerged into the center of Quest Campus.

But it wasn't the utopia he'd heard about in Nolan's podcast. It was an all-out war zone.

Half a dozen copters hovered low across the campus, their speakers blaring.

"This is your new quest: the voice, the fear, will stop when Hariri and every Yates on campus is dead."

Willis didn't know what the hell that meant, but he knew exactly who it was meant *for*.

Questers raced around the streets, their hands clamped to their ears, wide eyes hunting like starved animals.

A shadow passed over Willis. He screwed up his eyes to the clouds. It wasn't the drone or his nieces, but a giant white parachute that sailed overhead, cruising at a breakneck speed toward one of the jagged peaks. *Is that a space diver?* Then the sun glinted off a thick aluminum box. *No,* Willis realized. *Not a person. And not a parachute.*

It was a massive balloon, carrying a payload.

Had Jade and Crys found the shaking treasure?

Chasing after a landed balloon matched the lines he kept hearing the two singing on the hyperloop pod. *Look high, seek low . . . You will find riches greater than gold.*

Every instinct that had driven Willis toward the flames, back during the quake, now whipped at his gut, driving him toward where that payload was going to land. The coastal breeze picked up, sending dust all around him. Rubbing the sting from his eyes, he watched the payload spin faster and faster, like a metal trompo, before crashing on a sandstone peak.

Willis expected to spot the twin figures of Jade and Crys climbing the steep mountainside, but instead he saw platinum suits, cutting up through the cottonwood and sagebrush.

I've got to get the cure, Willis spurred himself on. *I've got to save my nieces and their family.*

Willis took off at a sprint. He reached the base of the rugged peak and realized there were no trails that led to the top. His legs felt like overcooked noodles. He was out of breath and out of time. The suits were halfway up the slope. He started scrambling, up and up, forging his own path through the tangled growth of evergreen chaparral, heavy limbed. His mind spun, thinking he spotted an inferno racing up the mountain just behind him.

Keep your head, he growled to himself, rubbing his eyes to clear the flames. *It's just the nano reform playing tricks.* He watched the backs of his hands and the tops of his feet as he navigated upward. Then his knees and elbows began to buckle before finally, on the edge of collapse, he crested the slope.

I peaked right on time, he thought, exhaustedly, as he spotted the deflated balloon.

The massive sheet, which looked to Willis like flimsy material you'd wrap your sandwich with, was snagged over a large slab of red rock. One platinum suit stood next to it, while another person-sized shape rummaged underneath the balloon before popping out with an aluminum box in his grubby hands.

The payload was deceptively small and lightweight for something that could save the whole damn world.

"Bet you think that belongs to you, huh?" Willis scoffed at the Conservators. "Like everything else in your Fortunate lives, you think if you want something, it's yours."

The Conservators spun. The female drew an object out of her handbag and held it up with a smug laugh.

One of their enamel pins with the fear symbol, if Willis had to guess. Which he had to, because these platinum scoundrels didn't realize that his vision had been fading. He was too blind to be scared. "Good thing I came prepared to take what I want, too."

He drew a BolaWrap device from the back of his pants and fired. The Kevlar cord wrapped around the aluminum box in the Conservator's hands, and Willis pulled. The steel cord retracted, and just like that, the treasure was his.

The woman hollered.

Willis ran. He didn't need his eyes to guide him. He used his ears.

Down at the base of the mountain, Jade and Crys were calling for him.

TWENTY-FIVE

As Maxen leaned against a glass wall of the floating elevator car, the words "move mountains" struck his unquiet mind. He would move mountains to get to Jade and his father. To Crys, *his sister*, even if she now went by a different last name.

Move mountains.

It was a good thing he didn't have to. He was passing *through* one instead, owing to his father's penchant for secrets. Damon believed he was the only one who knew about the private passageway that ran beneath this nameless peak to an unknown road outside the campus gates. Unlike with Asclepius, his father's illicit laboratory, Maxen had found *this* secret early on, when he was a second-year at the academy.

Magnetized coils ran along the elevator shaft's guide rails, making the car "float," similar to Quest's hyperloop technology. Maxen cocked a smile, knowing how much Jade would appreciate the exhilarating 360-degree view of the heart of a mountain.

Jade's screams jarred him back to the surface. To the here and now. On full volume, Ani was playing Jade's live audio stream from the Grove boards.

"Get back!" Jade commanded the infected Questers. "Fight the *voice*, not us! I know I'm asking you to move mountains, but fight back against the bot!"

Move mountains. So *that's* where Maxen had pulled the words from. Suddenly a voice overwhelmed Jade's.

"This is your new quest: the voice, the fear, will stop when Hariri and every Yates on campus is dead."

Maxen recognized no trace of his uncle in the sonorous recording. And neither would the navy suits. Or the rest of the sleuthing world. The Grove had yet to peg Hoi Szeto as the Buyer of Monaco.

The emerald. Maxen could kick himself for his hasty and ill-considered chucking of the invaluable gemstone into the bottom of the Pacific. It was their only solid evidence that his own uncle had Maxen's brother killed. *Half brother,* he thought fleetingly. But Palmer's murder still hit Maxen full in the chest.

"I can't believe the navy suits haven't raided campus yet," Wily seethed. "How many Yateses are they going to let die while they wait outside the gates? The *one* time I want their meddling, and they shoot us the middle finger."

"They believe it might be a hoax," Iris stated. "They won't force entry into Quest until they're certain."

Maxen still found it difficult to look at his cousin straight on, in her poppy-orange suit, her silken hair combed like his mother's.

These mountains had seen so much death. When would the atrocity ever end?

Carefully, Maxen rolled the beige nylon mask over his eyes and nose, yanking the elastic lining well over his mouth, in case there were any shrewd Questers out there who might recognize his Cupid's-bow lips.

Beside him, Vance tugged on his own black hosiery, his features bunching in what looked to Maxen like a frozen cry.

"I wouldn't pin you as a Yates if I saw you," Sage assured them.

They cut through Splendor Park on foot, Sage and Wily pointing out the flowerless patches where they'd fought Palmer and Vance the night the Conservators took Quest.

"My gun had incendiary bullets," Vance said, shamefaced. "With my terrible marksmanship, if I'd hit one of you, there was a chance it could have just been a flesh wound—"

"Oh, a *chance*," Sage scoffed.

"Why don't we take that chance on *you* next—" Wily rounded, but his heated threats ceased when they saw the helicopters hovering above the center of campus. The screams of Questers reached them on the wind.

"It's an invasion," Ani said, unsheathing her knife. She turned to Iris. "Your dad really has gone to war."

Iris led them in a full sprint.

They had to cross through the active *mind*field of fear to get to the base of Beelzebub Rock, where, according to Jade's livestream, she and Crys had already arrived.

"Do you think that balloon really holds the treasure?" Wily asked eagerly. They'd spotted the enormous balloon descending toward campus on their way in. "Did your dad *actually* bury a secret cure in the sky?"

Maxen shook his head. He'd no idea what his father did on Earth, let alone in space. He may have the Yates last name, but he had always been an outsider. An exile in his own family. Maybe that's why he gravitated to Jade so strongly. She knew what it felt like to be nothing but a disappointment to the ones who were blood-bound to love you most.

"This is your new quest: the voice, the fear, will stop once Hariri and every Yates on campus is dead."

The cries of the terrorized Questers grew louder as they reached the center of campus. Wily shot Vance a look like he'd be more than willing to take out at least one of the voice's targets. Vance blanched, moving closer to Iris, who'd stopped to take in the enormity of what her father had done.

Bodies lay strewn across the streets, writhing in agony, fists pounding their ears. Blood pooled around a few, and Maxen realized that they'd stabbed their own eardrums to make the voice stop.

"All right, I'm silencing this sick assault," Sage raged. "I'll have a speaker jammer rigged up in ten." She took off toward the engineering labs.

Wily followed her, his reclaimed knife drawn. "Be sure to give Hariri a punch hello for me," he called back over his shoulder.

"Right now, the payload is ours," Ani announced, listening to Jade's livestream. "Jade and Crys's uncle has it, but he's surrounded by Conservators. He needs backup."

Iris and Ani bolted for Beelzebub Rock.

Maxen and Vance remained rooted where they stood. Their father had just darted past, a shrieking mob at his heels. What was he doing loose on campus? In the elevator, they'd overheard on Jade's livestream that she and Crys had ensconced Damon safely inside a storage closet in an undisclosed building.

"We'll meet you there," Maxen shouted after Iris.

Without a word, Maxen and Vance chased after their father. As Damon ran toward the towers of the Forest, Maxen remembered being told that without his Quest Bot, his father would no longer have control of his Alzheimer's, his mind. His memories.

So Damon had probably forgotten why he was tucked in a closet and stumbled out onto campus, unaware that a voice was calling for his death from half a dozen invading helicopters and every speaker in every building across one thousand acres.

Maxen got to Damon first. Tackled him into the nearest building. Vance slammed the door closed behind them, bolted the lock, drew the window shades. They ripped off their nylon masks and dove behind a crowded display case, crashing into the glass. A row of diamond-shaped perfume bottles shattered on the concrete floor.

"I know that smell . . ." Damon panted. He smacked his hands on the shallow pools of sweet-scented liquid—notes of cedar and amber and a flower Maxen could never place—and brought his fingers up to his nose. Damon's pale blue eyes trembled. "The fear fragrance. Crys, don't breathe it in!"

Damon pitched forward. Maxen lunged and pressed a palm over his mouth, quieting his cries. The infected Questers were gathering outside the door.

"All that's over now," Maxen whispered to his father.

"What have I done?" Damon muttered. He repeated it, like a mantra, like one of his sacred words when he was lost in meditation at his Quietude. Then he suddenly yanked free of Maxen's grasp, charging for the front door, toward his Questers.

"Father, no!" Vance roared. He'd somehow clinched Damon's bare foot and slid him back behind the counter, his slack body like some morbid mop, wiping away the spilled perfume.

"Let me go," Damon said. "Let me go." His eyes were alert now, his voice smooth and calm as the ocean after a storm. *He's lucid,* Maxen realized.

The Questers were banging on the shop's glass now. Some had found rocks and steel chairs to hurl at the doors.

Damon gripped Vance's shoulder. He grasped Maxen's cheek. "Let me go," he repeated. "Use the distraction to run. Let this be the last thing I do. Keep my family safe."

Maxen's eyes welled, and he shook away his tears. "No," he breathed. "They'll kill you. You'll make them murderers." He swallowed hard. "You'll make me an orphan."

Damon closed his eyes. When he opened them, he blinked in surprise as Vance held a thin, crystal-clear vial up to Damon's mouth.

"What on shaking Earth is that?" Maxen gaped.

Vance gave Maxen a small, exultant grin. "Remember on the supermax yacht, when I told you I rifled the bot cabinets before the lab exploded?"

Swimming in that tiny vial was the nanoscopic cure for their father's Alzheimer's disease.

Maxen grinned at his brother, amazed. "Who knew you had half a heart?"

Vance laughed, even as the glass windows of the shop began to shatter.

But Damon hesitated. Maxen did not. He took the vial and poured the liquid straight down Damon's throat, determined to save his father's memories. His life.

Maxen sighed with relief as Damon swallowed his bot, licking at his lips to ensure he ingested every drop. "I'll distract them while you run." He smiled at Vance, then Maxen. "The back exit. Go. Save *yourselves.*"

And then, Damon Yates was gone. Vanished into a mob of desperate hands that sought to tear him apart.

TWENTY-SIX

Jade could see the treasure in Willis's hands as he raced down the mountain, dust and Conservators at his heels.

But Willis didn't spot Jade and Crys. He bounded past them, straight into Hariri's path.

The nano reform was blurring Jade's vision, too. But she saw Hariri lift the gilded saber above his head and swing it down at her uncle. Willis raised the payload as a shield, and the ancient blade bounced off the aluminum box made to survive the rigors of space.

Willis stumbled from the impact. The treasure flew into the air, and into Jade's arms.

It was surprisingly light, considering what Jade hoped it contained. They'd gambled it all on this small box. The cure, the future of millions of Unfortunates.

Their own lives.

"This is your new quest: the voice, the fear, will stop once Hariri and every Yates on campus is dead."

Bloodcurdling screams—"Crystal!" "Hariri!"—cut through the sinister voice recording blasting down from the copters circling above. The mob had caught up with them. And so had the Conservators.

The crack of their guns echoed across the mountains, the bullets jumping like fleas at Jade's feet.

Opening the treasure would have to wait.

"The monorail station," Crys shouted, grabbing Willis's arm and bolting for the elevated platform. They took the stairs two at a time and sealed the barrier gate closed behind them. The mob rammed itself into the gate, hands pushing through the slats in desperation to wrap them around Crys's throat.

And mine, Jade thought. The pitfalls of sharing a face. The hijacked Questers wouldn't be able to tell Jade and Crys apart in their frantic need to stop the voice.

"I tried to open the lid but it's stuck," Willis said, nodding to the dented treasure box.

"It requires a passcode," Jade said, sliding open a latch on its bottom. "Twelve numbers."

Crys's brow furrowed in thought, her hand stroking the tattoo across her ribs.

"Always higher," Jade and Crys said in unison.

Jade went to punch in the numbers that corresponded to those letters, but the keypad was too blurry. Her vision was getting worse.

"It's all right," Crys said, moving in beside her to tap out the passcode herself. The locks opened with a satisfying *click* and Jade flipped open the box's lid.

A single, thin piece of paper was folded inside next to a sealed test tube.

"To Hema: what has been done can be undone," Crys read aloud. "This will get you started."

Suddenly the barrier busted open, the mob screaming Crystal's name. More gunfire rang out, and bodies started dropping onto the platform.

The Conservators were shooting their way to the treasure.

"Onto the railway," Willis grunted, jumping down to the narrow ledge of the single rail track.

Jade sprang after him, but she faltered. Her legs were giving out, her muscles stiffening, her motor functions shutting down like Eli had warned.

Crys wrapped Jade's arm around her shoulder, held on to Willis's hand, and led her family down the track. They made it a hundred yards before they hit an endless wall of murderous Questers barring their path. They fell back, but the mob from the station had chased after them, pinning them in on both sides.

"This is what you call a shit sandwich," Willis said bleakly.

They were sixty feet up in the air, with nowhere to hide.

"This is your new quest: the voice, the fear, will stop once Hariri and every Yates on campus is dead."

Every Moore *on campus,* Jade thought grimly. At least they were together. Jade wouldn't die alone. She'd come into this world with her sister, and she was going to leave it with her, too.

"Over here!" a voice shouted.

Iris. Beckoning to them from an emergency ladder.

Crys dove for their way out, dragging Jade along. At the ladder, they reached for Willis, but just then a hooded figure charged through the mob, the Soaring Precious slicing through the air and stabbing into Willis's shoulder.

Hariri laughed, but the triumphant sound died in his throat when Willis, immune to pain, slowly drew out the blade. He tossed it onto the track.

"It has its disadvantages, doesn't it?" he chided. "Having such a famous mug." He unmasked Hariri and shoved him into the middle of the railway before lunging for the ladder.

Jade hung back while the others climbed down to safety. She watched as the mob converged on Hariri, crying out his name. Hariri picked up the saber and held it to his own throat. Just as he drew his first cut, the voice stopped. The fear message silenced.

The mob stood down all at once, gaping around in a daze. Free from their compulsion to kill. Only one figure didn't stop her charge.

Ani.

She barreled through the confused Questers, knives drawn, straight for Hariri. The saber lay at his feet, and he was shaking, his dark eyes staring down at his hands. In shock at what he had almost done. How close he had come to death. How close he was now.

In Extremis, Jade thought, watching Ani grasp the saber's jade handle and raise the blade to Hariri's stomach. Right where he had given Ani her own near-mortal wound.

But Ani didn't strike. She moved in close, whispering in Hariri's ear. He looked up from his hands and into Ani's face, the usual glint in his eyes extinguished.

Still clutching the saber, Ani turned her back on him and reached for Jade, who'd started to wobble dangerously close to the track's edge. Bright yellow stars flickered at the corners of Jade's vision. She'd lost too much blood.

"Jade!"

Was that her sister calling for her, or her mother?

"Jade, come down!"

Ani guided her toward the emergency ladder, where she could just make out Crys standing at the bottom. "Come down," Crys repeated. "There's someone here to see you."

"Take it slow," Ani said. "There's no one chasing us now."

Carefully, *slowly*, Jade descended the metal rungs to the ground.

"I hear you were writing me prison letters," Maxen said. "I'd love to hear them sometime."

Jade's heart leapt in her throat. "You're free—"

But then the world went dark, and she blacked out in Crys's arms.

TWENTY-SEVEN

The hospital ward in Sophia Ray Medical Center was alive with laughter. Crys's stomach, ribs, and cheeks ached from blissful convulsions. She closed her eyes, relishing the experience.

She could feel pain. She was no longer infected.

Hema had invented a cure.

Crys blinked away her tears. Cole's bright smile and hazel eyes shone up at her from his hospital bed. His sight had returned, and his lightness of mood. His body was on the path to a full recovery. *What has been done can be undone,* Hema had explained. The only permanent mark the nano reform had left were gaps in his memory. Cole couldn't remember the dark days of his disease. Crys was grateful.

"Wait." Cole grinned at Willis. "So you stormed campus from a *storm* drain? Odds are *high* that Nolan's listeners will write you a song for that one."

"Ha!" Willis laughed from an overstuffed armchair, patting at the gauze over his saber wound.

Cole aimed his smile at Jade, who was in her own bed next to his. "And *you* flew into campus dangling from a *drone?*"

A 3D skin printer was clamped around the burns on Jade's forearm, her whirlpool of chestnut curls veiling the bandages on her forehead and upper jaw. She didn't mask her impish smirk. "Taking trespassing to new heights."

Beside her, Maxen laughed. "Ever the common swift. Think we can keep you on land for a while?" He fiddled with the folds of his baggy suit jacket.

Jade stilled his hands. "If only to see the heart of a mountain."

Eli sat up from his bed across the room. "A secret floating elevator inside a mountain peak? You were *really* holding out on us, brother."

"Two Quest Campus break-ins in under two months," Wily said, leaning against the open door with Sage. "Who knew the Exiles would be such good intruders?"

"Well, we can't be burglars." Sage smiled, unclasping a hand from her waist to curl around Wily's. "Since we own the place now. A hefty percentage of it, at least."

Damon had named Crys and Jade as co-inheritors of all Quest enterprises. Maxen and Vance had encouraged them to sign the contract. The Yates brothers wanted to build something new, of their own. *Besides,* Maxen had told them, *we need to keep the business in the family.* Crys and Jade Moore's first act had been to share the wealth, shaving off their percentages for Cole, Eli, Sage, Wily, and Ani.

Ani appeared now at the door, wrapped in faux burgundy leather, multiple colors of paint splotched on her fingers. "Is everyone up for a little journey? I'd like to show you something."

"You don't have to ask *me* twice," Eli chuckled, springing to his feet. "I don't care if it's only been a week post-bot. If I don't stretch my legs, I'm going to scream."

"Glad this thing's portable," Jade said, nodding to the skin printer as Maxen slid his loose-fitting jacket over her shoulders to cover her thin hospital gown. She tapped at Cole's slender IV pole. "Take your wheels and let's ride."

Willis stayed in his cushioned seat. "You're not coming, Uncle?" Crys asked.

"Uh, Nolan's bringing me dinner," Willis rasped. His cheeks burned a faint red. "The food at this hospital's worse than a dumpster."

"Right." Crys smiled, knowing full well that there was a Michelin-star chef in the kitchen.

Everyone else pulled on pants and coats, joining Ani at the door. They ambled slowly down the hall, passing the room labeled OPERATION ANTI-BOT, where, side by side, Hema and Rhett were overseeing the distribution of the nano reform cure. The test tube Damon had hidden in his high-tech treasure chest had turned out to be an artificial strain of human prions, created in vitro. *What has been done can be undone,* his note had read. It spurred instant inspiration in Hema, and in a stroke of genius, they had engineered their own synthetic prion disease, programmed to counteract all the damage caused by the Conservators' nano reform by correctly refolding the misfolded proteins in the brain.

Hema's discovery had not only cured the nano reform, but it also provided a technological framework for curing all human and animal prion diseases. The scientific community that had once spurned them now called for Hema Devi to win the Nobel Prize.

Crys lingered in the doorway, watching the FBI agents in navy suits gathered around the lab tables, checking cases of vials to be sent off to unhoused shelters across the country. She'd made certain that Celene and the Unfortunates from the lighthouse be treated and protected first.

The infected Questers had already received their doses, and every floor of the campus hospital was filled to capacity. World-class doctors, flown in especially for their care, tended to the mental and physical trauma they had suffered when their minds were hijacked by Hoi Szeto.

Hariri was behind bars—*May he rot with no peace,* Crys thought— but Hoi Szeto still roamed free. Apparently, it would tip the scales of justice too far to hold two Fortunates accountable.

Rhett looked up from his work, throwing Crys a nod. He wore thick sunglasses to shield his eyes, which were healing from a surgery to repair the slash marks Palmer had seared onto the backs of his lids. Although Rhett no longer got a boost of courage when he blinked, he still felt a hit of adrenaline whenever he happened across three diagonal slash marks. Jade had forewarned him to use this wisely.

Damon Yates stood alone in a far corner of the lab. He waved hesitantly at Crys and Jade. His renewed Quest Bot had stopped the progression of his Alzheimer's disease, but his memories of the trials and reconciliations they had all experienced were painfully limited. Still, he'd chosen to stay at Quest and face what his earthshaking invention had unleashed on the world. Damon would face judgment, in the twin courts of the law and public opinion, for his experiments on the Adsum sibs, but Crys doubted if he would ever see a cell. The whole world wanted his and Hema's disruptive nanotechnology, the medical miracle that would heal and enhance billions of future lives.

Crys closed her eyes. Time flashed forward, and she gazed out at the future. Soon, she predicted, the world would be divided into the Have Bots and Have Nots. Where would she fall? She took a deep breath and opened her eyes to her own faint reflection in the glass door: sharp cheekbones, chestnut curls, curious brown eyes. An image she no longer recoiled from but embraced.

"Anyone want to rappel down the place like Rhett did?" Wily quipped. "Jade?"

"Maybe when I'm back in fighting shape," Jade laughed, gesturing to her bevy of injuries. "I promised Hema I would heal up before I pulled any new stunts."

Crys led the way to the elevator and then out of the hospital. The sun made a languid descent as they walked the calm stretch of campus toward Adsum Peak. By the time they crested the mountain, the golden light of magic hour bathed the domed glass academy in a brilliant poppy orange. In the garden, Iris lounged and laughed with the Adsum students, a priceless bond being forged between them.

"Angels Walk has the prime view," Ani said, guiding the group to the glass-and-steel overlook that jutted out a hundred feet from the peak's edge.

Crys took in the vast thousand-acre campus cast in dreamy sunset hues. Her eyes lingered on the monumental sculpture at the center of Splendor Park, a vibrant, sharp-edged *U*, surrounded by wildflowers.

"So everyone will know this is a safe place," Ani said proudly.

Sage and Wily leaned against the glass railing, nodding with watery eyes.

"It's marvelous," Maxen said. "A superb center point for the new Quest."

"Khari and Zoe would love it," Eli whispered, hugging Ani close.

Crys took Cole's hand with her left, Jade's with the other. A peace washed over her as she gazed out at her family's empire. The sunset's fire-gold glow hit the overlook at an angle that made it look as if they were suspended in midair, and Crys ached to hold this moment, this *feeling*, suspended in time.

She grinned, tilted back her head, and let loose an unrestrained roar. First Jade, then the others joined in, their collective scream echoing off the mountains.

They were no longer screams filled with fear.

But joy.

ACKNOWLEDGMENTS

Writing a novel is hard. It requires discipline, time, enormous amounts of focus and energy and sacrifice. *Intruders* was the hardest one yet for us, but while drafting and editing it, we fell even more in love with the process. We hope that, reading Jade and Crys's story, you felt even a fraction of the exhilaration we felt creating it. Thank you for joining us on our Exiles journey.

And thank you to those who make it easier for us to put in the hard work. Our parents, you have our gratitude and love, always. Allen and Rob, your endless supply of yerba maté and love means the world to us. Our editor Adrienne Procaccini, thank you for your continued support of these books and your belief in us. Jason Kirk, for your friendship and your guidance—this is book number five together, and we've enjoyed every minute of the ride. Our scientist extraordinaire, Ashwin, for your advice and bountiful knowledge. Everyone at 47North, for bringing your talents and expertise to our team. And Wyatt and Winston, our loyal writing mascots, who have been by our sides as we wrote every word of our five novels and counting.

And lastly, once again, to each other. We're lucky enough to create and dream every day with our best friend.

ABOUT THE AUTHORS

Photo © Neal Handloser

Twin sisters Ashley Saunders and Leslie Saunders are the authors of the Exiles series and *The Rule of One*, *The Rule of Many*, and *The Rule of All* in the dystopian series The Rule of One. The duo honed their love of storytelling in film school at the University of Texas at Austin. After just under a decade penning screenplays and directing commercials, the sisters deliberately stumbled into the world of novel writing. They vow to never leave it. The sisters can be found with their Boston terriers in sunny Los Angeles, exploring hiking trails and drinking entirely too much yerba maté. Visit them at www.thesaunderssisters.com.